COEXISTENCE

COEXISTENCE

A Thriller

DANNY RITTMAN

COEXISTENCE
A THRILLER

iUniverse books may be ordered through booksellers or by contacting:

iUniverse
1663 Liberty Drive
Bloomington, IN 47403
www.iuniverse.com
1-800-Authors (1-800-288-4677)

ISBN: 978-1-4917-6611-8 (sc)
ISBN: 978-1-4917-6617-0 (hc)
ISBN: 978-1-4917-6616-3 (e)

Library of Congress Control Number: 2015907762

Print information available on the last page.

iUniverse rev. date: 05/18/2015

Dedicated to a dear friend, Rami, who was taken away too early, by cancer.

CONTENTS

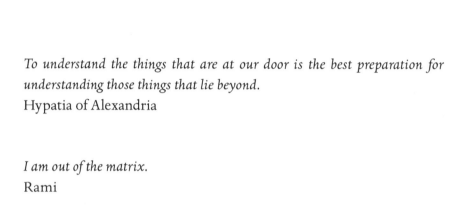

To understand the things that are at our door is the best preparation for understanding those things that lie beyond.
Hypatia of Alexandria

I am out of the matrix.
Rami

FORTUNE

The boat began to climb unexpectedly high on the crest of a wave. "Wow! What's this?" Samuel Daniels turned towards the wave and froze as he took in its enormousness. His small boat began to ascend the slope of the twenty-five foot wave and for a moment he was unable to move.

"Where did this monster come from? We are near the shore and no wave like this should be here. It's a fluke of nature and a violent one. Here I am. I must deal with it."

He glanced back to the shoreline in the distance and in an instant formulated a course of action.

He spun the helm hard to turn the ship to starboard and pulled the throttle to full. The sudden roar and surge beneath his feet gave him confidence. The more fuel that shot into the Mercury engine, the more RPMs the propeller had in the contest with the sea. The keel shuddered from the stress as the boat's bow climbed higher onto the foreboding slope of the wave. In a few painful moments the bow reached the crest and struggled to climb over it. The ship paused at the zenith, defying physics and nature, until the bow aimed down over the sea's threatening fulcrum and slid down quickly on the rear slope. A mighty smacking sound came through over the considerable din of the angry sea.

Samuel's elation disappeared as he saw the bow slice into the sea, deeper and deeper, until the entire ship had plunged below the turgid waters, seemingly never to rise again. He calculated that he had enough buoyancy to rise up again but then wondered how much of this was prayer, and not physics. He held his breath as the waters roared around him and tried to feel in his guts the almost sickening yet welcome sense of the craft rising to the surface. The planks creaked fearfully as the water pressed down on them, each sound sending a new challenge to his estimate. The roar of the sea became louder and louder until a sudden crashing sound and bright light told him that he and the ship had broken the surface. He spat the briny water from his mouth and watched the water race along the deck and back into the sea. Behind him the great wave rolled on toward the shore. Ahead of him lay calm seas and a pair of squawking gulls.

Samuel and his ship had endured the rogue wave quite well. Down below, however, an unusual chain of events was proceeding. The hatch to the cabin is supposed to close automatically on sensing the impact of a powerful wave. And indeed it did, just not as instantaneously as intended. The hatch closed quickly enough to save the craft from being pressed down to the seafloor, from which it could never have risen, but Samuel had brought some work with him.

Inside the cabin were petri dishes with unusual biological samples called HeLa cells. They were knocked to the floor where a light spray of seawater came into contact with them. Chemical processes began. Unexpected and unpredictable chemical processes began. The only visible change was a slight change in color that gave a subtle orange tint to the white samples. No one could have noticed it. Not in the laboratory, not in the cabin on a pitching ship. Samuel didn't notice.

Samuel shook the water from his hair and squeezed his shirt and trousers in a largely futile effort to dry out. He looked out ahead once more to see if another such wave was in the offing but he saw none. His relief was suddenly ended by concern with the cabin where his kitchen, bunk, television, and stereo system were. Then the matter of the petri dishes hit him.

He opened the automatic hatch and climbed into the cabin. The kitchen and its stove and refrigerator were all fine, as were the entertainment items and the semi-circular table fastened to the floorboard by sturdy titanium legs. The bunk was a little moist from the spray but there were dry sheets and blankets in waterproof bins.

On inspection, even the petri dishes looked alright. They'd been knocked about but nothing had broken or even cracked. He looked up at the aperture and saw blue skies and an occasional gull swooping by gracefully. He placed the specimens back on the table and felt grateful that all was well. Samuel's cancer experiment would proceed.

MYSTERY

Samuel was a researcher, a diligent one, and perhaps an obsessive one. That's why he brought petri dishes containing HeLa cancer cells with him on a sailing adventure. Obsessive and even quixotic. His research mixed hi-tech with biology and it had been underway for about two years. Colleagues were perplexed; some were amused.

As an undergraduate at University of Bridgeport, Samuel majored in electrical engineering—a field of study that prepared him for a career in the semiconductor industry. He had done remarkably well, finishing his undergrad work with a 4.0 average. While his professors and teaching assistants and fellow students thought of circuits and electromagnetic energy and metal oxides, he wondered of the effects of electromagnetic fields (EMF) on cell tissue, specifically on cancer cells. Teachers and colleagues wished him well, but thought him misguided. A smart guy who would eventually outgrow his youthful ideas or apply them to science fiction, not to real work.

Having sufficient credits in biology and chemistry, Samuel entered Yale Medical School and though immersed in the workload of preparing to be a doctor, he never put aside his curiosity about the effects of EMF on cell tissue. There were no courses on the question. Conversations with professors and colleagues led nowhere. Clearly, he was brilliant but no one he encountered at Yale shared his fascination, or obsession.

The same was true after finishing med school and taking a research position at Yale. They all thought him a smart guy who would eventually outgrow his youthful ideas or apply them to science fiction, not to real work.

Samuel found time for his interests outside medicine and hi-tech. His father, an entomologist by profession, had a boat, a twenty-five footer, and he taught his son to trim sails with the wind and sense changes in the weather. Sensing the coming of that rogue wave eluded him, but there's a reason they're called rogues.

The Connecticut coast is filled with sailors of varying skill and small craft of all description. One cannot look out to the ocean or one of the scores of brackish inlets without seeing white sails darting across the waters, some venturing well out to sea, like mariners from the days when whaling ships set sail from New England ports for years of searching.

Sam watched with wonder, then curiosity, and then with determination to go down to the sea again. He found an elderly couple, childless, who had once sailed to Europe and ventured up the Thames and into Norwegian fiords. Their sailing days behind them, they were reluctantly parting with their thirty-footer, and Samuel, with a comfortable salary and no familial obligations, eagerly bought it. He found a mooring in New Haven, just a short walk from his home and office. Samuel was now a seafaring man. Every weekend, weather permitting, he took her out. He called her *Nurit*, Hebrew for a tiny but bright light.

Samuel Daniels—Dr. Samuel Daniels as he was known in the research wing—was in his late thirties, tall, blue-eyed, and fit. He was in Syracuse, in upstate New York, and had spent most of his life there. Youthful athleticism and curiosity bestowed upon him a dynamism that all around him noticed right away and felt compelled to imitate. His dedication and energy made him see things through, despite doubts and criticisms from peers and rivals. Handsome and personable, Samuel remained too committed to his work for a meaningful relationship.

One Monday morning, after a pleasurable weekend on the sea, Samuel was back in his office and adjoining lab, looking over personal experiments in the hours before he had to deliver a lecture—one on a more conventional part of science, needless to say. His own work that morning entailed exposing a petri dish containing HeLa cancer cells to a powerful EMF. Samuel had built a chamber outfitted with two immense coils connected to high-power electrical circuits. The exposure would last two days, after which he'd study the cells for unusual changes in size. He'd done similar experiments but the results were inconclusive. This time the power would be higher and would last for two full days.

Placement of the high-power coils was crucial. Sam measured the distances to the millimeter between each coil and between the coils and the petri dishes. He adjusted the voltage and then the timer on the juice, and let physics and biology have at one another.

"You guys shall now get acquainted and have your fun for exactly forty-eight hours. No more, no less. No matter how much you complain or plead, that's it. Forty-eight hours."

With a flick of his fingers, solenoids clicked loudly and a surge of powerful electricity flowed into the coils, warming them, causing a low hum. Electromagnetic energy was washing over the HeLa cancer cells.

He didn't really expect anything remarkable this go around. But a research design is a research design. Science has its rules and they must be followed. Deviating from them invalidates your work and it may send you out looking for another job. He made mental notes of what exposures to make next time as he prepared to leave for his lecture.

He returned after class and after talking to a few first-years with eager minds and lots of questions. He'd been gone three hours and five minutes. He started to close up shop.

"Enjoy the evening, you folks."

And with that, he closed the door behind him and headed for home.

The term cancer is a broad category covering more than a hundred diseases. There are many variations in appearance and strength, yet all cancers involve cells growing at a rapid and uncontrolled rate—far more than the body can usually control. Normal body cells grow, divide, and eventually die. That is life. Growth is quite fast in an organism's youth, slower in its later years.

With cancer, normal cell death slows or stops and accelerated cell growth begins. Cancerous cells spread to other parts of the organism. That's not in the nature of normal cells. But cancer cells show no respect for that; they grow and spread and kill. Or try to.

The key to a normal cell becoming cancerous is DNA damage. If a cell is able to repair the damage, all will be well. If not, the cell may grow uncontrollably and its progeny will too be cancerous. They will spread. They will kill—or at least try to. It's in their nature. And it always has been. You might say it's in their code.

<hr />

The salinity, or salt content, of seawater is about 3.5%, with some variation caused by proximity to freshwater disgorged by rivers or ice melt or evaporation. Freezing and thawing affect salinity too.

Salinity affects organisms in the seas. Salt enters organisms through the process of osmosis. The water content and size of a fish will vary with the salinity of the water it inhabits. Science has studied the relationship between salinity and various marine life. Many studies of environmental influences on cancer cells have been done in the last fifty years. The effects of salinity and osmosis on cancer cells has been neglected. No one thought much of it. A fleeting thought here or there, a footnote in a forgotten journal article.

Seawater reached one of the petri dishes on Samuel's ship that day when the immense wave arose from nowhere. The cancer cells were affected. New bio-chemical processes were underway. Samuel didn't know it. Yet somehow, the cancer cells did.

The effect of electromagnetic fields (EMFs) on water and watery solutions is a growing field in science. Nonetheless, scientists don't know as much as they'd like. That's true of all scientific endeavors but more so here, as scientists are more intrigued about the field and more optimistic about its usefulness in medicine.

Although the precise mechanisms of the EMF effect are not been yet fully understood, some research has suggested that EMF may cause a colloid—a substance that is able to disperse its particles throughout another substance so it is almost impossible to tell that it is two substances instead of one.

Almost.

"Good morning, Sam. How are you this morning?" The tall, attractive brunette greeted Samuel as she walked into the lab.

"All is well, thanks. And how are you today, Alisha?" Samuel smiled more than professionally and poured them each a cup of coffee from the office brewer.

"Great, thanks." She flashed a smile and added. "Another day, another quest."

He smiled back and entered a common area shared by the two and a handful of other researchers. "How is your work going? I heard that you got impressive results with the new vitamin tests."

Alisha was working on an innovative research on the presence of certain vitamins in the blood as a signal of the cancer cells in the organism.

"I'm getting there. As you know, there's still the problem of finding adequate funding. I've gone completely through my budget as of last week and am presently using whatever meager resources the university will allow me to use." She gave him a meaningful look.

"Oh, you'll get your funding. Your research is too important and too promising. Early detection is a critical part of the fight against cancer."

Samuel took in Alisha's appearance and demeanor more appreciatively than before. That happens in offices and laboratories. She was in her early thirties, with long brown hair gently reaching her lower back. Her step was light and soft, as though her feet never touched the rude ground. Her green eyes had a penetrating quality that contrasted with her delicate face, which reminded many colleagues of a bust of Aphrodite.

More comparisons with the ancient goddess stemmed from her birth in the country along the Mediterranean and Aegean. Her family left an old Athens neighborhood about twelve years ago for Boston where her parents operated a restaurant. A little more than comfortable, they nonetheless put their daughter through Boston College then Yale Medical School. She did exceptionally well at both and was awarded a research slot in oncology, in the same building and on the same floor as Samuel. They worked together, nothing more than that, though both occasionally saw glances from the other that were of a decidedly more personal nature.

"I hope that you're right, Dr. Daniels. I'd hate to lose so many years of research trotting down a dead end."

Their eyes locked onto one another's for a moment, then another. He wanted to move closer to her and press his lips to hers. There was no mistaking that she felt the same attraction and the same urge. The moment hung uncomfortably, until it was gone.

"Well, I have to get back to my data, I hope you'll excuse me." He sighed at a lost opportunity and his backing down from the moment. There'd be other chances, he sighed. Their offices were close by and they saw each other at the kitchen most every day.

"Good morning, Drs Daniels and Weiss!" Bertha, a short, pleasingly zaftig woman, greeted them joyously carrying two sizable parcels which everyone knew to contain a noon repast. A dutiful administrative assistant, an excellent cook, and about fifteen years their senior, Bertha was well loved for her demeanor and culinary skills. In a hectic office where time often demanded they take in fast food, even though they knew the ill effects better than most, Bertha's bean salads and light pasta dishes were renowned. Words of appreciation directed to her led to her memorable response, "Workmates are a second family and I must take care of my family."

Nonetheless, her family members were known to speak off into New Haven for fast food. The best of medical doctors are not without their faults.

Cancer cells consume a great deal of energy compared to their healthy peers. Their metabolisms run at incredible rates. Rapid growth and frequent divisions demand more nutrients, especially iron. High iron levels cause the production of high levels of free radicals, which themselves are harmful. In response, cells bind the particles to "iron storage proteins."

EMF can affect iron storage proteins in cancer cells. Strong EMF blocks iron storage proteins. Free radicals are produced in exceptionally high values, this causes damage to cancer cells, killing many of them. The severely damaged ones mutate into other forms.

Mutated cancer cells were exposed to seawater on Daniel's boat and unusual chemical processes began to take place. Accidents happen in medical research. Sometimes for the worse, sometimes for the better.

The seawater dissolved within the mutated cells of the second petri dish and its constituent parts slowly diminished. A colloid was formed and there was almost no way to recognize the changes that had taken place in the cells. The other two petri dishes were unaffected by the events that followed from the freak wave.

The three dishes looked almost exactly the same. Almost. The cancer cells in the second dish had a slight orange hue. Very slight.

Placing all three dishes side by side would not allow many observers to discern the change. Only a trained observer could. No, only someone who had studied the contents, had come to practically know them, and had come to see them as part of his career and life could have discerned the change.

"What the heck is this?" Samuel scratch his head looking through the microscope at a specimen sample. "The color . . . it's changed."

He increased the microscope's magnification. Not only was the color different, the cells themselves looked different than the others.

"But why only dish number two?" he mumbled. "They all had the same HeLa cells. That's odd."

He placed the three small dishes near each other and studied them thoroughly. No doubt about the color change. A magnifying glass showed no difference. A microscope did, though. Something had happened and he determined to discover just what.

He studied the contents of the second dish minutely and for quite some time. He'd have continued to do so if he hadn't had to deliver a lecture that afternoon.

"I'll see you again soon and we'll get to the bottom of this. But for now, there are students awaiting me in Sterling Hall. Don't go anywhere! I'll deal with you more soon enough."

"You will deal with who later, Sam?" Bertha was amused at how researchers talked to their lab specimens.

"Oh, nothing out of the ordinary. At least I don't think it's anything out of the ordinary."

"Good luck with your lecture."

"Thank you, Bertha, I'll be back for a late lunch."

"Will hummus salad be satisfactory today, Sam?"

"Just perfect. Thank you, Bertha."

"My pleasure."

His lecture on basic cell structure to a college biology class went well. It concluded at four pm and he finished Bertha's hummus salad by five. Then it was back to the lab. Dealing with the anomalous change in the second dish proved to be more difficult than Samuel imagined. He examined the specimens and looked through the literature for any relevant findings or observations on change in color or appearance. Nothing. Nada. Zippo. Null set.

He had no recollection of such changes in previous experiments but any researcher knows that memory is faulty and that's why they take notes. Minute notes. Offices have stacks of them. He went over them on his laptop and found nothing.

"Okay, we have a change in appearance, but why only in the second dish? The specimens were identical at the experiment's outset and the EMF exposures were also identical. There should be no change."

He left the office at four am. Some people leave their work at the office and go home to routine lives. Not so with Samuel Daniels. Not at all. All the way home he kept thinking about the second dish and its change. He lay in bed for an hour and half with the same thought. He also wondered if cancer cells communicated with one another, in some way or another.

He left the office at four am. Some people leave their work at the

The governor received reports from constituent parts of the colony. It was routine and rather dull. Aide after aide said that the population was growing at satisfactory rates. Forecasts were not out of the ordinary and supplies of nutrients were good.

Governors are worry warts though. The upbeat reports made everyone comfortable. Everyone but one—the governor. His gut told him that an atmosphere of confidence was misleading. When everything looked good, something swooped down out of nowhere and upset things. Unexpectedly, unpredictably, unfortunately.

The governor was left with an inexplicable feeling of foreboding. In a few minutes, though, he was back at work and his mind was absorbed by the minutiae of governing the colony.

Samuel looked up eagerly from the coffee maker. "You are early today, Alisha." She breezed into the reception area and hung her blue woolen coat one of the hooks arrayed on a wall.

"And you look like hell, Sam. I hope you don't mind my saying so." Samuel noted her humor but there was an undeniable truth in her words. He thought of a Russian friend and wondered if he was becoming like him. "You look like you didn't sleep much. Anything going on?"

He handed her a cup of breakfast blend and nodded.

"I was here all night. I came across something yesterday afternoon. Something very peculiar. There was an anomalous chemical reaction in one specimen dish out of the three. Only one. They all have the same conditions, same specimen, and same culture."

Alisha weighed his words. Every researcher faces unusual phenomena. Sometimes it leads to throwing out a pet hypothesis. Sometimes it leads to refining it, making it better, one that leads to interesting findings—and sometimes to an important breakthrough. She thought that tossing out a pet hypothesis was most common, but she didn't share that with Samuel just then. She noticed that Samuel was paying attention to her and she had a pet hypothesis that it was due to her perfume. But it was too early in the morning of a busy day for flirting.

She took a long sip of her coffee and spoke.

"Well, that's odd. Do you need any help?" she asked in a flat voice that disappointed him.

Samuel remained transfixed. He saw her nostrils flare with each breath. He inhaled her perfume and closed his eyes in momentary pleasure. Momentary. He came back to a routine office encounter, suddenly and completely.

"No, thank you. I think I can handle it."

"Sure?"

He nodded.

She looked at him few more moments, amused and flattered by his attraction.

"Okay, off I go to my office then." She vanished from the room. His heart gladdened when she peered back in from the doorway. "Thanks for the coffee!"

Better than nothing. His heart slowed down. He came back to his senses. He knew there was an attraction but nothing like this, nothing like that moment that came and went like a summer front that passed without rain. He was so close to holding her close to him and pressing his lips to hers and telling her that he needed her desperately—thoughts he never thought he had until only moments ago. Calm but disappointed, he crept back to his part of the lab and stared at the petri dishes. Actually, he only stared at one of them.

He again looked at the curious contents of the second dish, this time under a stronger microscope. He noticed irregularities along the edges but couldn't think of any significance. Amping up the power, he noticed that the cells had become elongated, stretching out unexpectedly far and almost resembling wires. A quick check with the other two dishes showed no similar elongation.

The enzymes in the second specimen revealed higher sulfur content than the others. A fair amount of debris was visible but Samuel couldn't be sure this wasn't from the cotton material that the specimen lay on. He leaned back and thought.

What if we have a colloid? Something in which microscopically-dispersed insoluble particles are suspended throughout another substance. This would create a new substance.

But with what elements or substance?

Samuel looked over to the periodic table on the laboratory wall. So many elements, so little research money. Somewhere on that basic chart that high schools had in chemistry classrooms was a combination of elements that would compose a great breakthrough. Where to start?

He looked from the periodic table towards the large schematic of the electrical coils that hung on the other wall. It showed two large coils connected to a power supply and a variable resistor to control the power. The magnetic field generator was his own creation. The electrical and magnetic fields this array put out was amazing. Turning it on to full power dimmed the lights in the entire building. The sudden dimming caused colleagues to remark, good-naturedly or not, that Samuel must be at work.

Unlike high-frequency X-rays and gamma rays, which are strong enough to break chemical bonds (ionizing radiation), the electric and magnetic fields from 60-cycle electric current are extremely low-frequency (ELF) and thus low energy. No one ever worried about these fields because they are not strong enough to break chemical bonds—which was considered necessary to cause cancer or have other biological effects. Recent investigations, though, suggest that these low-energy fields may indeed be a cause of concern. During his last experiment Sam designed the magnetic field to be stronger than ELF range. Now it was defined as EMF. But the reaction that he found could not be entirely caused by the EMF.

"It could never create this type of change so fast! So it must be some sort of chemical reaction. Also the big question still remains about the one dish."

Samuel called up a paper that he published last month in the *Journal of Cancer Research and Therapy*, and skimmed it quietly.

"Biological cells have been shown to respond to low frequencies electromagnetic fields as well as in chemical and biochemical reactions. The energy of the electromagnetic field is too low to affect the cellular level to produce observable effects. Therefore, the physical mechanism of primary interaction between the magnetic fields and the biological target sites, such as electrical charge in motion, molecules structure with magnetic moments and the application of Faraday's law, generating local electrical current by a magnetic field has mainly concluded only amplification mechanisms can solve the puzzle.

The interaction should be very weak at field strength less than 10 Gauss and the frequency below 100 Hz. If considering the stochastic resonance model, the amplification of weak electromagnetic interaction signals can be modulated by external fields. By considering ferromagnetic transduction model, the minimum applied magnetic fields would produce a torque on a biogenic magnetite particle coupling via the cytoskeleton to the ion gates. The deformation of the cell membrane and the closing of the ion gates would occur quickly enough to compensate for the forced opening of the gate as long as the frequency of the forcing field was below 100 Hz, regardless of the strength of the applied field. When an EMF is applied, its magnetic strength may cause a different deformation of cells membrane. The final effect on the cells however is not conclusive and needs to be further investigated."

He mumbled the words he wrote just a year ago but was not convinced they pertained to the mystery before him. He delighted in watching the morning sunbeams gently sweep through his office, illuminating piles of papers and sending dust particles into riotous dances as the air warmed however minutely.

"Good morning, Sam! Good morning, Alisha!" The shrill but pleasing voice of Bertha woke Samuel.

"Yes, hi. Good morning. . . ." Samuel rubbed his eyes as he realized he'd nodded off at his desk, again. His heart gladdened on hearing that Alisha was nearby, until he realized how disheveled he must look.

Alisha peaked through his door. "Good morning, Sam? How are you this fine morning?" She seemed especially buoyant that morning, and who knows, perhaps capable of overlooking his appearance.

Her forehead wrinkled. "Are you still wearing the same clothes from yesterday?" She covered her mouth when it dawned on her. "Wait, you stayed all last night in here? Oh, poor you. You work too hard, Sam. Go home. Get some fresh air."

"Yes, I know. I'll leave early today." Samuel smiled. "I have a lecture to give at three. After that, off I go home to sleep—and later to change my clothes."

Bertha nodded approvingly. "Ah, but at least I have something very healthful for you both today. I made quinoa salad. Very good for you. I'll start to prepare it soon so you'll have it for lunch." She scurried over to the kitchenette to do her magic.

"Oh yes. Quinoa salad. How thoughtful of you." Sam and Alisha had sampled it before and found it, well, lacking. Its pungency was off-putting, almost disgusting. Almost.

"I know Alisha's day will be all the brighter after a goodly helping of my specialty. No worries, you two. I'll make plenty!"

"Oh . . . you're spoiling us. Please don't fuss. Not today. Samuel and I have a luncheon over at the faculty lounge."

"That's right!" Sam all but smacked his forehead to accentuate things. "We look forward to more hummus dishes though. For tomorrow, that is."

"There's always a tomorrow here at Yale!"

"There'll be plenty of leftovers for you tomorrow here at Yale." She leaned over to whisper a secret. "I'll make sure the others don't get it all."

Sam and Alisha took small consolation in putting off the unloved salad for a while. Later was later, and many things can happen until later arrives.

Samuel, still groggy and eager to get that first cup in, looked out the window and rested his head on the palm of his hand. Before he knew it, he was asleep again.

⟨⟩

"We have a problem with the perimeter, sir." A section leader gave a crisp report to the governor.

"What's the problem? A storm? A penetration?"

"No, sir. Neither of those. The problem is difficult to explain as we've never encountered it before. Our perimeter has changed, and for reasons we do not yet understand. We soon will, though."

As governor of the small colony he was responsible for its survival and growth. From the reports coming in, the change in the perimeter wasn't catastrophic. Its mysteriousness, though, had him worried.

"All we know at present is that the particle structure of the perimeter has been altered. We hope that it does not open a channel for other species to penetrate into our environment or otherwise cause us harm."

"This is my main concern. Please keep on it and get back to me promptly when you know more. It may be the opening of a new form of invasion. Have our history section look closely into the archives for anything relevant in our long and proud past."

"Valuable counsel, sir."

"Dismissed."

The section leader left with all of his five million assistants.

⟨⟩

They kissed each other passionately. Alisha wrapped her arms around his neck and he could feel her full lips pressing against his. Her tongue darted into his mouth and tasted his, and they became a fire. They were gravitated toward the office couch. She took off her shirt and skirt within seconds and he kicked his shoes into the air. They fell into the soft couch and pressed their flesh together.

Their passion grew, their caution vanished. She called his name, over and over. "Sam . . . Sam. . ." Her voice was strange, distant and uninvolved, though they were on the brink of fulfillment.

"Sam . . . Sam. . ."

He opened his eyes, reluctantly.

"Sam, wake up. It's past noon and we have to go to lunch." Alisha stood above him pointing towards Bertha's desk. She leaned down to him and whispered, "Unless, of course, you would like to have the notorious quinoa salad for lunch."

"Ahh. . . I was having such a beautiful dream." He murmured his words slowly and wistfully, unhappy to abandon the dream world just then. "I'll tell you about it someday."

"You can tell me on our way to lunch." She motioned with her hands to urge him to make haste.

"Not just now. I hope to soon though. I'll explain all to you then." Samuel was reluctant to stand up lest he reveal at least something of his dream. He concentrated on quinoa salad to help resolve the matter.

"Yes, you are quite right. Let's go have lunch, as we scheduled."

"Great. And don't forget you have to tell me about this dream someday."

He glanced at his reflection in the darkened computer screen, straightened his hair cursorily, and they both stepped towards the door.

"See you later, Bertha. We'll be back in a couple hours." Alisha gave her a sweet smile.

"Enjoy your lunch. I'll save you some of my salad for later." Bertha beamed towards them and turned to her little fridge.

With or without them, she was about to eat her healthy quinoa salad.

"This thing's driving me nuts."

Sam spoke ruefully, almost in resignation, as he took a bite from a thick cheeseburger. They sat at Louis' Lunch, a New Haven institution, and enjoyed exceptionally unhealthful cheeseburgers. The menu at Louis' isn't very large but everything is quite good. Only a ten-minute walk from the heart of campus, the small and colorful restaurant looks like it was taken straight from the streets of old New York City. Small, square tables, covered with checkerboard red and white plastic tablecloths, a bottle of ketchup and mustard, and even a little rose on each table. Loud music of the sixties was always in the background and the staff was already dressed in quaint attire. The food and atmosphere made it popular with students and professors as well. The place gives the idea that in the late seventeenth century a beer and burger lunch was common.

Alisha could see that Sam's mystery was bothering him. He wasn't going home and he wasn't sleeping well—and he wasn't enjoying her company as much as she hoped.

"Are you sure that you're not getting too close to science fiction?" She asked hesitantly. She knew that many times in the past he thought he was on the verge of a breakthrough but it turned out to be nothing but a simple technical matter.

He shot her a brief and less than serious scowl.

"Okay, sorry. . . . So you found higher sulfur concentration. What else?" Alisha took a sip from her Sprite.

"This is the main thing: why only one out of three?"

Alisha sank into her thoughts. "And you applied the same EMF to all three?"

"Yes."

"Let me look into the research design when we get back."

The promise of a partnership brought new appreciation for his burger.

"Sure. But you know something? Sometimes the fringes of science are a lot like science fiction."

Alisha looked closely at each of the three specimens under her Nikon microscope. She initially saw no difference in any of them. However, when Sam suggested focusing on the edges, she saw the irregularities in one dish and without any prompting identified them in only the second dish.

They reviewed the chemical analysis and the electrical information for a full hour.

"Sam, this time you did it," Alisha raised her eyes eventually. "You've given science another puzzle. Great work!"

He welcomed her humor as a break from lab tedium.

"But I'll solve this puzzle, even if it'll take me months or years. I have the feeling that this is a clue to something big. Something truly significant."

She smiled. "I love your enthusiasm."

"Thank you."

They sat there for a while somewhat uncomfortably.

"But at least we had a good lunch." Samuel mused.

A knock on the door.

"I heard someone mention lunch!" Bertha entered. Much to their dismay, she was holding two plates of a certain salad.

Samuel was glad that he didn't say too much. "Well Bertha, I meant we had a good time."

"That's what I thought would happen. So, I saved you both some of the *specialté du laboratoire*. I already ate mine. Trust me, it is delicious."

"I am sure it is, Bertha. Thank you, dear. We'll enjoy it a little later." Alisha nodded agreeably.

"And one important thing you have to remember," Bertha added with a look of an imminent word of importance. "You have to have few dashes of sea salt. Without it, the dish may be a bit bland for most palates. But only a small amount, and only sea salt. Not your run of the mill, cafeteria-variety salt. Oh no. That will *never* do."

Samuel was amused by her fussiness, yet intrigued. "My dear Bertha, why must it be sea salt? Salt is salt."

"Ah, not true. Did you know that sea salt has many more vitamins and minerals than regular salt? I will send you an email with the link to a wonderful health and cooking site. You'll be surprised. A dash of sea salt makes a world of difference."

Samuel marveled at the wonder of this woman. So endearingly chatty and well informed on many things, even if she didn't know the applicability of her remarks for science.

Bertha arched a brow at Sam's prolonged look. Had she said something wrong?

Samuel stood up, approached her, and gave her a big hug.

"Bertha, you are a genius!" He proclaimed joyfully. "You are absolutely right. A dash of sea salt can make a whole world of difference."

"Well . . . yes."

Samuel turned toward Alisha. "This is the answer. I completely forgot about the incident."

"Incident?" Alisha leaned forward to hear the story.

Sam leaned forward until their faces were no more than two feet apart and recounted the day the giant wave struck and upset the petri dishes below. "There is no other explanation, Alisha. It must be the exposure to seawater—and the salts therein that our gregarious cook here speaks so authoritatively of."

"So you would like to have my quinoa salad with or without sea salt?" It was all arcane science talk for Bertha.

Samuel kissed her on her cheek. "I am sure that this is the solution— or at least it puts us on the right track to find the solution. In return for your serendipitous help, I'll enjoy your quinoa salad, with sea salt. But not before I prepare another three dishes with the same specimen."

"I am glad to hear." Bertha beamed. "I am sure that you'll enjoy my salad—and it is good for you too. Unlike those greasy burgers at that dive people here like so much!"

Samuel and Alisha prepared three petri dishes with the same specimen. They took out cancer cells from the fridge and carefully placed them onto the dishes substrate.

"All we need are a few drops of seawater." Samuel was happy. "Off I go to the ocean. By tomorrow we should have mind-boggling results."

"I am impressed, Sam. You got me enthusiastic with your research. I hope you're right." She gave him a hug and he enjoyed the brief moment.

"Yes, by tomorrow we'll know."

"This is a complete copyright infringement!" The governor was furious. "Are you sure about your findings?"

The assistant leader was intimidated yet sure of what he saw. "Yes sir, we ran a thorough investigation and our results are conclusive. We also conducted the analysis on many regions and I must report that we are getting the same results there too."

"So it seems like someone is trying to steal our information. I can't believe this is happening. I am well familiar with our history and nothing like this has occurred before. Never! Not in millions of years."

"Indeed, sir. This is the first time in our long proud history that copyright infringement has been definitely identified. We also searched our generational documents and nothing similar could be found. It seems like someone is acting against our basic copyright law."

"Well, to tell the truth, I am both stunned and angered to see this. Any intelligent species that is developed as individuals and a community sooner or later figures out ways to mimic and copy." He sunk into thoughts. "It was just a matter of time. And now that I am thinking about it, it pleases me that it is happening in my time." He turned towards his assistant leader. "Aren't you?"

The leader was slightly uncomfortable. "Well . . . yes. We are working around the clock to find a way to block this penetration. Alas, we currently don't have any estimated completion time, sir."

The governor fidgeted nervously. "This leaves me no option but to alert all the others. Start a global transmission."

"But sir, are you sure? Global transmission is strictly forbidden unless there is a highly critical situation."

"This is a highly critical condition. Somehow our vital information has been compromised and we don't even know by whom." The governor looked determined. "But worse, currently we can't stop it. We are completely vulnerable. We have to alert the others, worldwide. Take note. This is the transmission: 'We've encountered global copyright infringement and do not have any way to stop it. Following are the incident's technical details. We are urgently working to find a way to block more of this. If you have encountered a similar situation, please send a transmission stating so.'

The assistant leader looked at him almost in panic.

"Start the transmission immediately."

"Yes, sir."

"Dismissed."

An extremely low frequency electromagnetic field (EMF) was activated on the signal pathway within the plasma membrane of the cancer cells. Electromagnetic field (EMF) radiation is the flow of photons through space. Each photon contains a certain amount of energy, and the different types of radiations are defined by the amount of energy found in the photons. The electromagnetic spectrum is the range of all types of EMF? radiation.

The cells were exposed to the EMF for about four hours before the effects started to show. After four hours and twenty minutes, calcium ions—electrically-charged calcium atoms—were released within the cells in a slow but growing rate. Calcium ions bound to the surfaces of cell membranes are important in maintaining their stability. They help hold together the phospholipid molecules that are an essential part of their makeup. Without these ions, cell membranes are weakened and are more likely to tear under the stresses and strains imposed by the moving cell contents. After all, these membranes are only two molecules thick. Although the resulting holes are normally self-healing, they still increase leakage while they are open and this can explain the bulk of the known biological effects of weak electromagnetic fields.

Leaks in the membranes surrounding lysosomes, tiny particles in living cells that recycle waste, can release digestive enzymes, including DNAase which is an enzyme that destroys DNA.

After about six hours EMF-exposure gene mutations started resulting from DNA modification. A gene is a section of DNA containing the information needed to make a particular protein or enzyme. The cancer cells that were already altered, were not damage as normal cells would endure, but the change's results were immediately noticed.

⟜➞

"Fascinating! Simply fascinating!"

Alisha exclaimed softly as she peered through the microscope. "I can see it. There is a development of orange pigment within the mixture. Your cells are responding to the EMF."

"Ah, not EMF only. The change was also induced by seawater and chemical elements that are in it."

Samuel felt like a lottery winner and couldn't hide his excitement. He walked back and forth in the room to help him formulate a next step. "The question is where do we go from here? There are so many possible directions."

"True, but we can start with the obvious and move forward. Like the EMF strength or providing the seawater chemicals artificially." Alisha was still glued to the microscope.

"So this is a joint project now?" Samuel's eyes brightened.

She lifted her eyes and faked a serious expression. "What else? Now you need to investigate in many directions. You need the help of another skilled researcher." She turned back to the microscope. "And besides, this is both interesting and challenging. I *have* to be involved."

"But I thought that you said my work is closer to science fiction than to medicine!"

"Well, it still may be a science fiction but at least I have to know where the story goes. I am too involved. And as you said, the cutting edge of science often sounds like science fiction. Let's see if we fit in one field or the other, or both."

Samuel help up a pile of papers more than a foot high. "I have it all in here." Pointing to his temple he added, "I have a plan too."

RESPONSE

"Good morning, Sam. Please have a seat."

Dr. Stanley Kraft, the young dean of Yale School of Medicine pointed towards the brown leather armchair that was in front of his desk. "Would you like some coffee?"

"No thank you, Stan. I already had two cups this morning." Sam took a seat, increasingly uncomfortable about what this meeting portended.

Sam looked out the window to the university grounds. The trees were in full color, and they were beginning to shed their leaves onto the manicured lawns of the campus. Stan tamped his pipe with an aromatic tobacco from a cylinder on his desk.

"Autumn in New Haven. . . ." Stan sat on his chair and turned towards the windows. "The trees are in a state of change. The air is chilly but not yet cold. Ahh, autumn." He then lit his pipe and drew in air until the tobacco was ablaze.

Sam knew this remark about the weather was simply a pat prolog. He knew Stan Kraft since they were in med school. They played chess quite often out in a courtyard, though neither was especially accomplished at the game. It was a break from the book and labs and an occasion to talk about aspirations. Sam spent many a holiday with the Kraft family and in many ways preferred them to his own.

Sam wanted to get to the point.

"What's going on, Stan?"

The dean released a long sigh. "Sam, I see on the report that you've recruited Alisha Weiss to work with you."

"Indeed, I have. And I'm pleased to have her on board. I am on the verge of something big, Stan. Really. Something earthshaking. You have to trust me."

Stan Kraft stood and walked across the office, releasing small clouds of smoke. "Of course, I believe you, Sam. Of course, I do. Nonetheless, you know that I am restrained by the board on the matter budgets here."

"I know."

Stan gave him a penetrating look. "I simply don't have the funds for this, Sam. I have to use the budget on more promising research or at least on something more in line with conventional research. Something that we'll be able to publish in the journals and deliver lectures about at conventions."

"And you will. I promise."

"Sam, I love you but you promised me so many times before over the last year."

"I am aware of that. Look, Stan, if Alisha is the problem then she doesn't have to work with me. You can assign her to another project."

"Yes, but she is not the only issue here, Sam. Even if I give her something else to work on, I still have to report what you are doing. What type of research you are working on. Something that will justify your salary and your position."

"This is a unique and compelling direction I'm taking. I am already getting significant results."

"Yes, I read about your EMF effect. But Sam, when I read your work I think it is more appropriate for engineering and not medical research."

"I know that I have a massive amount of engineering stuff with the EMF procedures but if you read the biological part, you'll understand the promise."

"Sam, I did. I read it and not only me. The problem is that others also read your material. Sometimes I wish that no one but me will read it but I am bound to this university's rules." He looked worriedly to his friend. "I have to say that the results do not speak in your favor. They are not convincing. There are too many question marks and the greatest issue is that it touches a very sensitive topic."

Stan sat back in his chair, hoping to find comfort. He noticed his pipe was no longer lit. "Sam, as a friend, listen to me. You know that your research is touching one technological field that should not be touched by us. The entire cellular communication world, which I don't need to tell you how many billions are invested in it, is affected by your research. You also know that our engineering research is also involved in the next generation of cellular technology development."

"Yes, I know, but I'll not touch cellular aspects. This one is pure electromagnetic field, pure EMF."

"Please let me finish, Sam. You also know that major industry cellular technology are contributing heftily to our university. We can't publish medical results that will harm this industry. Do you know what I mean?"

"Yes, and my research will not harm anything, Stan. You have my word."

Stan remained quiet. "Sam, I am sorry. I can give you only one month to show practical results. After that one month, I will assign a new research topic for you."

"But Stan, please."

"Sorry, my friend, this is what's best for your career and for the university as well."

Sam walked calmly into the lab where Alisha was poring over a journal, sat down, and announced, "We have to show some promise—and soon."

"What? Why?" Alisha raised her eyes in astonishment then dismay.

"Stan the Man doesn't think our work is essential research. In fact, he doesn't think it's going anywhere at all."

Samuel didn't sound defeated, more like motivated. Ticked off and energized. "He wants to shut us down. I am not worried, though. We will get significant results by the time."

"When is that?"

"Thirty days." He turned to the experiment table and saw what'd to be done. "We have prepared eight petri dishes. In each one of them there is a different culture. The cells have enough food to survive at least one to two weeks. We will split the next experiment to four parts. Two for you and two for me. Here are the specs for each unit."

He handed her printed sheets and turned towards the drawing board. He drew four boxes and connected them with diagonal lines.

"Each experiment, beside one, will be governed by a different dosage of seawater and EMF strength. The exceptional dish will be given seawater elements artificially. I want to see if we can find the exact cause and duplicate it artificially."

"Good thinking, Sam. I am proud of you." Alisha gave him an admiring look.

Encouraged by her reaction, Samuel smiled. "Thanks, Alisha, we need to catch this puppy and quickly. I have a feeling that we are on to something big. I don't know exactly why and how, but I can feel it. My instincts have never failed me."

Alisha squeezed her lips with a hidden smile. "I have to admit. As much as I was skeptical in the past consider me as one of your fans now. I do believe that you are correct. You discovered something that can lead to a breakthrough." She arranged her hair femininely. "I love the passion you have."

"Well, I was always considered very passionate. . . ."

There was tension in the air. Alisha's nostrils widened uncontrollably and Samuel's heart raced.

"Really?"

Beep, Beep, Beep.

The centrifuge alerted about completing the culture for dish number eight.

They exchanged looks of sheepishness and returned to their experiment.

"Wow, you guys are working too hard. Go home and get some rest." Bertha entered Samuel's room to see him and Alisha leaning over microscopes and taking notes. "It's already seven pm."

Alisha turned toward her with a smile. "Thanks, sweetie, but I am too excited. Don't fret. We'll go home shortly."

Samuel didn't even notice her. He was stuck above his microscope scrutinizing the cells.

"Sam, Bertha here is leaving. . . ." Alisha cleared her throat.

Samuel raised his eyes. "Oh, thank you, Bertha. What did you say?"

"Oh, go back to your microscope!" Bertha laughed. "I just wanted to let you know that I left you some of my bean sprout salad in the fridge. It's still fresh. If you get hungry, have it with a glass of organic milk—also in the fridge." She suddenly coughed uncontrollably for a few seconds.

"Are you alright, Bertha?" Alisha was alarmed by the unexpected onset.

"Oh, yes, I am fine, thank you. I think I may have a mild cold. No worries, and good luck with your research. I am sure people will benefit from it one day." She beamed towards them. "As for me, I am going home now. You have a great night and don't stay here too late."

"Thanks, Bertha, what would we do without you?" Samuel hugged her, albeit briefly. "I am actually a tad hungry so I'll try your salad now."

Bertha left, and they both took a break for a quick dinner. Although they didn't plan to stay too late, they ended leaving well after midnight.

Before they can cause biological effects, electromagnetic fields must generate electrical currents flowing in and around the cells or tissues. Both the electrical and magnetic components of the fields can cause extensive effects. The blood system forms an excellent low resistance pathway for direct current (DC) and low frequency alternate current (AC). It is an all-pervading system of tubes filled with a highly-conductive salty fluid. Even ordinary tissues carry signals well at high frequencies since they cross cell's membranes easily via their capacitance. In effect, the whole body can act as an efficient antenna for electromagnetic radiation.

Most biological membranes are negatively charged, which makes them attract and adsorb positive ions. However, these ions are not stuck permanently to the cell's membrane but are in dynamic equilibrium with the free ions in the environment. The relative amounts of each kind of ion attached at any one time depends mainly on its availability in the surroundings, the number of positive charges it carries, and its chemical affinity for the membrane. Calcium normally predominates since it has a double positive charge that binds it firmly to the negative membrane.

Potassium is also important since, despite having only one charge, its sheer abundance ensures it a good representation. Potassium is by far the most abundant positive ion in virtually all living cells. It outnumbers calcium by about ten thousand to one in the cytosol.

When an alternating electrical field from a current hits a cell's membrane, it will tug the bound positive ions away during the negative half-cycle and drive them back in the positive half-cycle. If the field is weak, strongly charged ions, such as calcium with its double charge, will be preferentially dislodged.

Potassium, which has only one charge, will be less attracted by the field and mostly stay in position. Also, the less affected free potassium will tend to replace the lost calcium. In this way, weak fields increase the proportion of potassium ions bound to the cell's membrane, and release the surplus calcium into the surroundings.

This surplus calcium when arranged in an organized pattern has a few effects on the cells.

One of them is discoloration.

"Sam, you have to look at this!"

Alisha couldn't hide her excitement the next morning. She quickly returned to peering into the microscope. "You must see this right now. I've never seen anything like this before. And I don't think anyone has."

Samuel rushed to her station and leaned over her microscope.

"Well, hello there!" Samuel exclaimed. "Where did you come from?"

"See the color difference? There's blue." Alisha impatiently pushed Samuel away from the microscope. "What do you think?"

"I don't know, but this is something new." Samuel looked over the notes.

"These dishes were under stronger EMF and the same amount of seawater."

"Did you see similar phenomenon with the other dishes?"

"Nope. I didn't see anything like this. My dishes are showing the orange discoloration which is consistent with previous results. This is good news. We can reproduce the same results."

"So we have the usual interplay between potassium and calcium which is induced by EMF." Samuel returned to the notes.

"This we've already known for many years." Alisha made some scribbles in her notebook. "This is not something new."

"Right, and we also know all the proclaimed effects of EMF on biological cells, the increase chances for cancer, fertility issues, metabolism, and so on, and so on." Samuel continued monotonically.

"Yeah, some of that is from cell phone studies. Like we will ever stop using our cell phones."

"Yes, but we have to remember that this is a field that is worth billions of dollars, as Stan said." Samuel gave her a meaningful look. "We should be very cautious about presenting any medical evidence that hurt this field."

"And like every multi-billion market, even if there are serious medical effects, they will be hushed. Money talks." She completed his thought.

"Given the world's economy and the ubiquity of cell phones, it doesn't matter what damage this EMF does. The world goes on."

"And we continue to develop cell technology without considering the EMF effects."

"Exactly so, I'm afraid. I told you that we are a good team." Sam was amused, though only a bit.

She turned away from her microscope. "So, what do we do? Do

we want to change the world? No one will ever let us. We may be able to publish few good papers and get some colleagues recognition, but that's about it."

Samuel was in deep thoughts. "Obviously, we will not be able to cause any conceptual change in the world's approach to EMF, but we may discover other useful things." He scratched his head. "For example, we may find a way to intervene with the growth of cancer cells. Maybe if we break the discoloration code in here, we may step upon some way to stop the vicious process."

"Well, it's a possibility. What else?" Alisha was intrigued.

"And there is of course the possibility of finding what actually is causing the damage to the DNA. If we can somehow put our hands on this factor, we can make something that no one has made before—a vaccine against cancer."

"Imagine that. . . ." She looked through the window. It was sunset and the skies were colored orange and yellow with hints of red. "A vaccine for cancer. It sounds even better than a cure. Imagine how many lives we will be able to save.

"Just think about how over-populated our planet will be." He wryly countered. "There are always pros and cons to every discovery."

"As for example our cell phones."

"And our microwaves."

"Virtually any electrical device that generates EMF—and we have plenty."

Samuel stood up and went to the central area to make a cup of coffee.

"A pick-me-up?"

"Yes, please."

He prepared two cups and brought them back to his office.

"But then again, we are living in a modern world. In a modern world there is technology that you can't live without and this include vacuum cleaners, hair dryers, air conditioners, and microwave ovens. All are immense EMF generators."

He turned towards the window and they both were taken in by the orange skies.

"I love the sunset." She murmured.

Samuel simply nodded.

"So what do you think? We may find a cure for cancer?" She looked into his eyes.

He sunk into her deep blue eyes and couldn't say a word.

"We have detected a change in our organizational structure, sir." The assistant leader reported to the governor.

"What are the details?" The governor was not pleased. "Are there enough nutrients for all?"

"Yes, we estimate that there is no problem with the food. The problem is not with the food but with our environment. It is changing rapidly."

The governor thought for a while. "Are we going to survive?"

"There is no way to know yet, sir. But we are witnessing serious changes in our climate. The climate is slowly warming. One thing is for sure. We are having these changes for long time now. These changes are consistent and we don't know their source."

"We can't take a chance of the others not knowing. We have no other choice."

The assistant's leader remained quiet.

"Send the emergency distress call."

"Yes, sir."

"Dismissed."

It was almost midnight when Samuel arrived home. He lived in a three-bedroom house in Easton, about ten miles west of New Haven. The neighborhood was set amid hundreds of tall evergreens which graced the community with a pine scent after a strong wind came in off the Atlantic. He had bought his home right after med school and enjoyed his half acre of green grass, which he diligently mowed in the summer and raked in the fall. He somehow enjoyed yard work and every weekend dedicated a few hours to his flowers and lawn.

His house was furnished simply yet with style. Pottery Barn-ish but he'd found the items in antique stores and flea markets. A brown leather couch and a reasonably matched coffee table sat in front of a wall window that looked out into a small pond surrounded by fir trees and crafted topiaries, giving the room a sense of being outdoors. European landscape pictures were hung in the living room and soft light provided him hours of relaxation in the evenings. He loved to fall asleep on his couch watching the stars in the skies almost every night.

He poured himself a glass of rosé and made an avocado sandwich with sourdough. He ate his late dinner beneath the stars. Samuel was not religious but he often had talks with "nature." He preferred the term to a more theological and anthropomorphic term. The stars flickered in the cold skies.

"What is the meaning of this? Color blue? Color orange? I do not understand." But the stars gently ignored his questions. He wondered if the problem had been solved on other planets. "Maybe. If there is intelligent life out there, which most likely there is. Can it help me to crack this puzzle?"

He looked to the skies.

"Is there anyone up there who knows the answer? Please give me a clue, whether you are little green men or something else entirely."

After moments of silence, he chuckled and partook of his wine.

He thought about Alisha. Her appealing blue eyes, her lips, nose, and long silky tresses. And of course her body. He closed his eyes with pleasure remembering how many times he imagined kissing her passionately. On many occasions in the office he had to remind himself that they are in a work place and not a New Haven student bar. He wondered if she felt the same attraction towards him. Once he thought so but then few months ago he heard her telling Bertha about a guy named Patrick, and his heart felt agony. She has a boyfriend. He never had the courage to ask her about her love life. They generally talked about her family, her hometown of Norwalk and her interests in life, but never about relationships or loved ones.

She is smart and he was happy that she joined him with the research.

The North Star flickered faster and he concentrated on it.

"Am I seeing well or I am too tired? Maybe the wine? Yeah, must be the wine."

He watched carefully again and the North Star returned to normal.

"I must be very tired,"

He lay back on the pillow and breathed deeply before looking once again up to the stars. There was a section in the skies that had so many. It almost look like a sparkly, white carpet. He had the strange thought that some of these stars may not even exist anymore and that they exploded into super novae or were swallowed up by black holes. Only their light is still arriving to our planet through many light years distance. Then he thought that the stars high resolution gave an impression of a white, lighted patch in the skies.

"What are you thinking about?" His tired mind tried to tell him. "I don't know but this is important."

All of a sudden he felt that a crucial idea was right before him. But about what? He closed his eyes and began to enjoy the onset of sleep. A glimmer of that crucial idea revealed itself to him.

"Wait, what if the stars were in colors? No, that's nonsense. This is leading nowhere. Still, this can help me with the puzzle in the office, but how? Many stars, high resolution, patch of color. . . ."

The idea flickered more brightly just before the blessed sleep gently took over. Fortunately, the idea embedded itself into his mind.

Somewhere.

"Good morning, guys," Bertha entered the office with her usual parcels of food. "How was your evening? Did you make any breakthroughs?"

Alisha liked up from her email. "Good morning, Bertha. No breakthrough yet but we're on task. Maybe today we'll get meaningful progress. Maybe tomorrow. Certainly within thirty days," he added mischievously.

"Oh, I trust you guys. You are smart as Einstein and Salk, if not more so." Bertha coughed, though more gently this time. "I brought all the delightful basics to make us a memorable lunch today. Did you ever see a documentary about processed food? *Food Inc.* was the movie name. Disgusting. There is nothing like homemade food and that's why I am here at the prestigious Yale Medical School—to see that its people eat right. Or at least some of them."

"Thank you, Bertha, we really appreciate that." Then Alisha decided to ask something she'd already asked. "Bertha, why can't we reimburse you for the lunches that you make for us? You are spending your money everyday on us. It's not fair."

"I won't hear of it. We are like a family here. You know that we spend more time at work than at home. That means that we are practically a family and my job is to feed you with excellent food. Besides, I feel like a mother in this wing. You guys are always busy trying to solve the most challenging medical problems in the world. The least I can do is make a little meal once in a while."

"You are a sweetheart, Bertha, thank you."

"Bongiorno, all," Samuel entered with a smile. He fondly pecked Bertha's cheek. "And how are you two this fine morning?"

"I'd say we're both just fine this fine morning. I'll just put this stuff in the fridge."

"You are a jewel, Bertha. When will you let –"

A darting look from Alisha cut him off. "I already asked her this morning." She sent him a soundless lips-only message.

"Off I go to my office. I thought about something last night but I fell asleep in the middle of my thought. I know it's stored somewhere in my mental cloud. I'll just have to head up there and browse around."

"Just don't get lost up there with all the debris!" Alisha jibed. "I'll help with the clutter in a minute."

"You two deal with cancer and debris. I'll start pealing the cucumbers"

CHALLENGE

"So what was running through your mind last night as you dozed off?" Alisha sat in front of Samuel, a pleasing look on her face. "That's the exasperating thing. I don't remember. I was very tired and had this idea—a great idea, in fact—but just then I fell asleep. When I woke up in the morning I forgot everything, except that I once had a great thought. It's like desktop icon that you click on and nothing opens."

"This happened to me once or twice." Alisha went to one of the microscopes and watched through the lenses at the specimen. "What is this?"

"Oh, that's the culture that changed its color to blue. I want to observe it thoroughly, maybe it will help get rid of some of the debris hiding my idea."

"Where were you when you were struck by this idea?"

Samuel peeled a banana and took a small bite. "I was on my couch, watching the stars. There's something. I was looking at the North Star." Samuel looked up to the ceiling with a bold expression. "And then the morning light woke me up."

"Okay. We have some material around your idea." Alisha patted his shoulder gently. "Beside the North Star what else were you looking at? The view? Something in particular?"

"Not really. I had a glass of wine and relaxed on the brown couch."

She was able to conjure up a memory of the place from a small gathering he held there a few months back.

"I was looking at the stars . . . the North Star. Hot damn, I got it! You are a gem, Alisha." He dropped the remnant of his banana and kissed Alisha, on the forehead. "The key word is 'resolution,' Alisha. 'Resolution'."

"Resolution?"

He turned to the microscope. "See? The culture here changed to blue. Before that it changed to orange. EMF strength being the determining variable." He looked up from the microscope with his amazed eyes. "What if this discoloration is actually a density message of some sort?"

"A density message?" She was confused. "What is a density message? From who?"

"Now I fully remember." Samuel stopped for a second and looked at her, wondering if she'd accept what he was about to say or leave the room in anger or fear or both.

"Last night I watched the stars and thought about the probability of having life-forms on other planets."

She had no idea where this was going and wondered if he was fully awake yet or in that liminal state between dream and reality, with the former holding the high ground.

"The probability is high. Given the fact that we have billions and trillions of galaxies and planets out there, the probability that some kind of life-form exists is high. Very high. Now, please do not think that I smoked something or had too much wine, but what if these discolorations are some sort of very-high resolution, high-density pattern or even binary message? What if they are collections of zeroes and ones in a very dense form so it creates an effect of discoloration?"

"Ummmm. . . So you are suggesting—that is, if I hear you right—that there are intelligent entities inside the cancer cells that are sending us messages in binary form?" Her voice conveyed bewilderment if not fear—fear of being in the same room with a lunatic.

"I know how crazy it sounds, but it is a possibility."

She exhaled noisily. "Sam, please. It's enough that the oversight committee considers your work more engineering than medical, and now you are trying to tell them about little green men inside cancer cells sending you messages?"

"Please! I'm not saying little green men. I'm suggesting that there might be a form of intelligence within the cancer cells that communicates with the outer world and with other cancers. What if they're trying to communicate with us? After all, looking at the equation from the cell's point of view, we are performing all kinds of procedures on them, adding or removing elements, constantly changing their environment."

"Sam, I understand what you are saying but I am telling you one thing." She stood up and shook her head as though to clear it of the nonsense she just heard. "I am not going to join you on this one. This is a little bit too much for me." She stepped forward and stood close to him, looking straight into his eyes. "This direction is crossing the line. Neither Stan nor anyone in oversight will ever support this. In fact, they'll get you out of here fast to save themselves the embarrassment."

Samuel held her gently by her shoulders. "Yes, I know what they'll think. What do you think? Do you think it's possible?"

She stood there for few minutes and then bit her lip. "I guess it could be, but it is so. . . so . . . unscientific or un-medical or un-anything else. For crying out loud, Sam, we work for Yale Medical School and not Hollywood. I am sorry, I am not in. You'll have to do it by yourself, but not for long. Stan will cut you off. I think you are committing career hara-kiri with this."

With that, Alisha all but stormed out of the lab. Sam stood there feeling more alone than he had in a dozen years.

The nucleus of a cell contains most of the its genetic material, organized as multiple, long, linear, DNA molecules in complex form with a large variety of proteins such as histones to form chromosomes. The genes within these chromosomes are the cell's nuclear genome.

The function of the nucleus is to maintain the integrity of these genes and to control the activities of the cell by regulating gene expression; the nucleus is therefore the control center of the cell. The main structures making up the nucleus are the nuclear envelope, a double membrane that encloses the entire organelle and separates its contents from the cellular cytoplasm, and the nuclear lamina, a meshwork within the nucleus that adds mechanical support, much like the cytoskeleton supports the cell as a whole.

Because the nuclear membrane is impermeable to most molecules, nuclear pores are required to allow movement of molecules across the envelope. These pores cross both membranes, providing a channel that allows free movement of small molecules and ions. The movement of larger molecules such as proteins is carefully controlled and requires active transport regulated by carrier proteins. Nuclear transport is crucial to cell function, as movement through the pores is required for both gene expression and chromosomal maintenance.

Although the interior of the nucleus does not contain any membrane-bound sub-compartments, its contents are not uniform, and a number of sub-nuclear bodies exist, made up of unique proteins, RNA molecules, and particular parts of the chromosomes. The best known of these is the nucleolus, which is mainly involved in the assembly of ribosomes. After being produced in the nucleolus, ribosomes are exported to the cytoplasm, where they translate mRNA.

Ribosomes were exported in a typical rate until the EMF affected their mobility. Since the nuclear membrane structure has been weakening, the EMF ribosomes were exported in much higher rates, causing different patterns. The addition of chemical elements due to the seawater created a defined organization within this pattern. This organization opened a channel for the colony's global transmission. Any transmission caused a unique structure of the RNA molecules which could not be seen using standard biological microscopes.

But one side effect could be identified even with a standard microscope.

A new cell structure was formed.

"This is it!" Sam bolted up from his microscope. "The deformed structures are creating the color change!"

Sweat was beading on his furrowed brow. It was one week after Alisha's walkout and he was working late again. Alone. The air conditioning was turned down at night and the coils from his electronics were like small ovens and he was the potato.

He observed his last experiment where he significantly increased the EMF to an extreme value, hoping to see something out of the ordinary. And he was seeing just that. The culture changed its color, but this time to an almost black pigment.

Samuel wiped his sweat and observed the cell's pattern. His microscope, which was one of the best on the Yale campus, magnified 3000X.

He sat down and thought out loud, as usual.

"This is not enough power," he grumbled. "I can see pattern change but I need more magnification in order to see the cell's membrane structure. Much more."

He opened the top buttons of his shirt and felt the office air warm his open chest rather than cool it. Turning up the AC all but required authorization from Yale's board of directors, so he opted to open a couple of windows. He stuck his head out into the autumn night and closed his eyes. He took deep breaths and felt invigorated. He opened his eyes and looked up in the clear skies. The stars flickered silently as though whispering a billion secrets to those below, almost none of whom were listening.

"If I could see you more closely, I am sure that I'd discover magnificent facts about you. Well, for that I guess I'll need a serious telescope. Same here, my cancer cell friends. I hope you don't think me forward to call you friends. If I want to get to understand you fully, I'll need an electron microscope." He remembered the capabilities of such microscopes and shook his head. "But an electron microscope cannot view live cultures. Well, maybe for a short time until it dies in the heat. Hmmm. . . . I'll have to give it a try anyway."

He knew of an electron microscope in Sterling Hall.
Tomorrow he'd use it.

An electron microscope uses accelerated electrons as illumination. Because the wavelength of an electron can be up to 100,000 times shorter than that of visible light photons, the electron microscope has vastly higher resolution than then finest light microscope and can reveal the structure of smaller objects. A transmission electron microscope can achieve better than 50 pm (a picometer = 10E-12) resolution and magnifications of up to about 10,000,000x, whereas most light microscopes are limited by diffraction to about 200 nm (a nanometer = 10E-9) resolution and useful magnifications below 2000x.

The transmission electron microscope uses electrostatic and electromagnetic lenses to control the electron beam and focus it to form an astonishingly clear image which is useful to investigate the ultrastructure of a wide range of biological and inorganic specimens including micro-organisms, cells, large molecules, biopsy samples, metals, and crystals. Industrially, the electron microscope is often used for quality control and failure analysis. Modern electron microscopes produce electron micrographs and tomography, using specialized digital cameras or frame grabbers to capture the image.

No doubt, the invention of the electron microscope was a breakthrough for many fields, including medicine. Yet, the light microscope that had much less magnification factor had one clear advantage. It allows the viewer to observe living specimens.

An electron microscope is usually used only on non-living specimens. The specimen must be coated in chemicals and put into a vacuum, a process which will kill any living specimen. Newer electron microscopes have the capability of using a very high frequency beam which enables observation of living organisms and biological specimen like cells, but only for a very short time. The heat that is produced by the electron beam will kill any living organism.

A corporation named AlphaTron invested a hundred million

dollars in the development of a unique microscope—the Photonic Microscope. With this device, photons are artificially accelerated to an immense speed then fired into the specimen, and from there, into a set of optical lenses that translated the information into a 3D image on a computer screen. Living cells and other live samples can be observed in heretofore unimagined detail, about one billion times greater than the best human eye can see.

Oddly, AlphaTron was not dedicated to medical research but rather to metallurgic research. Its Photonic device was intended for the development of advanced metallic material for space travel.

Samuel called a few friends and was able to get an hour-long session with an electronic microscope. He asked them not to mention any of this to Stan Kraft. He paced about the hallway outside the room that held the magnificent optical device and waited for a group of students to finish their lab routine.

As they piled out and headed for the next lecture, he began to talk to himself.

"Okay, Sam my boy, you have fifteen minutes for setup and an entire forty-five minutes for observation." He made last-second adjustments to the culture. "That should be plenty of time."

At last everything was in place—the culture and the viewer. He turned the electron microscope on and observed the images that began to appear. He figured that he had at least few minutes before all living cells would die from to the heat produced by the electron beam. He was reasonably sure that had enough time to discern what he was looking for.

"There is serious trouble, sir," The assistant leader spoke clearly despite an underlying sense of urgency that wasn't lost on the governor. "We have massive atmospheric change. We do not know the source. I can only say that temperatures have been rising at an alarming rate and I'm afraid the same is true of air pressure."

The governor wasn't wholly unprepared for such events. "Activate the enzyme protection. Lock the membranes."

"We already did this, sir. We did everything we could and thus far the results are null."

The governor ran through a hundred scenarios in his mind. He released long sigh. "Is there anything else we can do?"

"No sir, I am sorry."

The governor felt the heat and the pressure rising all around them. He knew that the inevitable was approaching.

"Launch the buoy."

The buoy was a biological molecular message to inform other colonies about the colony's fate. It would be flushed into the environment as a whole through routine waste channels. Critically, the message would retain all vital information in a molecular stamp. In time, this information will find its way back into the system where many other colonies can identify it. They will learn from the message and archive it as an historical document. This document will be enclosed to million others that were collected over the years and passed on for the next generation colonies.

"I'm afraid there's nothing left to do but that."

Nothing was left to be done. They all knew that their time was at hand. They joined together in a group structure and awaited their doom. A few seconds later they ceased to exist. Their only consolation was that they'd sent out their warning to others like them.

Samuel uploaded a program into his personal computer. It was early in the morning and he just received it from a friend in Cambridge, England. The program called "Genius" was well ahead of rivals and used by scientists to analyze geometrical shapes and patterns. The program included sophisticated algorithms of pattern-recognition mechanisms to identify the origin of ancient texts such as those found in Egypt and the Himalayas.

Samuel trembled with excitement and then increased annoyance as the program only slowly loaded into his machine. The progress bar seemed to move only a millimeter each two minutes. "Yes!" he exclaimed when a window announced the download was successful.

Then he fed a series of images that he took using the electron microscope over in Sterling Hall. That meant more waiting. The screen showed an hourglass and a time estimation for complete analysis. A scan line started to run through each image from top to bottom, searching for signs of intelligence or at least a meaningful sign of some sort.

Samuel released a long sigh. The hourglass showed almost two hours for estimated analysis time and he simply had no patience. Off to the library for a while, though that just made him think of a thousand books and articles he should read. Better head out for lunch. Louis' Lunch again.

A flashing screen grabbed his attention as he reentered his office. From the other side of his desk he could clearly see the results window:

Intelligence Probability: Higher than 90%

Sam just had to tell the news to someone.

DISCOVERY

"I solved the riddle, Alisha! I did it! I did it last night!" Samuel was beaming as Alisha entered the office. He wanted to hug her strongly but controlled himself.

She hung her coat and gave him a look of only mild interest. "You did?" She saw the look of joyful triumph in his eyes. It was seen often enough in the research wing. Truth told, she didn't expect to see it on Sam's face. She was still skeptical. "Just what did you see and do?"

"Last night, at seven thirty-two pm, I found out the reason for the discoloration."

"You recorded the exact time? Really, Sam?"

"It is a great moment in medical history." He held his head in resigned superiority.

"How? The electron microscope kills every living cell." She sat at her desk and placed a bag of English Breakfast tea into a cup of hot water, barely listening to him.

"I still had a short time to observe the cells and their structure before the end came."

She became slightly curious. "So what did you find out?"

He smiled superciliously. "I thought that you were out of this project."

She gave him a look that could kill. "You need all the help you can get. What did you get?"

He looked up at the ceiling with a haughty look. "Sounds like someone is a little more interested than yesterday."

"Maybe, but it isn't the Nobel Prize Committee or even Stan the Man and the oversight board. Whaddya got, Sam?"

"Here, let me show you the photos that I took."

He placed few images on the neon viewer on the wall where they observe X-rays.

"Perhaps a little introduction is in order. In the last decade, the discovery of a new cellular structure, the 'porosome', and the discovery of SNARE-induced membrane fusion, and regulated expulsion of secretory products, has provided us with an understanding of cell secretion at the molecular level."

Alisha listened carefully. She'd heard this in a lecture recently but it hadn't all stuck.

"The results that I saw last night clearly show an organized structure of the porosomes in the observed cancer cells. The presence of porosomes at the apical plasma membrane is ordered in a definite non-random fashion, where secretion occurs to the EMF and seawater is a catalyst.

"The electron microscope clearly identified porosomes at the apical plasma membrane. There are a number of fine elements that appear to connect or anchor the porosome structure with the plasma membrane, and most likely to the cytoskeletal network of the cell."

Samuel stopped and let her take it in. She ignored his look of supreme mastery.

"So what are you saying, Sam? This cannot be random or as a result of some chemical reaction?"

"The structure pattern has consistency. It has repeated forms. It has some meaning." He paused and took a long breath, unsure just how much she was buying. "It is my belief that this is not a result of chemical reaction. This is intelligent. It is planned, organized and executed accurately. Like for example binary language or programming language of some sort. I am certain to 99% percent that this was planned."

She looked shocked or appalled. "You think the cancer cells are alive?"

"Well, not anymore, but we learned from this specimen that the cancer cells have a definite form of intelligence. Unfortunately, the cancer cells died shortly after the electron beam hit them, but I was able to take these photos." Samuel showed another series of photos.

"See the dark colorization formed by numerous porosomes that were organized in a defined pattern and order? By being so dense and in a certain pattern they caused discoloration. If we look closely, we can clearly see that these are condensed structure of dots. The dots are porosomes, of course."

"Wow!" Alisha didn't want to admit it. She didn't want to show it. But she was impressed—or at least intrigued. "You're right. The dot's pattern has some organization. No doubt."

"We have to find out what it means. To be able to gain further understanding of this pattern of porosomes, we need much greater magnification."

"But we already used the electron microscope."

Samuel paced the room restlessly. "Well, it simply is not enough."

His elation had sagged and the signs of lack of sleep. More than that, there was obsession, and she knew that was not a sound frame of mind for scientific investigation. He needed a stabilizing influence. She began to see in his disheveled and grumpy look a bit of an idealist, a man on a quest. She felt the desire to hold him and to kiss him.

"I guess we'll have to search for a larger toy for you to play with. A toy with greater magnification. Then we shall see what we shall see."

They heard the distracting sound of a door opening and graceless footfalls.

"Good morning, Alisha and Sam, how is your morning going?" Bertha coughed lightly as she placed her bundles on the table.

"We are both just fine, Bertha, thank you for asking. And how are you today?" Alisha welcomed a break from the porosomes talk.

"Very good, thanks, just tired. Soon it's the weekend—and I can't wait to catch up on my rest."

Sam added how wonderful the extra sleep of a weekend would be, though he knew that there was no such promise for him in coming weeks. Or months.

"So Sam, what do we do next?"

Sam was taken by the use of "we."

"I already researched the matter of more powerful microscopes. A few universities have one of the largest electron microscopes. The University of Victoria, Canada has one. So do a small number of other places." Samuel took a large sip from his glass of water. "But amazingly enough, we have right here, under our noses, an innovative mechanical engineering company that has one of the largest electron microscope in the world."

"Really? Where?"

"Bridgeport. Half an hour away from here, there's a company called AlphaTron Research. They are conducting mechanical engineering research on metal atoms. Aerospace stuff."

"Actually, I know that Bridgeport is a major place for mechanical engineering research and development. I have family members that worked there. Do you know exactly where they're located?"

"I already checked with them." A look on his face betokened trouble. "They are willing to let me use their electron microscope, but since their entire lab is now set up for metal research, it needs to be reworked for biological research. That will cost money. Lots of money."

"Well, how much? We are Yale, for crying out loud. Just talk with your friend Stan Kraft."

Samuel moved his hand through his hair. "Not that simple. Not that easy. AlphaTron wants one million dollars per day. It will take about two hours to set up the area, six hours for my experimentations, and another two hours to reset their lab for their work."

Alisha squeezed her lips. "That's insane! What type of microscope can cost that much, even considering the set-up and chargeback costs?"

"Well, it is the best in the world when it comes to magnification but they don't even see what I see. The research of a live specimen without heating, without chemicals. Purely huge magnification. I need this microscope and only it will do."

"Still, you should talk with Stan. Show him your results and I'm sure —"

"I don't know. He already gave me the speech." Samuel gave her a look. "Do you really think that he'll look at my notes and sign a check for one million dollars to allow me to check a hypothesis about intelligent cancer cells? Even to me it sounds . . . unreal."

Alisha bit her lip. "It doesn't hurt to try. He is also your friend. Talk with him, Sam. That's the best thing to do."

"Sam, you are out of your mind!" Stan Kraft threw the notes on his table and looked at his friend. "One million dollars? For what, Sam? For a hypothesis that sounds like a made-for-television movie. Sam, please, I am telling you. We are medical doctors here. This is not Hollywood, with all due respect."

"Stan, listen to me." Samuel talked with more passion than he thought he had. "You see the pictures for yourself. These patterns cannot be random. Only an intelligent organism can be responsible for them."

"No, no, no. It can't be, Sam. The EMF may cause something, the seawater created a reaction. There are a million possible reasons for this color change. A microscopic intelligence is definitely not one of them."

He approached Samuel and lay a hand on his shoulder. "Look Sam, I truly appreciate your efforts and creative input in this research. Yes, sometimes you are really looking out-of-the-box, and this is a great thing. This is the only way to make real breakthroughs. With this, though, you are going too far. An *intelligent* cancer cells?"

"I analyzed the cells' membrane pattern using a state-of-the-art program to detect intelligent structure. This program is used to identify intelligence with old documents and artifacts, rocks engraving and similar. The program gave it probability of more than ninety percent of being created by an intelligent life-form."

Stan walked nervously in the room. "Sam, even if I at least partly believe that you have something, I can't authorize one million dollars for a microscope rental. It will not be approved by the committee. I also have to report to my boss and he'll demand justification for this type of expense." He lowered his tone. "Sam, you know that I can't do that. As much as I'd love to help you, I simply can't."

Samuel lowered his eyes.

"Look, why isn't our electron microscope enough? You know that this microscope will immediately kill every living cell. It is not justified for this amount of money."

"The technology's description is in these documents that I gave you. This is a one-of-a-kind microscope. It's unfortunate that it's not used for medical purposes, only for mechanical engineering."

Stan couldn't argue with that. He observed the documents that Samuel provided him.

Sam raised his eyes. "I'll have the ability to see things in cell structures that have never been seen before. That's all I need, Stan. Once I have a clear image of the pattern, I'll be able to analyze it further and to find the source of the message."

"I don't know. It still sounds far afield of anything in our world." He lit his pipe and released clouds of aromatic smoke into the air. "I know that I am not allowed to smoke in here, but there are special circumstances—such as when a friend asks for a million bucks to find little beings in cancer cells."

"I understand. But you see my point also, Stan? You see a glimmer of promise."

Stan didn't answer. He paced back and forth in the office, sending more clouds to the ceiling.

"Stan . . . you have to ask yourself, what if I'm right."

The AlphaTron Corporation keeps its great technological innovation in a specially-built hall in its Bridgeport facility.

The ten-ton, five-meter tall Scanning Transmission Photonic Holography Microscope, the first such microscope of its type in the world, was especially designed and built for the company in the course of four years. A team from Hitachi and GE, which constructed the ultra-high-resolution, spent another whole year painstakingly assembling the microscope in a climate-controlled lab in the hall that was designed and built especially for the device. The building walls are thick and embedded with isolation plates in order to provide maximum safety. The walls are coated with a non-reflective material to eliminate any light disturbance.

The device is used by the company's scientists and engineers for a plethora of research projects relevant to the advancement of mankind in the field of metallurgic materials. For example, engineers viewed titanium alloy atoms through the microscope at a resolution of fifteen picometers. One picometer is a trillionth of a meter.

This microscope allows researchers to see atoms in a manner never thought possible. It has full analytical capabilities that can determine the types and number or elements present, and high-resolution cameras for collecting data. The images are immediately translated into 3D holographic images using seven supercomputers that were especially designed by IBM. Five 52" screens present the images in real-time. A sample chamber, which is vacuumed cleaner than a surgery room, is used to contain the observed sample.

Soon it would hold its first biological specimen.

"Hey Sam, would you like to join me for a little horseback riding this Saturday?" Alisha saw the need to cheer him up. Since he stopped working on his research he was sullen and withdrawn.

"No, thanks."

She looked at his eyes. "Look Sam, I know how disappointed you are, but another opportunity will come and you'll be able to work again on your research. You can't shut out life. Since you stopped working on this topic you've become a zombie."

"I can't believe it. They gave me this ridiculous new topic that will never lead to anything. This, cell nucleus analysis. Any second-year med student can do it. That's a waste of my time." He threw a stack of papers on the floor and leaned back on his office chair, rocking back and forth, perilously close to falling.

Alisha sat in front of him.

"Sam, you are taking this too hard. Come with me on Saturday. You'll have a great day. You told me that being in nature inspires you. New ideas come at you from all directions. Well, maybe something will come to you during the outing."

Samuel looked into her almond-shaped green eyes and Mediterranean features. High cheek bones, proud nose slightly pointing up, full lips. Her brown hair gently fell on her shoulders, almost covering her half face. Who could not feel a burden life from his shoulders? Not Sam. Not even that day.

"Come with me tomorrow. You won't regret it."

"Okay, you win. What time?"

"Ten am. Breakfast at IHOP. My treat." She licked her lips naughtily. "I love the pancakes there."

"Count me in."

"I already did. Before I even set foot in the building!"

They breakfasted in a booth at IHOP. She had pancakes, he had an omelet. The stables at Glendale Farms in nearby Milford were uncrowded. Alisha and Sam saddled their mounts with some supervision and off they went into the yellow and red and fading green woods of the New England forest. The sun peaked through the thick branches overhead from which birds called out songs and warnings to one another. Coming to a fork in the trail, Alisha chose the one she knew that led to a pond about four miles away.

"My father used to take me out on hikes when I was but five. That was back in Greece. We hiked for an hour or more. I'm sure he must have carried me some of the way. We came to the village he grew up in. Even at my young age I could see a sense of peacefulness come across him as we sat on the patio of a village restaurant. He drank wine. I had something less potent, I'm sure!"

"It clears the mind. Clears it of noise and trash and clutter. All the unessential things. We should ride out here more often."

"You tell me this every time you get out of New Haven, even if it's only for an hour or so on your boat."

The path sidled a small stream that flowed out of craggy rocks on a soft incline. They halted their horses and listened to the gurgles and whooshes.

"Listen, Alisha. It's the sound of life."

Alisha nodded silently and decided to mention the natural forces animating him.

"I admire your passion, Sam. When you are into something, it's like the whole world stops."

"That's me." He agreed as his eyes transfixed on the flowing waters. "When I believe in something, it's hard for me to quit. I have a strong belief in a certain idea and I must see it through. It is almost an obsession."

"I can tell. But you know sometimes, and I am saying sometimes, you have to realize that at least a few projects may be too big or you simply can't complete them. Some topics you just can't handle because of reasons that are way out of the control of you or anyone else. Sometimes resources are just not available."

He released a long sigh. "Yes, I am aware of that. I do not have personal resources and the university budget is important for other things. Still I have this gut feeling that I am on the verge of something. A path that was never investigated before. A concept that no one ever thought about." He then looked straight into her eyes and his eyes were in flames. "A breakthrough that may give us a chance for something that was never seen before."

"What?"

"A cure."

Despite all his recent claims and assertions, Alisha couldn't keep from smiling. "A cure for cancer?"

He nodded silently. "Yes, Alisha. I do not know exactly where this will lead us but think about this. We discover that there is some intelligence within cancer cells. What if we could communicate with it?"

"Sam, I know that you are very excited but we are dealing with cancer cells. Although they are live specimens, they are still just cells."

Samuel got even more excited. "Exactly. We already found some kind of response under certain conditions. We can't rule out the possibility that—and I admit, it is just a possibility for now—that there are intelligent entities within these cancer cells. What if we can establish communication with them?"

"Sam, we are in the medical field!"

"Yes, I know, you are right and I admit it. It sounds crazy but . . ." he paused to stress his point, "but it might be. We can't rule it out. Exactly as we can say in almost certainty that there are intelligent creatures in outer space. With so many billions of stars and galaxies it would be only logical that there are some other life-forms out there. We just never established communication with them due to distance and technology. Same here with tiny cells all around us. We have the technology today."

Alisha took a deep breath and remained silent. Logically he was correct, if only barely so. They continued their ride.

As they arrived back to the barn, Sam smiled to her.

"Thank you, Alisha, for this outing. It was very inspiring and it strengthened my desire to continue this research. Now more than ever, I am sure that we've come upon something. It would be a shame to desert it before we looked fully into it."

He approached her and hugged her to his heart. She closed her eyes and enjoyed the moment.

A knock came on Sam's office door the next day.

"Sanjay! Long time no see. How in blazes are you?"

It was a friend from his undergraduate days—a chap from Bangalore who'd won a Marshall Award to study electrical engineering at Yale and who went on to earn a PhD in the same field. Sanjay was now an assistant professor at Yale, teaching chip design. He and Sam lived a block away from each other.

"Don't tell me. You're here at my humble office to have coffee with me this morning."

"Well, that would be pleasant."

Sanjay's downcast mood suggested he wasn't there simply for a cup of joe.

"Sam, I am here on a serious matter."

"What?"

"I found this little thing on my head and I would like you to have a look at it."

"Oh, Sanjay, I'm not in practice here. I do arcane research."

"I know, but I'm worried. You're still an oncologist and an expert in cancer research."

"Okay, pal. Let's take a look."

Sanjay leaned down, parted his thick black hair, and pointed to a red patch of skin on top of his head. "See, I've had this spot for a few months now. It itches and swells a bit. It's become more red in the last two weeks. Like I said, I'm worried."

Samuel inspected the spot on his friend's scalp, occasionally probing with an index finger. He looked at his friend intently. "Well, I can tell you that I am glad you came to see me. I can definitely tell you that you have a condition called seborrheic dermatitis."

"Is it serious?" Sanjay was ashen. He sat expressionless, his mouth agape.

Sam maintained a serious, clinical look then broke into a soft laugh.

"I'm not a dermatologist but I know that this is a simple scalp rush. Probably you changed shampoo recently or something like that." Samuel went to the coffee maker and poured two cups of coffee. He handed one to Sanjay.

"Indeed I did change a shampoo recently."

"Then change it back. If the problem persists, go see a dermatologist, not me."

Sanjay took a deep breath. "Don't do that, Sam. You scared me to death. I thought I had the Big C. You know, everyone is scared to even hear the word. This is probably one of the biggest fears we have. For you it may be a daily topic, but for us average humans it means very bad news."

"You're right." Samuel looked through the window at the falling leaves. The lawn outside his window was covered with orange and yellow signs of autumn's lateness. "You know, Sanjay, I have a feeling that I found something exceptional regarding this topic of what you so quaintly call the Big C."

Sanjay's eyes lit up. "Really? This is great news! Knowing you, a bright promising doctor, you can definitely do it. Imagine that, my good friend Samuel Daniels, found a cure for cancer. Wow! Can you imagine how many people you'll save? Not just here in America, all around the world."

"Sorry, but I won't be doing anything like that soon. They cut my funding, Sanjay. They blocked my research. All we have is some odd ideas running through my head."

"But why?"

"My hypotheses are, well, unconventional. They're out there. Maybe way out there. But perhaps more importantly, in order to proceed I need the use of an exceptionally powerful microscope. Something far more powerful than that device over in Sterling. What I need makes that device look like a Gilbert microscope that our dads gave us for our birthdays."

Sanjay remained silent, expecting more information.

"There is only one such microscope on the planet. Amazingly, yet frustratingly, it is right just down the road in Bridgeport. It belongs to a metallurgic research firm called AlphaTron. They'll let me use it . . . for a million bucks a day."

"And your oversight committee won't cough it up, I presume."

"They won't cough it up, in large part because they think I'm . . . well, *meshugenah*."

"I didn't know you knew any Hindi. I wish I could offer some help."

"Not as sorry as I am." Samuel was weary of this old story. "This will be a breakthrough. I just know it. I have to find a way to use this microscope. I have to find a sponsor."

Sanjay's face showed wittiness. "You know, Sam, I will quote something that a good friend of ours said a long time ago."

Samuel's forehead wrinkled with curiosity.

"The closer you get, the less you see." Sanjay smiled. "I love that quote. Do you remember who said it?"

"Wait a minute. Yes, I do remember—Nikolai Nechaev. How is the old joker doing?" Samuel's face illuminated. "Did he return to Russia? He was a brilliant fellow, conversant on so many things."

"Oh, yes. I recall him the same way. As a matter of fact, I am still in touch with him. He returned to his home town of Novosibirsk. Crazy guy. I never understood why he went back to live in Siberia. He could have it all here, nice and cozy. I can still remember his words every time when he got an A+ in a test."

"As I recall, he'd say: 'Extraordinary times demand extraordinary measures.' Funny guy. He always treated an exam like a battle he had to prepare for. Can't say I'm completely surprised he went back to Siberia. He was always talking of the mountains and streams. He yearned to leave the US. Anyway, what he is doing back there now?"

"He's a researcher at Novosibirsk's school of technology. A computer genius of some sort. Well, the reason that I mentioned him, Sam, is because of the hobby he spent his free time on. Remember?"

"Of course. He enjoyed hacking into servers around the world. I remember once he hacked into a travel agency and booked a Caribbean cruise for him and his girlfriend. Free. He also always had a good taste in women. They sensed genius and mischievousness."

"Exactly. Well, he was caught a few times by the police but always found a way out of it." Sanjay stood up and straightened his shirt. He gave Samuel a meaningful smile. "Thank you, my friend, for the scalp diagnosis. I'll definitely change my shampoo." He patted Samuel on his back and winked. "I'll send you an email with Nikolai's contact information, including his Skype ID. Get in touch with him. You never know what may come of a chat with an old Russian friend."

Samuel looked at him in a most puzzled manner as he left.

"What's wrong, Bertha?"

She noticed that Bertha entered the office without her food baskets and didn't boast of the healthy lunch that she was going to make them. She simply entered the office and sat on her chair with desolation clearly shown on her face.

"I don't know how it could have happened to me."

"What couldn't have happened?" Alisha sensed something dire.

"I eat healthy foods, maintain a healthy life style. I don't smoke or drink." Bertha murmured her defense. Her face was ashen. She was on the verge of tears.

"I went to my doctor for a checkup. You noticed my constant cough, I'm sure. I thought that it may be allergies or some sort of cold. They took an X-ray and it turns out I have lung cancer—stage four."

Alisha gasped, then pressed her to her heart.

"I mean, it was just a simple cough. And it was just a routine check. Who would imagine that with such a simple doctor's visit would lead to begin told that I have only a few months to live."

Alisha now had tears in her eyes. "I am so sorry, Bertha. We'll help. We'll take you to our lab and run some tests."

Samuel burst into the office. "Good morning, everyone." His uncharacteristic exuberance came to a sudden and unpleasant stop when he noticed Alisha hugging Bertha. "What happened?"

Alisha shook her head quietly. "Bertha has lung cancer. And it's stage four."

"I was diagnosed at the Medical Center yesterday by Dr. Brown." Bertha wiped her nose with paper tissue.

"Dr. Brown? Stage four?" They all knew Dr. Brown. He was head of oncology. Other doctors sent their patients to him for a second opinion. If he said Bertha was in a late stage, there was little doubt that she was. And there was little doubt she had not much longer to live. Nonetheless, no doctor is infallible. "We'll check you again." Samuel was upset he hadn't sent her to a doctor long ago.

"No, it is confirmed. Dr. Chen, the assistant at oncology, has already confirmed the diagnosis. I already went through the best doctors around. They all did the same tests. They all came back with the same diagnosis and the same grim prognosis."

Samuel slumped back in his chair. "I am so sorry, Bertha. I wish there was more I could say or do."

"No need, Sam, I love you both. You are my family. I was in shock myself for a while. But everyone has their time I guess. I am okay now. I chose not to pursue treatment. The chances are slim anyway. I just want to have the next few months to be happy ones, not wasted fighting side-effects."

Bertha found a way to smile. "Everyone dies. After all, death is part of life. I have no fear of death. It just caught me by surprise. But I guess it always does."

"No, no, no, Bertha. You are not there yet. There are treatments, experimental trials." Samuel refused to give up but he stopped talking after Bertha motioned to him with a hand.

"You are the best workmates that God could give a person and I am very blessed to have you. When I am gone, you have to remember to continue to eat healthy."

"Of course," Alisha smiled through the ordeal. "But we still have you here with us for a long time."

Bertha released a long sigh. "I really don't know what I'm going to do. I'll think about it for the next few days and let you know."

They both approached her and gave her a long hug.

Sam kept thinking of finding something to save his friend.

A thin young man with a three-day beard and an overall disheveled look appeared on Sam's Skype window. Behind the scraggly fellow was an array of screens, video cameras, and ethernet cables. The image was one of an eccentricity and dodginess. The image was of Nikolai Nechaev.

"Good to see you, Samuel. How is my old college friend?" A warm smile contrasted markedly with the air of the illicit.

Sam needed some humor and warmth just then.

"Hey Nikolai, good to see you. You still have the same impish look on your face. It makes me think that you're doing things that you ought not be doing. I'll refrain from asking for specifics."

Nikolai laughed. "Me? Of course not. However, we should nonetheless not explore the subject in any depth."

"I hear you. Ahh, remember when Skype encryption was thought safe?"

"It never was. We just thought it was. Anyway, Sanjay tells me you are a famous doctor now. True?"

"A doctor, yes. Not so famous. At least not yet. I'm working on things though. And you?"

"I am professor of computer science at Novosibirsk University. You know the usual computer stuff for large numbers of students who want a way out of Novosibirsk. Nothing that I can't handle."

Samuel laughed. "Modest as always. You do have ingenious skills and I'm pleased that you are imparting at least some of them to younger people."

"Yeah. Some of them. I was just helping a good friend get an airline ticket, first class, to visit his parents."

"How considerate of you, Nikolai." Sam pondered momentarily how he got the ticket.

"Well, what can I say. The poor guy studies in Prague and really wanted to visit his parents in Ekaterinburg. They are not well to do by any means and they spent so much of their money for his education. So . . . I found him a ticket, an electronic one of course, to visit his parents. He was so happy. I like making people happy, especially good friends, you know. It's a calling."

"And however did you find him a ticket?" Samuel braced himself.

"Well, you know the airlines' ticketing systems are not as secure as they should be."

Samuel shook his head. "Yes, of course. And they can't trace you?"

"Oh, every transaction is traceable. Unless you operate from a global server that has millions of share points. Then tracing becomes exponentially more difficult, especially if you are using a fake IP address. What a shame." Nikolai's face expressed profound and contrived sorrow. "But then, we do not need to worry too much for the airlines. They make enough money. Besides, they will learn from me."

"It's comforting to see such compassion."

"Indeed. Hey, Sanjay told me that you are involved in tremendous research and may need my compassion. What is it all about?"

"Yes, I am on to something that, in my opinion, can be crucial for cancer research but I hit a major snag. I need to ramp up my visual power by an enormous amount."

Nikolai's gears were turning. He grabbed a snack bar and took a bite. "And?"

"I need to use the strongest microscope on the planet, Nikolai."

"Okay. I remember that Yale Medical has one. My girlfriend Alina—ah, my beautiful Alina—she mentioned one in Sterling Hall. She's probably a beautiful doctor now."

Sam saw a look of fond nostalgia come across his friend's face. Sam had no time for it though.

"Nikolai! Earth to Novosibirsk! Earth to Novosibirsk! The scope in Sterling Hall is a toy compared to what I need. I need something vastly stronger. There is one of such power right here near us, in Bridgeport. It's called a Photonic Microscope. It uses photons instead of electrons and more importantly for my purposes, it can observe a live culture for a significant amount of time without killing the culture."

"Cool! Then why don't you use that Photonic device." Nikolai finished his snack bar and was searching for another on the desks around him. "Where is something to eat when I am hungry. Oh wait. Do I fit into this somewhere? You don't think I can find you one out here in Siberia, do you? We still use horse sleighs in winter."

"The Photonic Microscope is used for metallurgical research and while they will lease it out to me, the cost is prohibitive. Way beyond what I have and way beyond what dear old Yale will pay. The company wants one million dollars per one day rental."

Nikolai choked on his snack bar and coughed to clear his throat.

"Nikolai, be more careful. Russia needs all the hackers it can get. And for what it's worth, my advice is to eat better food."

"Well, thanks for the dietary advice, doc. Now about this super-duper microscope with the exorbitant fee, I'm beginning to see why Sanjay told you to get in touch with me. But I'm not sure there's anything I can do. A million bucks is a lot of money and the banks and the federal government aren't as careless as they once were. And they're much more vindictive, I can assure you."

"Yeah, but you're in Russia. And you're smarter than they are. You went to Yale. Their security people didn't."

Sam heard his objections yet saw wheels turning in his mind. Nikolai was seeing a challenge set down before him. Banks? Government? Yes, they were better than before. But were the better than he was? Part of Nikolai was saying, "Hell no!"

"Well, maybe I could but this is nuts. A million bucks is a little more serious than a ticket from Prague to Ekaterinburg. This calls for a hack of great majesty."

"It calls for a hacker of great *talent*—and *daring*."

"I don't know, Sam. I've never done anything like that." Nikolai opened a bag of chips and started to eat one after another. "This is, how do the Americans say? It's the major leagues."

"The money has to come from a Yale University account or at least appear like it did. I don't care where you take it from."

Nikolai mumbled trough a mouthful of chips as he began to type away on the keyboard. Sam saw the reflection of a Yale website in Nikolai's glasses as he paused to read. More keystrokes, more reading. An occasional nod and "hmmmm." Nikolai adjusted his glasses and typed and read some more. At length, he turned back to the camera.

"Okay, I may be able to do it."

"You mean you *can* do it. You mean you *will* do it!"

"Sam, you have all the subtlety of one of Putin's security people. Here's what you Americans call the lowdown. I can create an anonymous ghost IP and from there, log into a few fat bank accounts in the Persian Gulf and send a wire. Yes, I can do that." He turned back to the keyboard and blazed away. "When do you need it, Sam?" Without giving Samuel a chance to answer he repeated quickly. "When do you need it, Sam?"

"You are even better than I dared think, my Russian friend—I mean my Russian tovarich!"

"The name of the company to wire to, Sam. Quickly. I need the name of the company not a demonstration of your rich Russian vocabulary."

"AlphaTron. The name is AlphaTron. All one word."

"AlphaTron . . . Yes, AlphaTron. I see it. It is in Bridgeport, Connecticut, 1200 Fairfield Avenue, zip code 06604. Just a few more minutes, please, while I find their Swift Code. Yes, they are banking with Citibank. Good bank. Average security though. Yes, I can see everything. We're in good shape. I don't know why these AlphaTron people have to be so greedy about renting a microscope but then again, this is not my business. Yale has it easy. They just earned one million dollars for a very short time. It will still show on their account though. And . . . yes! We are good to go, Sam." Nikolai then moved his eyes from the screen directly into Samuel's eyes. "Do you authorize?"

"Too fast for me, tovarich. Do I authorize what?"

"Do you authorize one million dollars to be wired to AlphaTron Corporation by Yale University? Yes or no, Sam."

"Uh, yes, yes. I authorize. I mean *da, da.*"

"Good." Nikolai's eyes moved back to the screen. He silently typed for few more minutes and then hit the enter key and wiped his forehead. "Done. You know, Sam, I always believed in your capabilities and I want to be part of this, but you have to promise me one thing."

"Anything."

Nikolai gave him a very serious look. "That you'll bring me cigarettes when you visit me in jail." Then he laughed wildly and lit a cigarette. "American cigarettes!"

"I may be in the cell with you, so I'll have to find someone to bring us both American cigarettes."

"But as I recall, you don't smoke."

"I may pick it up in prison."

The new colony was large and had plenty of food. The governor was satisfied. The glucose was plentiful and they could multiply and grow. The assistant leader was pleased.

"We are at optimal condition, sir. All activities are conducted as schedule."

"Good, good. This is always good to hear." The governor observed the colony's activity. "Dismissed."

Although everything looked normal he had a feeling that something was not right. Things were just too perfect.

⌒

That morning they received a message from Bertha. She'd been hospitalized at Yale Medical Center. The news was troubling but not enervating. On the contrary, it added a sense of urgency to what was at hand. It was not simply research, nor was it simply a feather in their resumes. It was an urgent matter. A friend's life was slowly ebbing away as cancer spread from her lungs to other parts of her body—her body that seemed so healthy only two weeks ago.

"Yale must think highly of you, Dr. Daniels. I've never seen them handle a financial transaction of this size so quickly. You must have promising research. I'm sure you do."

"I like to think so too. But it helps to have friends who can expedite things."

Samuel's hand was almost shaking as he performed the final adjustments on the Photonic Microscope's lenses. Alex, AlphaTron's lead engineer, helped him with software on the controlling Cray 7000 supercomputer. Alisha prepared the specimen and placed it in the tray beneath the mighty device. She had chosen to hear only the vaguest outline of how AlphaTron was paid for the day rental. The research program would go on, somehow or another.

Nikolai was reasonably sure that it would take Yale at least a month to find out just what had happened. That was a month for Sam and Alisha to get somewhere. Somewhere big and important in the field of cancer research. Even if his tovarich was right, and even if the research was highly successful, Yale might not be amused.

The Photonic Microscope was housed in a spacious hall, roughly the size of an old movie theater or one of the churches that graced the towns of the Connecticut countryside. Computer gear and power units lined the white sides of the eerie interior. The floor and walls were made from finely honed metal that would greatly reduce ambient interference with the device. The device itself was sealed inside a cylindrical chamber about fifteen feet high and ten feet in diameter.

Those permitted to enter had to wear contamination-proof garb reminiscent of that worn in semiconductor plants or by medical personnel treating deadly diseases such as the Ebola virus. Before entering, Sam and Alisha entered an access hall in which high-power vacuums sucked the tiniest of impurities from them and their suits.

They looked in wonder at the Photonic device. It was as though they were seeing a sacred relic or a gift from an advanced civilization that had mysteriously come and gone from the planet, known to only a few initiates who kept its amazing attributes far from public attention.

On a large, almost barren desk were two tablets which would be used to control the precise details of the experiment. Sam and Alisha would be assisted in this by AlphaTron's lead engineer, Alex Karpov, who gently took the petri dishes from Sam and Alisha and placed the first of them into the inspection bay beneath the cannon-like tube that fired photons into the cancer specimens. Alex signaled that everything was ready to go.

"All set?" Samuel asked Alisha.

"I'm ready, Teddy."

Samuel turned on the magnetic coils that created a powerful electromagnetic field, causing a low hum to build in the photon cannon.

"Alex, activate the cannon, if you would."

Alex keyed in a few commands on a tablet and lights atop the cannon glowed and the hum rose in pitch an amplitude to an unsettling level. The lens moved slowly toward the cancer specimens until it was only inches away. At that point, the device began firing photons in copious quantities and then extracting precise images that were burned into a pair of 4 terabyte hard drives that Sam borrowed from the office. Simultaneously, an AI program analyzed the images and converted the binary based information into 3D and 2D images as a sliced cut of the specimen.

The Photonic Microscope's main advantages are that the photons are emitted in pairs and at high velocity. The pair is significant because the detection of one photon is an unambiguous sign that another has also been emitted. It's like a time stamp that says a photon is on its way. Second, these pairs are fired in a very high frequency which provides astonishing and unrivaled sampling rates.

As the first photon hits the sampled specimen, it bounces into a deflector, which analyzes the photon speed and energy lost. Feeding into real-time software, the program builds a two-dimensional image of the specimen. This image will be translated into 3D image later. Hardly a task for even the finest desktop, or even a dozen of them linked in series, a supercomputer had been designed and built by Cray.

The second photon acts as an "error protocol corrector." It repeats the same operation as the first one to ensure that the data was saved correctly. The scope's photon canon emits billions of pairs of photons per second. The wavelength of the photons can be changed by heating or cooling the main crystal and thereby changing its size. This enables a rainbow of colors that can be painted over the sample for better detail.

This microscope can be tuned to various different atomic transitions allowing investigation of a variety of different atomic structures and patterns. Together with advanced computer software, 2D and 3D images are formed. The images can be rotated and viewed from all angles due to the software's simulation capabilities. The enormous magnification factors opens a whole world of possibilities in many scientific arenas.

But the most important feature is the ability to observe live specimens without killing them.

"Sir, we noticed a disturbance in our environment. It doesn't have any danger to us but still I believe that we should alert the others." The assistant leader was concerned.

"What is the nature of this disturbance?"

"It's hard to tell. It's in our perimeter." The assistant's leader reported to the governor.

"Is it some kind of attack?"

"It doesn't look like an attack. There are no signs of any disaster or dangerous conditions but it has caused particle changes."

"We can't take any risk. Alert the others."

"Are you sure, sir? It may be something minor."

"Alert the others." The governor was not willing to take any chance.

"Yes, sir."

"Dismissed."

"I got something! I got something!" Samuel almost screamed out the news inside the glass cylinder.

"Yes, I can see it also." Alisha beamed in astonishment and wonder.

The three of them looked at the 52" monitors as colorful patterns formed. Areas of the molecular structure were taking on differences in color and shape.

"What do you know? I never saw anything like this before."

"You should look at something besides metal for a change," Alisha quipped.

"Metal rules!" Alex shot back.

The display became even more alive as the image continued to generate from the mighty Cray supercomputer. No more quips, only silent awe. More and more detail. More and more resolution. More and more changes in structure and color. They could see straight lines of black dots that seemed to extend to infinity. The lines occasionally waved about as though they were wheat shoots touched by a gentle breeze that came and went.

Samuel turned off the coil's switch, ending the EMF flow.

There was no immediate response. The waves of dots were unchanged. But two minutes later it happened. The dots stopped their waving motions and straightened into fixed structure.

Sam restarted the EMF flow.

After two minutes, the waves of dots reorganized themselves into a different pattern.

"Absolutely amazing." Alisha spoke in a low almost reverent tone. "You were right, Sam. This is a response and not a random one. Not purely chemical. It does look like something is making the changes on purpose." She turned towards Samuel. "Let's try a few more times. I want to be sure."

"With pleasure."

They implemented the changes in EMF several times, each time with the same remarkable results. The molecular structure changed in a regular pattern. They increased the EMF strength but this didn't seem to affect the pattern. As long as the EMF was activated, the molecular structure reorganized itself in the same pattern. When the EMF was turned off, the cells returned to their normal structure.

"I don't know exactly what I'm witnessing. However, I sense it's something remarkable. But what is it?" Alex was all but pleading.

"These are cancer cells," Samuel explained. "When we put them in certain conditions, they change in a certain way." Then he looked straight into Alex's eyes. "I believe this is sign of a form of intelligence."

It took Alex few seconds to comprehend. "Are you saying that the cancer cells are intelligent?"

"There is no other explanation." Samuel squeezed his lips and pointed to the screen. "How else would you explain that?"

"It may be a simple chemical reaction."

Alisha shook her head. "Not like that. A chemical reaction would show in a different way. The molecular structure change would be irreversible. For example, chocolate melts with heat but will not return to its previous form after cooling it off. Here we see an accurate change that is completely reversible."

"It's like turning a light bulb on and off." Samuel murmured. "It's signaling."

"Exactly."

Alex still had difficulties to understand. "But these are microorganisms. How can they do such things?"

"That's exactly what I am trying to find out." Samuel nodded towards the screen. "How can they do such things?"

They stared at the screen for a while.

"Can you record the screen shots?" Samuel broke the silence.

"As a matter of fact the entire session is being recorded on a JPEG4 movie file. You will have it by the end of the day." Alex smiled. "You paid for it. It's yours."

"Yeah." Samuel shook his head. "And at what a price."

"Wait. Can you please take a printout of the dots patterns with and without the EMF on a file, even graphic file? I have a software that will recognize patterns. I would like to feed it to this program." Samuel was excited. "Maybe it's binary code or similar."

"Sure, I'll create a few files for you."

"Thanks, Alex."

They continued their experiment the entire day. Samuel changed the EMF strength and polarity, with and without seawater and other elements. The basic results remained the same.

⌐⌐

"I am not gone yet!" Bertha spoke defiantly from her hospital bed. "I'm getting tired of all these needles that they stick in me, though." She looked weak but her spirit was strong as Samuel and Alisha visited her at Yale Medical Center. "How are my two darlings doing?"

Alisha tried to keep her own spirit strong. "We are not the ones to worry about. Bertha, our doctors are trying to help you. Please cooperate with them."

"Yes, but they keep sticking these IVs in me and plying me with medicine. It just doesn't do anything."

"Have any family members been by to see you?" Alisha asked.

"Yes, my sister was here two days ago. She flew in from in Portland, Maine, and poor her, it took her two days to get down here. The train made countless stops and it was hard on her."

Alisha looked at her chart that one of the doctors gave her. She bit her lips quietly.

"Not that good, eh?" Bertha looked at her eyes. "Ah, I don't want to talk about it anymore. How are you two doing? Are you getting somewhere with your research project?"

Samuel sat near her and held her hand. "Yes, Bertha. As a matter of fact today I think we managed a significant step forward. We are on to something that may change the way we think. Please hang on for as long as you can and I am sure that we will get more findings that will help."

"I am not going anywhere, Sam. I'll be right here." Bertha smiled frailly. "I'll try."

Samuel gave her a hug. "Just hang in there, Bertha. Hang in there for a little bit more time."

"There is something . . . very peculiar with the recent condition's change, sir." The assistant leader was hesitant.

"Peculiar?"

"Yes, as you remember we had active perimeter changes recently. We've never experienced so many of them. They were not harmful. Still, we didn't take any risk and transmitted warning signals to all colonies. I conducted a research of my own, sir. It seems like these changes are exactly the same and repeating. Some of them are slightly different environmentally but they are all of the same nature and concept. They repeat themselves many times it's like. . . ."

"Like what?"

"Like they are done intentionally."

The governor was puzzled.

"I hesitate to say so but it's like these changes have some meaning, sir." The assistant almost whispered.

"Meaning? What kind of meaning?"

"We don't know. It is just an assumption of course, sir. These repeated changes look like a message—one sent by intelligent life-forms."

"Intelligent? But this is impossible. We already know from years of experience that these are environmental changes caused by climate and other perimeter conditions."

"Yes, but these ones are different, sir. They consist of the same nature and pattern. I think—as do my assistants—that these changes are done intentionally by an intelligent life-form."

"Aliens. . . ." The governor had difficulty in comprehending the idea. He knew about all the phenomena that were recorded over many years—the deadly clouds and the storms. There was never mention in all of their historical documentation about alien life-form.

"I am not sure about aliens but we suspect an intelligent life-form that is creating these changes."

The governor remained silent. "What do we do about it? We need a plan."

"Well, for now, we can't do much. These changes are causing us no harm. They may in the future though. In any case, there is nothing that we can do. This is a greater power than ours."

"Indeed. Keep investigating. We need more information. Much more. Let me know immediately about any new event."

"I will, sir."

"Dismissed."

"I made you a cucumber sandwich. You'll love it!" Alisha entered Samuel's office as he was sitting in front of the computer screen. It was midnight and he was still working on encoding the patterns that they printed from the Photonic Microscope. "How are you doing here?"

"I can't figure out the pattern's meaning." Samuel took a large bite of the sandwich. "Thanks for the snack. I *do* love it."

"Sam, you should get some rest. You are working days and nights. Take a break for a while."

"I can't, Alisha. This is the key thing to the entire theory. If I find the meaning of this changing pattern, it can be the biggest thing to hit medicine in the last century."

"I know, and you are right, but you have to rest your brain sometime. Then get back to it with a renewed mind and body."

Samuel released a long sigh. "Yeah, I guess you're right. Maybe I am done for the night." He gave one more look at the screen and shook his head. "I tried so many approaches. I tried binary language, all kind of bases, logarithms, and even integrals and differential pairs approach. The program I am using is one of the best in its field for pattern recognition and yet, I have no conclusive results. There are no meaningful repetitions, no consistency to assemble some type of logical message. I tried all kind of mathematical formulas and analysis but nothing seems to work."

Alisha could see near despair on his face. She couldn't hold herself. She hugged him to her heart. Samuel closed his eyes and simply treasured a very pleasant surprise. The attraction built until he couldn't hold himself back. He kissed her. Her soft, warm lips sent sparks of passion throughout his body and he held her tight. At first she slightly resisted drifting away, obeying her logical sense, but then the flames of love caught her.

Their hands found their way and heedlessly explored each other's bodies. Samuel tossed all objects from his desk and she lay down there immediately. She moaned as he kissed her passionately. Within seconds they had shed their clothing and the passion that was held back for months erupted and only when they were truly satisfied and exhausted did they lay next to each other, covered with sweat and breathing heavily.

"Do you know how long I've wanted you?" Samuel whispered into her ear.

She giggled. "No!"

"From the first moment that I saw you."

"Really?"

"Yes, really."

"So what took you so long?"

Now it was his turn to laugh. "I don't know. The office setting . . . rules . . . norms."

"Still, you should always listen to your heart."

He looked deep into her eyes. "Yes, I know the cliché but there are always logical reasons for not moving forward. I don't know, all my previous relationship were not shining successes."

She played with his curly hair. "Well, I can't blame you much. I wanted you also and didn't do anything about it."

"Really?"

"Aha!"

He sealed her lips with a kiss and soon they were drifting in the passion of love again.

Bertha coughed uncontrollably in a dry, pointless manner.

Alisha poured water into the hospital cup.

Bertha took long sips to relax her cough reflex. "Thank you," she said softly, hoping her bout had passed.

Samuel was struck by how wan and frail she looked. Her skin was almost translucent and her eyes were red and swollen. The joy of life was taking its leave from her eyes. They were now dim and almost vacant.

It's like life has left her. Samuel thought.

He looked at Alisha and wiped a tear. As doctors, they both clearly saw the signs. Bertha was dying.

Bertha summoned her vitality. "And how are my two favorite, brilliant doctors doing this fine day?"

"We are doing well, Bertha. How do you feel? That's more important."

"They keep changing the story everyday. One time they say it spread all over my body, and one time they say it's only spread to my kidneys and liver. Does it really matter?"

Samuel hugged her and sat on her bed. Bertha sensed his good heart and simply patted him on his head. "And how is your research going, Samuel? Are you going to be the most famous doctor in the world soon? I'm sorry if I keep asking you about your work, but I think about it always."

"Thank you, Bertha, but I don't want to be the most famous doctor in the world. I just want to save lives, one at a time."

"I always loved this feature in you, Sam. You are such a gentle and wonderful soul. You are not looking for fame and glory, only to save lives. That's the sign of a true doctor, you know."

Bertha held his hand in hers. Samuel lowered his eyes to fight off the tears.

Bertha touched his chin, lifting his eyes to hers. "There is no need to be ashamed of crying, Sam. I am crying almost every day. I am looking at the sunshine through my room's window and I cry when I eat my food—every meal. But I want you to know that you both are my family and I love you dearly. You gave me the love and the care that only family does. No one is immortal, it is just a matter of time."

"I feel so close to having answers, Bertha." Samuel's voice was scratchy. "If I could have a few more months, I am sure that I could help."

Bertha shook her head with a smile. "Sam, don't take it personally. We both know that I'll not be here in a few months, and this is fine with me. I came to closure with this. It is important that you'll help many others with this same sickness."

Alisha wept quietly.

"I heard this quote somewhere but I can't remember when." Bertha's face all but illuminated. "Don't cry because it's over, be happy that it happened." She gave them a heartfelt look. "I am happy that you both are in my life. I am happy that you both happened to me."

Alisha and Samuel held Bertha's hands and couldn't say a word.

Nikolai sat on his chair and looked expressionlessly into the Skype window at Sam's image.

"Say, Nikolai, did you even move from your chair since the last time that we talked?" Samuel scratched his head. "I think you were even wearing the same clothes."

Nikolai didn't answer but continued staring at Samuel.

"Never mind," Samuel continued. "I need your help one more time."

Nikolai turned to his computer and typed rapidly on his wireless keyboard, completely ignoring Samuel.

"Nikolai?"

After a few minutes he looked into the webcam at Samuel. "You forgot the magic word."

Samuel's forehead's wrinkled.

"And yes, sometimes, when I am in the middle of a life-changing, awesome challenge, I can't even go to the bathroom. But no, these are different clothes and I took a shower this morning. I do appreciate your concern."

"I'm truly glad to hear that. What is the magic word?"

Nikolai grinned alike a mischievous child. "Please."

"Sir, we are getting the same perimeter changes as we had in the recent past." The assistant leader was agitated. "You can come with me and I'll show you."

The governor and the assistant moved quickly to the boundaries. And there it was.

Biological cell membranes are selectively permeable, which means that the ease and rate of small molecules passing through membranes vary widely. The plasma membrane regulates exchange of nutrients, oxygen, inorganic ions, waste products, and water. The cellular membrane's molecular organization controls permeability. A cell's plasma membrane consists of a bilayer of lipid molecules, which allow certain molecules to pass more easily than others. Additionally, transport proteins may aid certain molecules to cross the plasma membrane. These proteins either provide a channel or physically bind and transport the specific molecule across the membrane.

The governor and the assistants watched how molecules and ions re-organized in what looks like random order.

"See, these particles are moving in a certain way and pattern." The assistant leader referred to a series of molecules that were defusing through the membrane. "It seems like they move randomly and without any order, but if you'll look closely you'll see a consistent pattern."

And indeed the molecules quickly arranged in many structures alternatively. After a while some of the structures repeated.

"No doubt about it. These are repeated patterns." The governor moved gently with the plasma's layers.

"I have an idea, sir."

"Yes?"

"With your permission I would like to change our global transmission. We'll still transmit the same message but the method will be different. Since there is a very strong tendency for particles to move from higher concentration to low, just based on thermal energy. Particles at normal conditions have very high speeds and random motions. We will change our boundary condition regarding particle size, polarity, and other features. This will keep transmitting the same message but with different conditions. Do I have your approval to do so, sir?"

"Make it so."

"Thank you, sir."

"Dismissed."

Accelerated by the production of enzymes, the cells started to pump sodium from a region of lower concentration to a region of higher concentration. Other cells transported energy to pump ions like calcium, amino acids, and other electrically-charged molecules either into or out of the cells.

Ions carry positive or negative electrical charges so that the gradients have two components: a concentration gradient and a voltage or electrical gradient. This potential difference across the membrane was used as an energy source to move other charged molecules. Positively-charged molecules were attracted towards the inside of the cells and the negatively charged molecules, so they were attracted to the boundary's molecules of the cells. It was the electrical potential that caused positively-charged potassium ions to enter the cells, even though they were moving up their concentration gradient.

The potential energy of the gradient was used to produce glucose to transport other molecules across membranes. The glucose created gradient that appeared to be a pattern. This pattern was aimed to transmit a message. Although the pattern was different than before, it still transmitted the same message.

"This is different than before. Do you see that, Alisha?" Samuel was fascinated as they looked into the large screens of the Photonic Microscope. "We used the same culture and the same specimen as before, yet we are getting different pattern."

"No doubt about that." Alisha was transfixed on the image. "What can it be?"

"I don't know . . . I simply don't know." Samuel murmured. "But we have to find out."

"Well, maybe you two are drifting too far into the inner galaxy of these cells." Alex, the AlphaTron adviser, chided good-naturedly.

"No, we are not drifting at all. As a matter of fact, I think that this change is done on purpose and it will bring us to a new understanding."

"Not sure why you think that. I really don't."

"Sometimes even science has to operate on hunches."

Alex nodded as he started to pack their specimens. "One thing I must say. Your feelings cost your university a bundle. I hope one day all of these efforts will be justified."

"Yes, but all I need to know is the language."

"Language? What language?" Alex raised a brow.

Samuel didn't hesitate even for a second. "The language that the cancer cells use to communicate."

Samuel and Alisha kissed gently as they lay on the shore near Mystic after a full day sailing on the Atlantic. The campfire was down to embers and the pine logs crackled and flared. The ocean waves slowly lapped the beach and the lights of ships gently flickered on the horizon. Samuel and Alisha cuddled inside their sleeping bag.

"We must do this more often." Alisha whispered into Samuel's ear.

His first response was a soft kiss. "You'll never know how long I waited for this moment. There are so many places we should see. This is only the first of my ideas."

She laughed. "You have great ideas then. It's a shame that we wasted all these past months. We could have done this many times by now."

"What's in the past is in the past. Let's live the present and ponder the future."

"Hallelujah! Tonight is probably one of the best nights I ever remember."

"I love to watch the ships on their way to and from ports. For some people I am sure it is their first visit to New York. I wonder if people still call it the Big Apple."

"For some it may be a new beginning." Alisha added.

"New York—I love that city. It doesn't matter how many times I go there, every time my heart races with excitement. The city itself has a heartbeat. Really. If you stop and listen you can hear the city's pulse. Yes, I know, it is probably the giant air conditioning fans on top of the buildings or maybe the subway system rumbling underneath, but still, to me it sounds like the city's heart beat."

Alisha smiled. "You are such a romantic guy, Samuel. I never would have guessed it, until recently."

"I save a few more surprises for you."

"Can't wait for the others!"

Samuel sealed her lips with a kiss and the flames of love caught them. They let their passions take over as the firewood grew from embers to flames as a seaward breeze came in. They made love passionately into the night and then laid together, enjoying the night, enjoying the moment. Until.

"This research is very important, Alisha. I'll give anything to see it's completion."

"You already have. You are breaking the law—seriously. You don't give up and you're doing everything you can to overcome this challenge. Sometimes I don't know where you get the powers from, Sam. I consider myself motivated and passionate, but nothing like you.

You're made of unique people-molecules. People-molecules like those in Einstein, Edison, and Madame Curie."

"Thank you, sweet one. I am not sure about Einstein though. I sure hope not to go to jail one day."

"You told me that Nikolai is the best in his field—whatever exactly that is."

"Yes, he is, but even he said that every scheme like this is eventually discovered. The question is how long it takes. I am hoping that by then we'll have big news and the university will forgive me."

Alisha smiled in the dark and caressed his head. "And pay the money back."

"Yes."

"I love you, Samuel."

He kissed her and they became afire again.

The stars above flickered in billions of lights as though applauding the passionate couple below.

Samuel was alone on a small island. He didn't know how he got there. All he knew was that he was soaking wet and freezing. He looked around. The island was very small, maybe a hundred feet in diameter. He could see seawater surrounding it. It was almost dark. The western horizon was still orange from the last sun beams but darkness progressed rapidly. There were no trees or bushes. It was just a little piece of land in the middle of nowhere. He was alone and he was shivering. His brain worked fast.

How did I get here?

Where is Alisha?

What's going on?

As much as he tried to think what happened he couldn't come to any logical explanation.

The seawater looked clear and an extraordinary cyan color. He never remembered seawater to be that bright and clear. He couldn't stop himself from entering the water. It was warm and felt unusual.

He dipped his hand in the water. It was as though the sea called upon him to feel it, to interact with it. He moved his fingers inside the blue water and closed his eyes.

And then he knew.

This is it. It is the sea.

He opened his eyes and took a deep breath.

It is the sea. It was always the sea. From day one. The sea started this chain of events.

The sea is the key to find the way to communicate with the cells.

Samuel woke up breathing heavily and raised upright in the sleeping bag. Curled near him was Alisha, sleeping calmly. It took him a while to return to reality.

I am with Alisha, on the beach. . . .

He looked at the ship's lights in the distance. They flickered as the ships moved towards their destination.

"Alisha, sweetheart, I think I found a new direction." He kissed her all over her face and she opened her beautiful green eyes.

"What?" She reluctantly became alert. "What are you talking about, Sam?"

"I am saying that I think I know the key to the language. I just had a beautiful dream about it."

Her eyes rounded in curiosity. "What is it?"

"It originates in the sea."

"The sea? Why the sea?"

"The seawater caused this breakthrough, Alisha. Without that tiny drop falling into the petri dish nothing would have happened. The key to this puzzle is seawater. Remember the patterns we saw? I believe that with some clue from the sea, we'll be able to proceed. We have to investigate this."

Alisha was fascinated. "You may be right. Everything started because of a drop of seawater. Otherwise, we would have not be here today.

"After so many languages and options that we already tried, we must take a different direction." He gave her a quick peck. "Now, come on. Let's get dressed and go do some real research."

Alisha didn't like the idea just then.

"Now? You want to leave this romantic moment and go do research?"

Samuel prepared for the worse.

But then something happened and her face became cheerful. "Seawater. . . . Wait a minute. I just remembered that my father knows an elderly Chinese fellow. He calls him 'the master of the sea.' Since I was a child I always wondered why he called him that. 'Well, my child, this is because this wise Chinese man is an expert in the wisdom of the sea'."

"The wisdom of the sea?" Samuel raised a brow.

Yes, he is the master of the sea."

"Well, let's go. What we are waiting for?"

"In the middle of the night? No." She pulled him to the sleeping bag. "But I'll take you to him tomorrow. He lives in Chinatown, in New York City. He owns a seafood restaurant."

"Don't look so disappointed. I know how to make this go away." She covered Samuel's face with kisses.

She was right.

They arrived in Chinatown just after the morning rush hour. The weather was cold but unthreatening and the streets were full of tourists from all around the world. Smoke from local cooking was seen everywhere. Colorful jewelry and bric-a-brac filled every shop window. People filled the little stores looking for things that they probably didn't need and would never use. But the atmosphere was cheerful and joyous and many a wallet and purse opened eagerly.

They parked on Mott Street and Alisha led them to a restaurant at the end of Canal Street.

"You're going to love this place." She beamed towards Samuel. "There's no place like it."

As they entered the restaurant, a short woman with pearl earrings took them by their hands to a large oval table. They didn't have any time to say anything. She sat them on two small chairs and vanished into the kitchen, promising that a man would soon be arriving.

Samuel noticed something. "Check this out."

In the center of the table there was a pile of green bean pods. A very old woman sat near them, opening each pod and tossing the peas into a porcelain bowl. She never looked at them or spoke. She simply pealed the pods and tossed the peas into the bowl.

"How long do you think it will take her to do that?" Samuel whispered. "I never saw such a humongous pile of green beans in all my life. Look here. She is old but she does her job quietly and diligently."

"It will take her all day long to peal these green beans but she's been doing this for years." A man's voice sounded.

They both turned and saw an aged man smiling at them. He was short and bearded, dressed simply but for a necklace with a large, blue stone. They were both transfixed by it.

"Ah, you noticed. This is a blue emerald of the ocean. It can be found only in certain locations of the China Sea." He gave them a smile. "I have a feeling that you are not here for the food."

"Ah, yes." Alisha found her voice. "We came here for your advice. My father used to visit you and he took me with him. It was many years ago."

The old man's eyes squeezed until they couldn't see his eyes. "Yes, your father is from Greece. He used to come see me every time he visited New York. I remember you. You were a child then. Yes?"

Alisha smiled. "Yes, that's me."

"How can I be of an assistance to the daughter of an old friend?"

Alisha and Samuel looked at each other. They just realized that they didn't prepare for this conversation. What would they ask from him? About what? It was Samuel that found his words. "Well, we are both doctors that are conducting research on cancer. We got a significant breakthrough when a drop of seawater dropped on a specimen."

"Amazing! Then you must want the Ancient Code of the Sea." The old man said in low voice as he was holding his blue emerald. "You need the code."

He remained quiet for a while and they stared at him without understanding.

"Come follow me, please." He led them to a small room which had presumably been used for special events but which was empty. A faded picture of an old fisherman and another of a craggy coastline were hung on the wall and that was it. There were no other decorations or windows.

"Please sit down." The old man sat on a small stool.

"I was waiting for this day for many years. No one came to me, asking for the Ancient Code. I am seventy-nine years old and soon I'll be eighty. I'll die when I am eighty. I am happy that I'll be able to do my duty and provide you with the code before my time comes."

He seemed encouraged as Alisha and Samuel remained silent.

"What is the Ancient Code of the Sea?" Samuel couldn't hold himself from asking.

"This is the code of all living things on earth. Only a few people know about it. I received it from my father and he received it from his father. See, my father was a monk and received the code to keep as a secret. We only knew it had some great intrinsic value that would benefit the world someday."

"And what is the code?" Alisha's eyes sparkled with excitement.

"I don't know." The old man answered quietly.

Samuel and Alisha were confused.

"But this stone holds it." He watched their confusion in amusement.

He removed the necklace and showed them the blue emerald. "This doesn't have tremendous commercial value, but I think for you it will be worth everything."

They both looked at the stone as it gently shone in the old man's wrinkled hands. It didn't sparkle as a diamond would. It glowed from an internal light. It was as though the stone had an inner source of energy.

"One day, my father told me, one day someone will need this code to benefit the world. Then, and only then, give it to them. Until then you are to keep this stone in your possession at all times."

He looked at them with a smile and handed them the stone. "The day has come. I give this stone to you today, to benefit the world."

With shaky hands Samuel took the stone. "Thank you but . . . how do we use it? What do we do with it?"

"I don't know. You'll have to find the way. My father said, 'Give them the stone. They'll find the code within it. They'll know what to do'."

Samuel and Alisha looked at each other.

"How do you know that we are the right people?" Samuel had to ask.

"I've kept this stone almost seventy years now. No one else will claim the code. You are doctors looking to help the world. You are the people. My name is Hai, which means 'sea' in Chinese. The last name is not important."

Samuel and Alisha didn't know what to say.

"One thought I can leave you with."

Alisha and Samuel's eyes rose to the old man.

"My father mentioned one thing about the code. The stone has to be underwater but not any water. You need to go to Palawan."

"Palawan?" Samuel all but exclaimed.

"Palawan is an archipelago of many islands in the western Philippines. You may enjoy your stay there." He smiled. "But the most important thing to remember, you'll need to go to Miniloc Island. When you get there you'll have to find a place called the Cliff of the Sea. You need to take the stone there. I don't know exactly why, I just remember that my father mentioned this place. As a child I grew up in this area so I visited that reef. Of course, I didn't do anything special about it. This will be your task."

"But . . . what shall we do with the stone there? I mean, I don't know! Going to where? China?" Samuel was confused. He held the stone, observing it without knowing what to say.

"Actually, it is the Philippines." The old man smiled again. "Go there. You are both young. You'll enjoy. Trust Hai."

"Thank you, we'll go there." Alisha smiled. "Any other useful information that may help us, Hai?"

"Oh yes. Be with the stone under the reef's gap early in the morning, when the sun rises. It has to be directly under the cliff as the sun rises. Look at the stone when the sun rises, but don't look too close. This is important."

"Don't look too close? I *completely* don't understand. Could you please explain why not to look too close?" Samuel scratched his head.

"Because the closer you are, the less you see."

Samuel looked with great disbelief at Alisha. "What? It doesn't make any sense. Alisha, please. Going to the Philippines to put this rock under a reef in the China Sea?"

"Do you want to know the Ancient Code of the Sea, young man, or not?" The old man spoke without a hint of mirth.

"Well, yes I do."

"Then do as I said." The old man looked at them quietly for a while. "And that's all that I have to say, except that I wish you both good luck."

"Thank you, Hai. We truly appreciate your help. We'll come and see you after we are back, hopefully with the code."

"Thank you but it will not be necessary. I'll not be alive anymore. I shall be eighty very soon." The old man smiled. "Go and good luck."

"Thank you." Alisha stood up. "We are leaving, Sam."

"Yes, thank you. Alisha can I ask you something please?"

"Not now, Sam."

They stepped out into the sun and din of Canal Street.

"You guys are going where?" Nikolai cleaned his smudged glasses and took a bite from a red apple. "Manila? The Philippines? Man, can I come with you? No, they'll never let me go now. It's mid-terms here."

"This trip almost cost me my job, Nikolai. Stan didn't like it very well but for this Ancient Code of the Sea, we have to go."

"Yes, I read your email. This is fascinating stuff, Sam. A reef at sunrise. Very mysterious." He took another loud bite from his apple. "How exactly are you going to do that?"

"I leave this to Alisha. She's the one who got us in touch with this idea." Samuel role his eyes. "I mean, what are the odds that some adventure in China Sea will get us the information to break the code? Science this ain't."

"Yes, but the whole thing is very unscientific, Sam. Give it a chance. Enjoy a vacation on those beautiful beaches." Nikolai gave him a big grin. "Hey, would you like me to arrange you a free flight?"

"No, thank you, Nikolai. We don't want to take any more risks than we need to. But the reason that I'm calling you is to ask your recommendation about what to take for this experiment? We need to find a code. Some sequence that can lead us to understand the cell's code."

"But of course. I'll give you an entire list of souvenirs to buy me."

"No, Nikolai. Digital equipment. I am going to need your help solving this."

"Yes, of course. You know the main clue that grabbed my attention when you described the meeting with the Chinese guy?" Nikolai was typing as he talked.

"What?"

"The closer you are, the less you see. Read your email. I sent you an exact list of what to take with you."

⌒

Samuel and Alisha took off on a 50-seater ATR aircraft from Manila to El Nido, Palawan. As they disembarked, the heat and humidity hit them. Connecticut it wasn't.

"We should mark this spot for vacation." Alisha kissed Samuel happily. "I love traveling, even if it does take us into tropical climes. We have to get to the dock for the next part of our journey."

The next fifty minutes were unpleasant. The high wind and wild waves tossed the small ferryboat about, making them both queasy. Sometimes more than that. They concentrated on the views of islands and fishing craft and the dock was soon in view.

"This is the beautiful Miniloc Island!" The ferry captain announced over the scratchy PA system. "Enjoy your stay and do take part in ocean activities and be sure to see the spectacular limestone cliffs overlooking vast schools of tropical fish and coral reefs stretching for miles."

"First, I need to settle my stomach, but thank you." Samuel mumbled weakly as he walked down the creaking gangplank.

Everything was ready early the following morning. They hired a guide to take them out just before sunrise. They rented scuba gear and listened to the guide's safety instructions.

Alisha shivered in the night air as the small motor boat made its way to the cliff. It was rather far away from all tourist attractions. The water was calm and clear blue and colorful fishes and sea plants could be easily seen in the moonlight.

After half an hour, they arrived at a black cliff shaped like a hand stretched toward the sky. A gap, no larger than a small car, lay at the base and from it stretching out into the sea was a land portion of the reef.

"We're expected to go inside that opening?" Sam looked at Alisha worriedly.

"Well, that's part of the challenge, Sam. Now brace yourself for adventure and let's prepare the electronic gear that Nikolai mentioned.

Nikolai had suggested documenting the event with underwater cameras. He recommended wide-angle lenses and a computer-controlled sequencer. A still camera would take continuous shots at very short intervals.

As the sun began to glow beneath the horizon, Samuel and Alisha put on their scuba gear and went under the gap in the cliff. They looked back at the red skies then swam under the cliff. There was a very small gap underwater and the water was very shallow, only a few feet.

Samuel looked at Alisha and shrugged his shoulders. She motioned for him to hold up the necklace and he did so as cameras fired intermittently. They looked above to the surface and saw the red streaks of sunrise flashing and darting with the tide.

Samuel held the blue emerald toward the surface and in a moment the sunlight found the stone and illuminated the waters with scores of blue flashes and rays. Extraordinary blues lit up the rocks around them and the sandy floor beneath them. They felt part of an ancient rite from a long lost civilization and they were the high priests in a ceremony they felt part of but did not fully understand.

The rite continued to their amazement and wonder until the sunbeams no longer struck the emerald as directly and the dazzling lights faded away. Samuel moved the stone about hoping to restore the magic but soon realized the moment was gone, perhaps forever.

They rose to the surface and returned to their hotel with the cameras.

They transferred the data to a laptop and prepared to try to understand what had happened in the waters beneath the hand-like cliff. The images and footage were spectacular but just what it meant for cancer research eluded them.

They went over the material again and again. Room service brought them sandwiches and soft drinks and they ate as they watched the sunbeams strike the surface and then the emerald. Alisha lay back on the bed and began to stew.

"The Ancient Code of the Sea," mumbled Alisha with more than a measure of sarcasm. "A mysterious old man in a restaurant might just have led us on a fool's errand." She looked at the emerald on the night stand and thought it just another junky trinket from a New York souvenir shop.

"Wait a minute! I think I see something!"

"What?" Alisha got up and stood behind Sam.

"The light sparkling on the rocks are forming a pattern. This pattern is not random. I can identify repetitions."

"Really? I'm afraid I don't quite see it."

"Well, I'll need a computer program to analyze this. The pattern might be turned into a code. A binary code. This is definitely work for one of Nikolai's programs. The old man was right. The data cannot be analyzed from close distance. The digital camera had to be fairly far away in order to catch the accurate ray pattern."

"As he said, the closer you are, the less you see. And the use of a digital program from Russia puts us even farther away from the stone and light than we thought."

"My dear, we have work ahead of us."

The return flight seemed much longer than the one out there. A thousand thoughts raced through their minds but couldn't be meaningfully evaluated. They landed at JFK, took a commuter hop to New Haven, and made a beeline for the office where the data was fed into the lab's Cray computer.

"Ready?"

Alisha nodded and Sam began to run the analysis program. A progress bar started to show the resource-intensive process.

The pattern-recognition program initiated an analysis trying to imitate the human visual cortex. The program was based on geometrical engine algorithms and analyzed large amounts of data within picoseconds. An incomprehensible number of complex computations were executed for the purpose of quantitative information extraction. Each ray and sparkle was analyzed, matched, and compared in real time to all known communication methods. Billions of computations were made, calculating coordinates of shapes. An advanced version of a scan-line algorithm scanned the data and assembled an internal database for analysis. Quantitative descriptors like length, points, and area were extracted and stored in large arrays. Object edges were scanned to identify its purpose and image segments were categorized to produce meaningful characters.

After long hours of computation that caused the PC fans to run on high, a surprising result came. The program identified a known communication method. It resembled DNA code in many respects but it had discernible extensions to it.

Since the program had a high reliability factor, it launched another set of experiments and analyses just to increase the authenticity of its findings. The new set, which included another few million comparisons, matched the previous set. The program reached a final conclusion and announced, with a probability of 99% accuracy, that there was a pattern.

It was an ancient DNA code that had been extracted from artifacts such as mummies found in burial chambers beneath the deserts of Egypt. The code was complete and ready for use.

Samuel and Alisha looked at each other in awe.

"We cracked the code, Alisha. Can you believe it? That old man sent us all the way across the world for a reason. Who would have believed it—besides us! The Ancient Code of the Sea. Sounds like nonsense but there it is."

Alisha gave him a hug. "I didn't have any doubt. Well, not too much."

Samuel looked at the message that appeared on his screen with great disbelief. The program identified a clear message—one that repeated itself endlessly.

Copyright infringement identified in colony perimeter.

"Copyright infringement? What the. . . ." Alisha stood behind Samuel and when she saw the message, she burst into laughter. "Copyright infringement? Now that's a good one. Are you sure this is actually coming from that super-microscope?"

Samuel didn't know what to make of the message. He stared at it without the capability to comprehend its meaning.

"Yes, the message is translated directly from the images," Samuel mumbled. "But what is the meaning of it?"

"Well, sweetie, with all due respect, I don't think that cancer cells will talk about copyright stuff. Don't you see that it doesn't make sense? This must be some type of mistake or malfunction. This message was produced from something else, maybe some ad on a magazine, newspaper? Anything that deals with business? It might just be from those lawyers in Hartford who advertise everywhere!"

"I know it doesn't make any sense, but still, there it is. It is authentic and was produced directly from the data that we took from the microscope. That's what I fed to the program. There is no other data the program could take it from." Samuel was defiant in the face of the absurdity of the message. "We must figure out the meaning."

Alisha gave him an amused look. "Sam, please, I know that you are very enthusiastic about this idea and want to find some answers, but please keep two feet on the ground and realize that this doesn't look right. I would expect gibberish or any unidentified language of some sort, but not this."

"It was gibberish first and then the program detected a pattern that matches the old DNA code. There must be a logical explanation for this. The fact that the message has a clear meaning tells us that it is correct."

"Yes, well, you just took me from a beautiful time on the beach, and for what? What's next from your program—a Wall Street announcement? A juice machine? Ab toner? I'm going home!"

"No, please, Alisha. I'll think this out. Please!" Samuel hugged her.

"That's okay. I'm not mad, I'm just tired. Sorry, I didn't mean to make fun of you."

"Oh, no need to apologize. We had a wonderful time on the beach and we will have many more in the future. I promise." Samuel kissed her.

"Get some sleep, maybe we'll do something tomorrow? It's the weekend."

"Of course. I'll call you in the morning."

"Late morning, please."

"Hey, maybe we'll go for brunch at the Market Grill. We loved the chicken kabobs we had there."

"Sounds good." Alisha gave him a kiss and left.

Samuel returned to the screen and checked the time. It was six in the morning.

"It's either something that is completely wrong, as Alisha said, or I am up to something beyond my understanding." He realized he was talking to the screen. But the screen didn't answer. Instead the message still appeared under the translated window, bright and clear.

Copyright infringement identified in colony perimeter.

The cells were surrounded by selective permeable membranes which regulated what gets into and out of the cells. The membrane allowed some types of molecules and ions to diffuse across the membrane and prevented other types of molecules and ions from crossing the membrane. Since the perimeter phenomenon occurred consistently, the cell operators, by the governor's order, initiated a distress warning. It was important to follow the protocol since it was created many millennia ago. It was called the Oxygen Protocol. Oxygen was allowed to cross the selectively permeable cell's membranes, but large molecules like proteins and DNA were not allowed to cross. The operators moved molecules from an area where they are highly concentrated to an area where they were less concentrated. By creating areas of low concentration and high concentration, the operators enabled a process called *diffusion*, which was the flow of molecules across the membrane separating the areas of concentration.

In the human body, this action occurs in the lungs. When we breathe in air, oxygen gets into the tiniest air sacs of the lungs, the *alveoli*. Surrounding them are the tiniest blood vessels — capillaries. The capillaries in the lungs, pulmonary capillaries, contain the lowest concentration of oxygen in the body, because by the time the blood gets to the tiniest vessels, most of the oxygen has been used up by other organs and tissues.

So, the tiniest air sacs of the lungs have a higher concentration of oxygen than do the capillaries. That means that the oxygen from the *alveoli* of the lungs can spread across the membrane between the air sac and the capillary, getting into the bloodstream. A colony's messages can be transmitted via a variety of organs using a similar method. This time, since there was no defined organ, the message was transmitted globally.

The message were transmitted to all other colonies, as the ancient code dictated.

Samuel reached a conclusion.

"This is it. We activated another experiment with the same and different conditions and we are getting the same results."

They were at the Photonic Microscope site one more time. This time Samuel experimented with a few EMF conditions and samples of chemical solutions. Although some conditions were different, they were still getting the same message. Samuel connected the program directly to the output of the microscope so it automatically fed the images into the pattern-recognition software. The results were direct messages. Some of the messages arrived with spelling mistakes but Samuel explained them as image blur in some segments.

Alisha stared at him without understanding where this was going.

"This message is real. We don't know what it means, but it is real. This is beyond doubt."

"How do copyright infringement and cancer cells connect? I don't get it." Alisha was still not taken in.

Alex rolled his eyes but remained quiet. He was assigned to help them with the Photonic Microscope, so he did. Anything he might say would just be the opinion of an outsider.

"We don't know what these words mean for them." Samuel spoke quietly. "For us, it may refer to something that is different to them. If we think about it, the word 'copyright' may mean one thing to us and something else entirely to the cancer."

"I have to admit that this possibility. As odd as it sounds, it makes sense." Alex admitted after a while. "It is definitely a different direction and way of thinking. Theoretically at least, it can happen. The word 'sky' can mean different things to different species. It sounds the same and may be spelled the same, but the meaning may be different."

"Exactly. Given the fact that cancer cells have been with humans since the dawn of our species, and assuming that they are an intelligent species by their own, who says that they couldn't adopt some ideas which they express as words of some sort?"

"That really steps out of science, Sam, don't you think?" Alisha shook her head. "I am with you on cracking the riddle, but sometimes . . . I really don't know."

Samuel brushed aside the skepticism. "Yes, it does make sense. I know it sounds crazy but this is the only explanation."

Alex clicked some buttons and slid some controls on the control panel. "I have recorded here thousands of samples for you. You can analyze these results later with your program. One thing I must say, the university must really believe in your research spending all these millions using our microscope."

"Oh, yes. Of course."

Alisha rolled her eyes.

Nikolai looked the same as the last time. He was seated on a comfortable armchair with his wireless keyboard. Same clothes.

"Say Nikolai, just out of curiosity, do you ever go to the kitchen or the bathroom, or do you just work on your computer all day? I know I already asked you, but you really seem in the same position every time I see you."

"Occasionally," Nikolai never lost his wit. "And the reason is because this is my computer station when I talk via Skype. Of course, I'll be seen in the same position. But I forgive you for you being handicapped by what you see only. How are you, Samuel? What do you need today? Another microscope session? You know that the bill is getting up there." His eyes looked to the ceiling and he made a brief, shrill whistling sound.

"Not today, but I am sure I'll need one soon. Today, I need another favor from you."

"Sure, anything. After what I've been doing, it should be easy."

"I have hundreds of thousands of results from the microscope sessions that must be analyzed for pattern recognition. I already used it with my program and it found that a modified old DNA code is the key cryptography. But I am getting many odd words as results. I originally thought it was due to blurry images but now I am not sure. I suspect that these may be different messages that got corrupted."

"Okay, since I was going along with your theory about intelligent cancer cells, I'll continue my support. What do you need?"

"We already know that the message uses old DNA code. I need a smarter program that can run much faster and analyze many samples with more accuracy. Can you write one?"

"I am an expert in geometrical engines since they are key to all advanced computer games. I can definitely write a much better recognition program but I am not sure about analysis time. Advanced programs of this nature require thorough analysis. It takes time. But it can be done."

"Time is a second priority. I need to know the message content. This is the main thing. I have another idea. I'll provide entirely different conditions to the cells and see if the messages are different. If they are, this will prove that they are coming from an intelligent entity. Do you agree, Nikolai?"

"Hmmm, it does make sense. I have a few free days starting tomorrow. Put all of your files on the FTP server and write me the details in an email. I'll see what I can do."

"Nikolai, you are the best. I don't know what I would do without you."

Nikolai grinned. "Yeah, I don't know what I would do without you either, Sam. Maybe I would not be in such trouble with the law one day? But hey, I always go with my gut feelings and I think that we are doing the right thing."

"Thanks, Nikolai. Just out of curiosity again, where are you taking all the money from?"

"Somewhere in the Emirates. That's the only place that wouldn't notice millions vanishing for some time."

"I see. Along with the program I'll need one more Photonic Microscope session."

Nikolai raised a brow.

"Please?"

Samuel couldn't believe his eyes. Alisha also covered her mouth in great surprise. The message was clearly displayed on the large screen. Even Alex stared at the screen as he understood that something was different.

Deadly clouds are on the perimeter.

"What did you guys do that caused this?" Alex scratched his head.

"I added another ingredient to the specimen." Samuel's voice was clear and steady. "I added alkylating agents."

Alisha's mouth opened.

"What's the hell are alkylating agents?"

"It's a class of chemotherapy drug."

Alisha and Samuel walked hand by hand down a well-worn footpath in a wooded area not far from Mystic.

"I still cannot digest it, Sam. This proves beyond any doubt that you are right about communication. We are communicating with an intelligent entity that is responding to our drugs and other external stimuli. As you said, we use different terms for different phenomena. We have to bring this to people in cancer research. Big names. This is probably the breakthrough of the century. " Alisha looked at him in admiration.

"Still, our results will be marginalized due to disbelief or insufficient data. It is not conclusive that the cancer cells are the source for the messages. Many arguments can be developed against these results. But our discovery today makes me much happier. Now I know that we are headed in the right direction. We just have to continue to the next step."

"What's going on? Now I'm the one who believes in the idea and you are skeptical?" Alisha stopped him and kissed him mischievously. "Take that my skeptical colleague!"

"No, Alisha, I believe that this is significant but we need more convincing data before we bring it to the big shots."

"But this is already convincing, Sam. We treat the culture with chemo drugs and they report clouds on the horizon. What more do you need than that?"

Samuel looked at her with joy. "This was only the first stage—what I called only fifty percent of the breakthrough."

Alisha's forehead wrinkled with curiosity.

"Now we have to communicate back with them and have them understand us. Once we get two-way communication, we'll be able to get much more information—and ultimately advancements."

She looked at him without understanding where his mind was heading.

Bertha lay on the bed, Samuel and Alisha standing near her. Alisha's eyes were red from crying and Samuel was haggard. Bertha's face was extremely pale and wizened. Although it was early in the morning and the sunshine entered the room, the atmosphere was gloomy. Alisha and Samuel spent the last few days at the hospital. Bertha asked them to be with her as her condition became worse.

"She's waking up." Alisha leaned down.

Bertha slowly opened her eyes. As she saw Alisha and Samuel, a faint smile spread on her face. "Thank you for being here with me." She coughed into a hospital towel which soon bore bloodstains. Alisha brought her a fresh one from the bathroom.

"No need to thank us, Bertha." Samuel held her hand and tried his best to look hopeful.

"They drug me so much now . . . I guess my time has come."

"Bertha, is there anything that I can do?"

"No, thank you, Sam. You did everything a family member could do. I am blessed to have you and Alisha with me now."

Bertha gave them a good look. All three held her hands.

"I feel that my time has come. I wanted you both to be with me in my final hour. I don't have many family members and they are too far away. I was never close to them anyway, well, beside my sister, but she is old and far away. I love you both very much. Please remember that."

Alisha wept quietly and Samuel fought his tears.

"I believe that you are going to find the cure for this, Sam. I really do. I wish that it would save me but things are not always as we want them to be. That is okay. We must accept it." Bertha smiled faintly. "But I want you to continue with your research. People like you help all humankind. Your dedication and persistence will pay off one day. If not for me, then for the rest of the world. You will find the cure. I just know it in my heart."

"Thank you for your faith in us, Bertha," Samuel's voice cracked as tears took over him. "I'll try my best."

"What do you say at a time like this?" Bertha whispered. "I am glad that it is a sunny day. The light is a sign of good things. It is the symbol of purity and hope. I have hope. I know it's funny to say this, but yes, I have hope. Not for myself but for all the rest of the sick people. You bring them hope. You will cure them."

The sun illuminated the large room, welcoming the new day. The flowers that Samuel and Alisha brought responded and presented their scent to the room and all in it.

"Don't cry because it's over. Be happy that it happened," Bertha whispered to them. "Please do not be sad. I want all of us to be happy that we were together."

Samuel and Alisha felt joy and sorrow intermingling freely in their souls.

"You are amazing, Bertha. Even now you are a light to all of your loved ones." Alisha kissed her forehead.

"I love you both, as though you were my children, and I am very proud of you. And now, I would like to watch the sunshine."

They held both Bertha's hands as the sun lifted her gentle soul and took it to the greatest light of all.

Samuel found Alisha weeping quietly as he arrived to the office on a rainy morning. It was almost three weeks after Bertha had passed away and Alisha was still having difficulties not seeing her there in the morning with her cheerful look and luncheon treats.

He hugged her quietly.

"I still can't believe that she is not with us anymore. I am so used to her gentleness and kindness every morning. I miss the food that she used to make us, even if sometimes we didn't like it. I miss her health tips and sincere concern. I just miss her presence. The office is so empty without her."

"I feel the same, Alisha. The office will never be the same without her. Stan said that he'll look for someone to replace her. I told him that I'm not ready for that yet. It will take me some time."

"But we have to remember her words. Be happy that it happened. She wanted us to continue this research. She wanted us to find the cure. You know, I believe that we do have a good chance to find it. And we have to do it. Unfortunately we didn't have it on time for Bertha." Samuel's voice cracked but he summoned the will to go on. "We have to continue, no matter what's happened. We have to do it. For Bertha's memory."

"Here is the letter Bertha left us." Alisha took a few yellow note pages from her purse. "She gave it to me in the hospital."

They read the letter quietly. Alisha wiped tears.

"She was so sweet. She even left us instructions how to make her health foods. Look, here are some recipes for her hummus dip and quinoa salad. She was a jewel."

Samuel shook his head. "I have some ideas this morning that I want to try. Now our main goal is how to communicate with the cells."

Alisha wiped her nose with a napkin. "When I think about the meaning of what you just said, it sounds unreal—communicating with cancer. This is more appropriate for science fiction than science."

"I have to admit that you are correct there, but we've already received clear feedback from cancer cells. The probability that this feedback is due to random phenomena or chemical reactions is very slim. That points towards intelligent cells. We now have a way to receive their transmission and translate it into our language. We're still not sure what they mean but we can find out, with time. The second part of the breakthrough is communicating back with the cells and having them understand our messages. This is most likely much harder than the first one. Much, much harder."

Alisha poured two cups of coffee, handed him one and sat near him. Going back to their daily life routine helped her get past her grief.

"What is your idea, Sam?"

Samuel took a sip from his coffee, leaned back, and released a long sigh. "We now know that they created molecular structure with a pattern of old DNA code. I don't know why or what is the source of this code, but this actually makes our life easier because we know the basics of DNA code. Now we have to find a way to create a pattern that they will understand. Then we need them to realize who we are. After that, we can actually talk with them about some ideas." He rolled his eyes. "Oh man, it sounds like sci-fi to *me* now!"

A Skype tone woke up Samuel. He rubbed his eyes and looked at the digital clock in his office. It was past midnight.

I probably fell asleep while looking at the computer—again.

For the past few weeks he'd been searching for ideas but he simply wasn't getting anywhere. One idea entailed adding elements to change the molecular structure of the specimen. Another idea was to use food coloring to create an understandable patterns. His most recent idea was to adjust the seawater purity and the electromagnetic field polarity. That didn't lead to anything significant. He didn't want to add chemo drugs to the specimen as that would harm or even kill the cells.

The Skype tone demanded answering. Samuel rubbed his eyes and clicked accept.

Nikolai's face showed on the screen. Samuel thought that he looked tired and somewhat worried but he noted to himself that Nikolai wore a different shirt for a change—and that was a welcome sign.

"Hey Nikolai, what's up? You look tired, my friend."

"Sam," Nikolai skipped the preliminary talk. "We got traced."

Samuel was awake now. "How long?"

"A few days ago, maybe earlier."

"What are we going to do?"

"Oh, I would not worry about me. They can't reach me. I lost my European virtual IP links but I will get new ones later. For now, I had to destroy all my camouflaged ports. It took me years to build these but I am not worried. It is you that needs to be worried, Sam. How are you doing with your research?"

Samuel raked a hand through his disheveled hair. "I still haven't found the method to communicate fully with the cells. We can read and translate their messages. There's more, though. Lots more."

"Oh, I agree with you there, Sam. Did you try to convince your colleagues or your boss? Maybe this can buy you the get-out-of-jail card that you may be needing."

"Eh, as much as this is a great achievement, Nikolai, it is not enough. I'll need to prove two-way communication and even this will be doubtful. It isn't easy. This is not your typical medical research. I'll have to find a biological way to prove that my communication with the cells can result in molecular alteration of some sort. Otherwise, why do we do all this?"

"What do you mean?"

"Ultimately, I am hoping to find a way to cure or prevent cancer— or at least provide some sort of possible treatment. I didn't think about this topic yet but this is my ultimate goal."

Nikolai was in thoughts. "I see your point. You can communicate with the cells trying to find some facts that can help you develop a new treatment—or ultimately a cure."

"A cure. Yes, that's my hope. I'll have to prove it to higher authorities in order to get continued funding—from more conventional ways. I know it. I am in this field and know what it takes to prove yourself and keep the funds coming in."

"Or something to save your ass from jail."

"Yes, saving my ass from jail will be nice. That, my friend, is another topic. I haven't thought about it yet."

Nikolai wiped his forehead. "I would start thinking about it. What are you going to do?"

Samuel looked at the screen. He was tired. "First I am going to erase your contact from my Skype account. I don't want to leave any trace leading to you."

"No worries. My user name is a ghost. They can't reach me. Next time when we talk, I'll find you."

"That's good to know."

"You also looked tired. Get some sleep."

"Yeah, I've been working for weeks now, trying to find ideas."

"What I am also unhappy about is another important fact."

"What?"

"In case you need more funding, how you'll get it? I really believe in your ideas and want to help you to complete the research."

Samuel smiled." Thanks Nikolai, I truly appreciate it. I guess we'll have to wait and see. In the meanwhile I am not giving up. I am going to try any idea that I come up with in order to find a way to communicate with these little guys."

Nikolai laughed shortly. "I am with you, buddy."

A knock on the door came. The knock was loud enough for Nikolai to hear.

"Who is that? It's after midnight your time." Nikolai was tense.

"I don't know."

Samuel turned his face towards the office's door. "Who's there?"

"New Haven police. Please open up."

Samuel gave a last look at Nikolai and clicked "disconnect."

The governor looked at his assistant leader with great disbelief.

"What do you mean you believe that they are trying to communicate with us? Who are they?"

"I don't know, sir. All I know is that we came out with this idea investigating the repeated pattern changes. Since they are not only repeated but consisted of certain structure changes, one of our theories is that it was made by an intelligent life-form. We also measured our food appearance schedule and I have good reason to believe that we are being fed."

"Being fed? By the same entity that tries to communicate with us?"

"I don't exactly know, sir, but it may be. These are assumptions and theories but all signs lead to some kind of intelligent life-form that we are interacting with. From our historical records we learned that we were hosted in the past by intelligent hosts. In our case it is hard to clearly say. The only sign is our feeding time. It may be that we are under intentional condition changes, for some reason."

The governor thought about this idea. "You know, I studied our historical documents and I believe that you may be correct. Take for example our message code. It was learned from a host long ago. He hosted a few large colonies at the time." The governor needed to show his superior knowledge. It was essential for a governor to have such knowledge in order to protect the colony. That was his mission.

"Interesting. Sir, one of the ideas that we are looking into is that we are a part of greater being that is affecting our lives. We don't have the particle structure that tells us about a host. This greater being may be feeding us and watching over us. We are not sure of this but it is something that we should consider."

"So we are a part of greater entity as what? As a symbiotic relationship?"

«I suspect so, sir."

"So they can't communicate with us. Do you know why?"

"No, sir. One assumption is that they may not be able to reach out to us. Maybe they do not have a method to communicate with us. Maybe they don't know the code, sir."

"Another possibility is that they may not be able to fully understand our messages."

"Indeed, sir. This is also a possibility."

"Yet, I suspect that they somehow can read our transmitted message about the perimeter. You said that you notice different patterns in the changes."

"Yes, but this is only an assumption, sir. We don't have any way to know for sure, yet."

"Hmmm. . . ."

"Sir, I was thinking about something. Maybe we can test our theory. Maybe we can help them communicate with us."

The governor was intrigued by the idea. "How do you suggest we do that?"

"I was thinking about a few ways. It also depends if they can read and understand our transmission or not. If they are capable of reading and understanding our message, then we can try transmitting something like 'We need food.' And then we can see if there is a change in our food supply."

"This is assuming that they are not hostile. If they are hostile then they will not give us any food."

"This is correct, sir. Also this is assuming that they have control over our food."

"What are your other ideas?"

"Assuming that the initial communication proves successful then we will have new friends out there."

"Indeed. And since we never know when we'll be in worse circumstances, we need any friends that may be able to help us to survive."

"I truly appreciate your help, Stan." Samuel sat in the boss's office and drank a cup of Earl Grey tea.

"You better, Sam." Stan sat on his desk and gave Samuel a fatherly look. "I used my pension fund for your bail. I still can't believe that you would be involved with such a scheme. Hacking into foreign bank accounts to rent a super-microscope in the name of the university? You went too far. What did you think would happen?"

"Stan, trust me." Samuel took a deep breath and spoke calmly. "I would like to show you something. Please?"

Stan shook his head and calmed down. "It better be good, Sam. My tolerance level is close to zero at the moment."

"Not here. Let's go to my office."

"I don't want to go to your office. Nothing can justify such irresponsible behavior. You used a hacker you knew long ago to steal money? I must say that this is a very creative way of financing research."

"Oh, thank you." Samuel sensed praise. Briefly.

"It's also a creative way to get you in jail for quite a while. This is a serious felony. This is twenty years."

"Sorry, but this is done for the greater good. Trust me."

Stan drank from his tea. "I don't care. Still, this is not the way to go about it."

"You didn't give me any funding."

"Then you don't do anything until you *do* get funding."

Samuel shook his head. "No, I will not stop until I find the answer. I thank you and truly appreciate what you've done for me, but I must continue. I know that this can save millions of people lives."

Stan remained silent. After a while he sighed. "Alright. Show me your research."

Samuel smiled joyfully.

Within minutes they had walked from the admin building to Samuel's office.

"See, we already have two significant results. One, we have a way to read their messages. I do not know whom they are sending them to, but I assume they have a certain way of communicating with other cancer cells. Maybe in other parts of the body. This needs to be investigated further but I can read their messages. Second, we applied a chemo drug to the specimen and we received a different message. A clear message that they recognize trouble. This means that the cancer cells have knowledge of the means we are fighting them with. They call it 'deadly clouds,' we call it chemo. Of course, they are not aware that we are the guys who are launching these bad things. Don't you see? We create a biological condition and they respond to it." Samuel's eyes sparkled. "This proves that cancer cells are intelligent. My assumption is that they are a living, cognizant entity that is not aware of our existence. Maybe they know we exist but don't know the harm they cause. What if? What if we establish bi-directional communication with them, making them aware of what they do to us? Maybe we can make some changes? Maybe we can find a cure in a nonconventional way."

"Ha! This is crazy, Sam. They'll put us in straitjackets if we tell this theory."Stan shook his head. "Talking with cancer cells?" he took out his pipe. "I know I am not supposed to smoke in here but you are getting me stressed out, Sam."

"That's okay. No one will notice and it doesn't bother me. Look, we can already read their messages."

"Yeah, but who will believe this? It can be any type of transmission. It will take decades to scientifically or technologically prove that these transmissions are coming from the specimen. Be realistic, Sam."

"Not if we can communicate back and forth with them."

Stan stared at him as he puffed aromatic clouds into the air.

"If we find a way to communicate with the cells then we'll be able to establish two-way communication and we'll be in much better shape."

"Sam, Sam. Again it sounds too science-fictionish. Given your background, no one will believe this." Kraft walked back and forth in the office. "Besides, we don't have this yet."

"Give me a few more weeks."

"And then what? I'll have to put a few more million for your bail? No, Sam. No!"

Samuel released a long sigh and lay back in his chair. "Then here is the data on my computer screen. You can kiss it all goodbye. Is that what you want, Stan? Tell me, after what you've seen here, do you want me to trash everything? You know that I am up to something big, you know it. Otherwise you'd never have bailed me out for so much money." Samuel's almost whispered. "You know I am right."

Stan sat on his chair and lit his pipe again. It burned out as he listened to Sam's plea. White smoke clouds went up in the air and the gentle smell of pipe tobacco spread in the air.

"And how will you get the additional funding to complete the second phase? I assume that you'll need to use this, whatever it's called, a Photonic Microscope, in order to see if you are able to communicate with cancer? I can't believe I just said that." Stan held his head with both hands in great disbelief. "You will need a few more million for that. How do you plan to get it?"

"Can you help me?"

"Oh, no. I already helped you enough, Sam. All my money is gone. You'll have to think about something else entirely."

"Good. This means that you believe me."

"No, I didn't say that. I just said that . . . that . . . I don't know. Oh, all right, I don't know why I am doing this but I guess I do believe you." Stan shook his head and exhaled more smoke.

Samuel nodded. "I'll use any help that I can get in order to complete my research. When it's done, we'll pay back the money somehow."

Stan grinned nervously. "And how exactly you plan to do that while you are in jail?"

Samuel smiled calmly. "Somehow I don't think I'll be in jail. I am thinking more about another place."

"Like what?"

"I don't know, the medical hall of fame? The Nobel Prize ceremony?"

Stan rolled his eyes.

Alisha and Samuel rode the same stable horses as before into the forest on a chilly but sunny Saturday. The sun was weaker than before and they both wore thick fisherman sweaters. They dismounted at a slow-running creek that curled through a rock-strewn bed before emptying into the Mystic River.

"I can't stop thinking about our findings, Sam." Alisha watched her horse gulp down creek water.

"Let's not talk shop just now." Samuel looked up to the sun sneaking through the branch cover. "Look at the harmony in nature. Everything is in balance. The trees are consuming water and nutrients from the soil. Some animals feed off the vegetation, others feed of other animals—and all live together in harmony."

"Yes, we humans also blend into this harmony somehow."

"I am not sure that we blend in all that well, though." Samuel frowned as they headed uphill from the creek. "We think and therefore we change. We develop technology, science, and medicine. All these are good but they also interrupt nature."

"And by interrupting nature, we introduce harmful phenomena that cause diseases."

"Correct. But then we can't live without technology and advancements since these make our lives more pleasurable and comfortable. We get used to it."

"At least that's what we like to think," Alisha interjected.

"Agreed. But still our lives today are much better than a hundred years ago."

"Yes, but with what price?"

"The price is damaging our planet, our nature, our forests, and our oceans."

"Also our air."

"Indeed, Alisha."

They reached the top of the hill and looked out on the forest below and a small town to the west, complete with a quaint white church and the signature steeple. A small lake was to the left and the blue water added to the pastoral vista.

"So the big question is whether this is worth it?" Alisha stopped her horse and watched the view.

Samuel stopped near her.

"I believe that this question is too late to be asked now. As a society we can't go back in time. We move only forward. Can you imagine a life without your cell phone? Or your microwave oven?"

Alisha nodded. "True. But then what do we do with the bad side effects that we brought upon ourselves. Ultimately they cause diseases."

"That's why they invented us—medical doctors. Since early times, humans invented medicines and treatments. Now, we have us. We need to provide the fix for the progress. We need to cure the sicknesses that we've caused."

"Well, not all sicknesses are due to progress and technology." Alisha released a sigh. "Some get sick for genetic reasons."

"True, but what are genetic reasons, Alisha? Are they genome stamps that were created along many years? Who said that we didn't warp our genome structure due to advancements? Yes, probably some are based in human biological history, but I am sure that many of these malfunctioned stamps were created along the years because of our interference with nature."

Alisha nodded silently.

"Now we are onto something that was never even thought of before. A new approach, a new understanding."

We always thought that diseases are something that we just have to find a medicine for it. A cure," Alisha continued.

"Indeed. Now we are observing the topic from a different point of view. What if some diseases are actually intelligent entities?"

"Yes! Living inside us. We are their hosts."

"Yes. Well, we know this for many years regarding parasites for example. The human body can be a perfect host for many living organisms."

"And it is. Bacteria, germs, and many other living forms."

"Not all hurt us, of course. And if we could somehow talk with them, we may find a new way to find a cure."

"Some kind of resolution maybe?" Alisha smiled in awe at the idea.

"Some kind of cooperation or finding a peaceful way to handle the condition. Sharing life resources. To exist separately or independently, but peaceably. There is a name for this phenomenon."

"Yes, what is it but I forgot the term. Typically it is used in politics." Alisha tried to remember.

"Coexistence."

"No, no, no. I am not doing this again." Nikolai was adamant.

"Nikolai, I must have it. I am very close to something. Something big. We have some ideas that we want to implement and we need that microscope again." Samuel was more pleading than ever. "Look, I know I've said this before but this time it's different. My boss, who is also a friend, believes in the idea. He'll back up the story. He'll let AlphaTron know that this transaction is kosher."

"But still, we'll need to swipe this million dollars, Sam. I can't do it. This is a huge risk for me. I don't have those linked IPs anymore. I need time to build them, otherwise they will not be credible. Do you even understand what I'm trying to explain?"

"Vaguely. All I understand is that you really have to make some efforts to get us the money." Samuel paused. "We really can crack the riddle. Then it will be all backed up. I promise you."

"And if not? Then I'll be left alone to deal with my illicit activity. This is a serious crime, Sam. This time I cannot hide behind ghost IPs. This time I have to go almost live. That means that the chances of tracing me are almost a hundred percent."

Samuel took a deep breath.

Can I really ask him to do this? This means that I may send him jail. This is going too far. What if this gets discovered too soon? No. I can't do this to a good friend. He's sacrificed enough for me.

Samuel released a long sigh. "I am sorry, Nikolai. I appreciate all that you've done for me so far. I was caught up in my eagerness. Truly sorry, my friend. I'll have to manage something."

"No."

Nikolai looked transfixed into a spot in space. "I am sorry, my friend. On further thought, I personally like this research—and I believe in you." He nodded and took a long sip from a large plastic soda cup. "I'll get you the money."

"No, Nikolai. I don't want you to go to jail or to get in serious trouble. I have to draw the line somewhere. Please, it's okay."

"Sam, you and I know that without my help, nothing will move forward. You need this microscope. You need this money."

"Yes, Nikolai, but this doesn't justify putting you in prison. I'll have to find some other way."

"You don't have other way. Your boss already spent all of his money. You don't have such money and you don't have any way to get it. At least not legally."

"True but still. Thanks again for your help."

Nikolai typed quickly on his keyboard as he was talking. "Sam, I am willing to take the chance. It's worth it."

Samuel smiled. "Not today, Nikolai."

Nikolai's lips pursed as he completed something on screen. Then he took another long sip of soda. "Well, too late."

"What? No! Nikolai, I told you not to do it."

"I got you ten million dollars in your budget. This should be enough to cover your second stage. What do you say?" Nikolai looked amused.

"Nikolai, but I asked you to skip the idea. Who knows what's going to happen now."

"Sam, our entire lives revolve around 'who knows what.' Don't worry. I'll be fine." A confident look spread on his face. "You just focus on the puzzle."

Samuel nodded. "Thank you, Nikolai."

"Now you have ten sessions for your microscope. Use them wisely."

"Thanks again, my friend. Off I go to schedule a microscope day."

"And Sam?"

"Yes, Nikolai?"

"We need more doctors like you. You guys are doing things that will benefit us all."

"Will try to do so, Nikolai. Got to go now."

"Good luck."

Remarkable chemical processes were underway in the HeLa cancer cells prepared for the Photonic Microscope.

Ribosomes contain the nucleic acid RNA, which assembles and joins amino acids to make proteins. They can be found alone or in groups within the cytoplasm. This process is known as protein biosynthesis. Biosynthesis is an enzyme-catalyzed process in cells of living organisms by which substrates are converted to more complex products. Some proteins, such as those to be incorporated in membranes, known as membrane proteins, are transported into the cells during synthesis.

An electromagnetic field was activated and a seawater solution was added to the petri dish. As a direct result, the protein biosynthesis process was accelerated. For an unknown reason, a succession of tRNA molecules charged with appropriate amino acids were brought together with an mRNA molecule and matched up by base-pairing through the anti-codons of the tRNA with successive codons of the mRNA. The amino acids were then linked to extend the growing protein chain, and the tRNAs were no longer carrying amino acids. This whole complex of processes was carried out by the ribosome, forming two main chains of RNA, called ribosomal RNA and more than fifty different other proteins. The ribosomes latched onto the end of an mRNA molecules and moved along them, capturing loaded tRNA molecules and joining together their amino acids to form a new protein chain. This formed an unusual molecule pattern.

Beneath the Photonic Microscope, the pattern was immediately detected by the photon stream and translated into a two-dimensional image that was viewed on the five 52" LCD displays. In parallel, the image was fed into an AI program with pattern-recognition algorithms which scanned the image and divided it into sectors. Each region was assigned to a specific processor core to be identified according to vectors and coordinates. A hundred thousand threads were launched and the program started its recognition and identification flow. This required vast amounts of mathematical calculations which were directed to the Arithmetic Logic Unit section on sixteen quad-core microprocessors. These chips processed the data into MIPS—million instructions per second. The microprocessors temperature rose dramatically and large fans started up. The CPUs sent the data into output registers which produced a message on screen.

"Alisha! Do you see that?"

Alisha was too astonished to speak and Alex shook his head in great disbelief.

The three were transfixed by the message translated from the cell structure pattern. A single brief message filled the big screen.

We need food.

Samuel was the first to recoup. "Alisha, please put one drop of glucose on the HeLa cells in the dish. We'll give it a few minutes and then we'll look again at the pattern.

Shortly later, a new message appeared.

Food received. Thank you.

"Ah, do you know what this means?" Alex breathed heavily.

Alisha and Samuel hugged each other with joy, then Alex joined the celebration.

"I can't believe it. You guys did it!" He sat in a chair and wiped his brow.

Samuel returned to a calm research mode—more suddenly than he thought possible. "So, they are capable of understanding that we affect their lives. They asked us for food. We gave them food. They thanked us."

"We still cannot communicate with them." Alisha continued logically. "We cannot send messages that they understand."

"Well, not directly." Samuel added "We can communicate with them through chemical signs. And that's a promising start."

"The question is if they know that." Alex was starting to feel part of the team.

"True. But the fact that they transmitted to us a clear message, we responded, and they acknowledged it, proves that they know about our existence. We have beyond any doubt proof that we are communicating with cancer cells."

Alisha held her head between her hands. "It's so hard to believe that this is really happening."

"Yes, it is." Alex said quietly. "And I still can't believe my eyes."

"What do we do now?" Alisha asked after few minutes of silence as they all grasp the meaning of their discovery.

Samuel looked at the specimen chamber in the Photonic Microscope. "Honestly, now I just want to sample their messages for hours and hours. Maybe it'll provide us with more information about who they are."

The governor was very pleased with his assistant leader. "We've discovered two important findings—thanks to you. First, we are controlled by a greater entity. Second, the entity can read our messages to other colonies. It knows our transmission code. Remarkable findings. We've never communicated with any other entities besides our colonies."

"With your permission, sir, we have discovered one more important thing. The entity is not hostile. In fact, it has provided us with food."

"Very true—and that is of critical importance."

All became quiet as they felt themselves on the precipice of a new understanding of the outside world.

"What now then?" the assistant leader asked.

"One unknown remains."

"What is it, sir?"

"We don't know if they are capable of communicating with us. Until now we sent them messages but they never sent us any."

"That is correct, sir."

"Based on the fact that they are responding to our messages but not sending any, I am concluding that they can't communicate with us. The fact that they responded to our message with an action, and not with a transmission, tells us that if they could, they would have sent a message. The only conclusion is that they somehow can't send us messages."

"Perhaps they do not know how to alter particles as we do," the assistant leader suggested.

"That's what I suspect also. We are fairly advanced regarding transmitting through particle patterns. I am not sure that they are capable of that."

"What do we do then, sir?"

"For now we can communicate as we did so far. We'll send them a message and they can respond with something like 'Yes' or 'No.' Something simple. An affirmative or negative will suffice."

"Another option is to train them how to use particle patterns to produce messages for us."

"With all due respect, I think this processes is more complicated and will take some time to learn."

"What's the rush? We have the time, sir. They are obviously on our side and friendly. We can try at least to consult with them to determine if they are interested in learning our communication method."

"Yes, good idea."

"We'll do this immediately as their interest is keen right now."

"Dismissed."

Do you know how to communicate with us—More Food—Yes.

Jaws dropped in the photonics microscope chamber. Three jaws to be exact.

"What are you guys waiting for?" This time it was Alex who spoke first. "Give them more food!"

Alisha dripped another bit of glucose onto the specimen. Samuel performed a scan few moments later.

Understood—We can teach you—More Food—yes.

"Hallelujah, I've lived to see this." Samuel jumped up and down like a child. "I have to bring Stan in to see this."

"Sam." Alisha's voice conveyed unmistakable caution. "I agree, this is a great achievement but there are still many unknowns. We don't know if these guys are going to be friendly. We don't know how the teaching process will go. We have to have more information before we bring this to the board and the general public."

"Yes, yes, but first please show little approval by giving our new friends another round of glucose."

"I hate to spoil the party but it is almost the end of the day. And my company insists that you guys have only one more hour of microscope time." Alex took off his glasses and rubbed his eyes. He looked up in a sympathetic manner. "I am really sorry, guys. I enjoy your research but I have to kick you out in an hour."

Samuel looked straight into Alex's eyes. "Alex, at this point we really consider you part of the team. We need your help. We need a few more hours to try to see if we can communicate with them."

"You two just don't understand." Alex looked upward and sighed. "Okay. I guess no one will know. We can stay a few more hours after five."

After several hours, as midnight loomed, they had tried scores of ways to communicate, but to no avail. The eagerness and optimism of the late afternoon was all but gone. Exhaustion was setting in.

Samuel leaned back in his chair and looked at his watch. "We've been working almost seven hours. Nothing to show for it. Absolutely nothing."

Alex scratched his head. "I thought we reached a milestone when we were able to order the molecules in a certain way, but it's less than I thought. The task is too complicated to perform at this point, biologically and engineering-wise."

"I agree," Alisha admitted after stifling a yawn. "I don't see any progress. We'll have to take a break and think about a new approach."

Samuel released a long sigh. He hated to admit failure but this time he knew that they needed to close down for the night and rethink things.

"What about the cells?" Alisha asked. "I hope that they won't think that we've abandoned them."

"No, I think that these little guys are pretty smart." Samuel smiled as he realized he was thinking of the cells as people now. "They'll figure out that we're just calling it a night."

Alex nodded.

"Alex, I would like to ask you to keep all this confidential. We are taking huge risks with this."

"Of course. I am with you guys. Although I belong to the engineering world I fell in love with your research. I'd love to be part of the team."

"You are!"

The three held their hands out and joined them together.

"We are one team now and we have to break new ground when it comes to cancer."

"Let's name our team." Alisha's eyes sparkled.

They all looked at her.

"I have an idea. You gave me the idea, Sam. When we went on a horseback ride the other day."

"What is it, Alisha?"

"Team Coexistence. Ultimately that's what we'll try to do. Establish a relationship with cancer so that we can all coexist."

Samuel nodded. "I like it, Alisha. We are Team Coexistence. With time, when we find a cure, we'll call it the Coexistence Serum."

"Team Coexistence it is." Alex concluded with excitement.

A knock on the lab doors sounded. The AlphaTron manager didn't wait for a response. He walked right into the microscope control room. With him were two policemen. They didn't wait to exchange introductions and pleasantries.

"Dr. Samuel Daniels?"

"That's would be me," Samuel said in a steady voice that he was somehow able to summon.

Alisha covered her mouth, expecting the worst.

"You will have to come with us, Dr. Daniels."

Samuel nodded quietly.

Alex entered the sequence code to shut down the Photonic Microscope.

The steady humming sound in the background slowly diminished and the image of the last communication remained on screen until Alex shut it down.

"I conclude that they can't communicate with us, sir." The assistant leader was resigned.

"Based on what?"

"We definitely noticed many irregularities along our perimeter, sir. I think they're trying to communicate with us, but simply don't know the code. They're too primitive, perhaps."

"So the only way that they can communicate with us now is through food?"

"It appears so, sir. We are experiencing food infusions right after our requests. The good thing is that we have plenty of food for quite some time."

"Yes, that's a positive sign. However, we have to find a way to communicate at a higher level."

"Agreed, sir. It would be very beneficial for us and our species. It was never done before. We've learned a great deal over the millions of years from our hosts, but we've never actually been in direct contact with them. Our existence is dependent on hosts. They are our providers."

"If we are able to talk with them, maybe they can help us deal with the disasters that our species have had to face for generations."

"Indeed, sir. That was my thought also. The deadly clouds, the storms, the massive colony extinctions, and the rest. Maybe with their help, we can learn about these disasters and somehow counter them or evade them."

"Or affect particles changes to overcome their devastation."

"We've transmitted all the necessary instructions how to create structural changes but nothing's happened. I don't think they can do it, sir."

"When was the last signal we received from them?"

"Quite some time ago, sir."

"I hope they didn't give up."

"I hope so too, sir."

"Dismissed."

Alisha entered the visiting room at the municipal detention center and sat across a glass barrier from Sam, an uneasy amiability on her face.

"How goes it?"

"Well, not too bad, as you see. As I *hope* you see." Samuel looked ridiculous in orange prison garb, but was in fairly good mood. "The only thing is that now we'll have to figure out a way to get me out of here."

"Stan is on his way. I hope that he can do something. Oh, I am so sorry."

"It's okay, sweetie. I expected this to happen sooner or later. Well, it happened sooner rather than later. Remember, I told you that right after my latest talk with Nikolai. I just hoped that we would be able to reach more conclusive results about communication before the long hand of the law grabbed me by the scruff of my little neck."

Alisha sent her hand to press against the glass barrier and Sam returned the gesture.

"I wish I could share your joy." Stan walked in behind Alisha. He gave a look of optimism then turned to Samuel. "I can't believe that you are in here again. I already talked with them and I can't get you out this time, Sam. Although they can't trace it fully yet, they said that eventually they'll get their hands on your helper or *helpers*." He breathed heavily. "I am sorry, Sam."

"That's okay, Stan. Thank you for all of your help. I'll have to look for another way to get out." He looked down the hallway to the row of cells. "These places look scarier with every generation. I remember in the old time movies the locks were simple mechanical affairs. Today, everything is electrical."

"Furthermore, Sam, the locking mechanisms are computer-controlled now. I saw a sergeant entering data onto a laptop and opening a specific cell."

Samuel shook his head as a wild idea formed. "Did you say computer-controlled, Stan?"

"Yes, why? Oh no, Sam, don't even think about this. You are not getting in deeper trouble with your computer-wizard friends. Let me handle this. In the morning I have a meeting with a capable attorney—a friend of mine. He'll advise us how to get you out as soon as possible. Please don't do anything stupid that will bury you deeper."

"Of course, Stan." Samuel didn't show any more interest in the topic.

"Besides this, you are well? Do you need anything? Food? Anything at all?"

"No thanks, Stan, I'll be fine. Besides, Alisha is right here with me. Sort of."

"Good. I'll see you in the morning then."

"Thank you for coming over. I truly appreciate it." Samuel braved a smile.

"Ah, don't mention it. But please, do me a favor, stay out of trouble. You have enough on your plate now. Do yourself a favor."

Samuel and Alisha looked on as Stan exited the visiting area.

"He's a good fellow," Alisha said quietly. "He really cares about you."

"Yes, he is. It's good to know there are two people looking out for me."

Samuel pressed his hand against hers. "You need to go home and get some sleep, sweetie."

"No, I'll stay here with you a while longer."

Samuel thought about something. "Could you please do me a favor? Could you ask for the wireless password here from the guy over there?"

Alisha looked at him suspiciously. "Why?"

"I just want to check my email and at least have an internet connection on my phone."

"I'll try."

Alisha struck up a conversation with the guard and returned after a few minutes. "That was easy. Here it is. He wrote it on this little note."

"Thank you, sweetheart." Samuel entered the code and smiled as his Galaxy 6 smartphone became alive with an internet connection.

"You can go home now, Alisha, I'll be fine in here. I want you to get a good night sleep. We have tough days coming up. Be back in the morning?"

Alisha released a long sigh. "Of course. I hate to leave you here by yourself though."

"Well," Samuel gave her a smile. "I'm not entirely by myself. There is always one of these public protectors with me just a few steps away."

"Oh please! Alright, I'll be back in the morning. Be good." Alisha blew him a kiss and left.

He looked after her and his heart rejoiced.

She is so lovely and I am so lucky!

Samuel smiled. They forgot to search him for a cell phone.

"No sign of our host, sir." The assistant leader reported to the governor with obvious disappointment.

"What is our food status?"

"We still have plenty of food but we also grew significantly after being given so much food. Now we are a much larger colony, sir. Our needs are greater."

"Yes. Are we transmitting anything?"

"Not at the moment, sir. We are not in any crisis, there are no disasters, and everything seem to be well. Still, I am concerned that all communication with our host has come to a halt. After all, our lives depend on the food that they provide us, sir."

"Yes, I know. Continue to transmit that we need more food. That was the last communications that we had with them. Let's hope that they'll get back to us as soon as possible."

"Yes, sir."

"Dismissed."

"Are you out of your mind? Are they putting hallucinogenics in prison food over there?" Nikolai looked almost frightened through the Skype window on Samuel's phone. "You want me to do *what*?"

"You heard me correctly, Nikolai. I want you to release me from this cell. It's a computer-based lockup in the police station in downtown New Haven. All you have to do is locate its IP. You can't miss it. It'll be a piece of cake compared to the accounts in the Emirates."

"I can't believe you are doing this. You are crazy, Sam." Nikolai talked as his hands were already typing on the keyboard. "You decided to put yourself in jail for the rest of your life. That's okay, but why are you dragging me into this? Why me?"

Samuel smiled. "Because I have to solve this puzzle, Nikolai. That's why. It's for the good of the world."

"Aha, and in the meanwhile, my ass is on the line." Nikolai shook his head. "You are crazy, my friend, but I think I am even crazier than you, helping you with this."

"No, Nikolai, you have a vision, like me. And that's why you are helping me."

"I am not sure anymore. Soon I'll have to move away from here, if I don't want to end in jail like you. . . . Okay, I found the New Haven police and you are right. They do have computer access to your locks but they are better encrypted and secured than you'd think. It will take me some time to hack this."

"Call me when you have some news."

"Maybe you'll just hear the cell open up. Later."

"Later. Oh, Nikolai?"

Nikolai raised his head from the computer screen. He was already on task. "What?"

"Thank you."

"We don't have enough food for all, sir. I would like to initiate the food priority procedure, with your permission."

The procedure was one the colony tried to avoid at all cost. It meant cutting the food supplies to the oldest cells to maintain the younger ones. The old cells would die.

"Did you send messages to our host?"

"Numerous times, sir. No response."

"It seems that we were abandoned."

"I am afraid so, sir."

"Initiate the food priority procedure."

"Immediately, sir."

"Dismissed."

Samuel was almost asleep when he heard the metallic click of the solenoids opening the cell door.

Good old Nikolai! He is the best!

He looked at his watch. It was almost two am. He could see the officer down the hall napping in front of a TV with a program on UFOs on.

This is it. This is the time.

He stealthily opened the cell door a foot and a half, closed it behind him, and walked quickly to the front door. He passed in front of the reception table where the policeman snored loudly. In front of him was a paper plate with a half-eaten jelly donut.

Looks Yummy, but alas I cannot stay for a bite.

Within seconds, Samuel was outside. The cabbie looked briefly at Sam's orange jump suit then told him to hop in. Sam called Alex from the backseat.

"Good news, sir. We just now got an infusion of food. It seems like our host is back."

"This is very good news for all of us. Please continue with the efforts to train them how to communicate with us. Try to make it as simple as you can. Primitive, as I said."

"That's what we are doing, sir. We developed a simple method to formulate and convey understandable structures. It involves basic particles so I am hoping that it would easier to understand. Primitive, sir."

"Good, very good."

"In the meanwhile we are growing again. As always, we try to immediately compensate for lost members."

"Yes, of course."

"With your permission, sir, I would like to continue the communication efforts."

"Yes, please do so. Dismissed."

"I appreciate your help, Alex, especially this time." Samuel was at the microscope station as Alex adjusted the photon beam.

"No problem, Sam. We have about four hours until the station is needed again. These four hours can be very productive." He couldn't prevent a mighty yawn. "Sorry about that."

"That's okay. It's totally understandable. Oh, before I forget. Thanks for paying the cab. My wallet's still back at the station. I owe you."

"Don't worry about it."

Samuel noticed messages on the screen. Many messages.

"I can't believe it. They've transmitted to us. Look, they need food." Samuel put two drops of glucose on the HeLa specimen in the petri dish.

"Unbelievable." Although Alex was very tired he couldn't hide his excitement. "The cancer cells know that they depend on us for their living."

"Yes. Now let's wait for their message back."

And it arrived quickly.

Food received—Thank you—We are well.

"Now *that's* what it's all about. Yeah! Samuel couldn't stop himself from shouting in elation for a moment. "Yet, all of the work is still ahead of us. How can we communicate with the cancer cells more extensively and not just through feeding? This is the challenge that we have to overcome."

"I agree." Alex nodded. "This looks like a tough one."

"Nothing is ever too hard to do. All we need is funding and time."

"I didn't know that you were such a philosopher," Alex jibed.

"I didn't know either."

"Well, we have a few good hours. Let's get rolling."

Samuel scratched his head. "Agreed. The only question is where do we get the money from?"

It was almost six o'clock in the morning when the police arrived at AlphaTron.

"Not you guys again! I am making such good progress." Samuel complained in resignation when he saw the two policemen at the door.

"Sorry, Sam. I don't know how you got away but this time it will cost you. You'll need a very good lawyer to bail you out now." The policemen cuffed him and within an hour he was in a more secure jail.

"Well, at least we're on a first-name basis now."

"I can't believe it. You really want to get life in prison, don't you?" Alisha had to wait for visiting hours to see him on the next day. They could meet only in a booth for half an hour. The light treatment was gone.

"I am sorry, Alisha, I just have to complete the research." Samuel was oblivious to his cinderblock environs. His concentration was as it was in his Yale office.

"Sam, can you stop for a moment and think about others?" Alisha sobbed softly. "Like me, for example? The way you're going, you'll ruin your life."

Samuel smiled to her through the window. "Do you have any news from Stan?"

Alisha wiped her nose. "Yes, a lawyer will visit you today. Stan said that he can get you out in a few days."

"As soon as he can, Alisha." Then Samuel thought about something. "There's something very important. You have to take the specimen that was in microscope and keep it alive. It needs its food and elements. This specimen is key to our success. We have to keep in contact."

"I already called Alex about the petri dishes but he said that the police confiscated all our material in the lab."

"What? Alisha, please! You have to leave now. Go to the police station and ask for these dishes. You have to get them back. You have to save that specific colony. They are already working with us. We have to keep them alive."

"Okay, I'll go now."

"Please do that for me now and visit me again today or tomorrow. I need to know that these specimens are safe. If they die, we lose all the time that we invested in them. We'll have to retrain a new colony from scratch."

"Off I go then." Alisha sent him a virtual kiss. "I love you!"

"I love you too, Alisha."

The clerk at the police station was not cooperative.

"Miss, I told you a few times now. I can't give you this equipment without a judge's order. It's evidence and it will stay in police custody. I am very sorry but that's the law."

"But please, these are biological specimens and very important for our research. They have to be kept alive. I have to feed them." Alisha begged.

"I am sorry, Miss. There is nothing that I can do without that order from a judge."

"Obviously something happened with our host again. We've seen breaks in communication before but then the host returned." The governor faced reality.

"Yes, sir. We didn't have any communication for a long time now," the assistant leader reported. "This time it's different. We didn't hear from them for much longer time."

The governor weighed the situation.

"As you know, sir, our food resources are at the end. It is a matter of only a short time until we face extinction."

"I am wondering what happened. We had a promising relationship. We were fed and everything seemed on the right path."

"Yes, sir."

"Maybe they were stricken by one of the disasters."

"The fact that we can't establish communication makes it a mystery. We'll never know, sir."

"That may well be."

They knew that they had only a short time to live.

"Well, we have no other choice. Send our final message." The governor, the assistant leader, and the entire colony were not afraid. Death was part of life. It was part of their destiny but they were always on a mission to grow and repopulate. Ultimately this was the mission of every colony. It was in their code.

The assistant leader gave the order and the structural pattern of their particles changed and started the transmission to all other colonies in their vicinity. The colony's cells slowly died one after another. But those who were still alive continued their task, transmitting the final message. Even when the entire colony died, the message would be distributed through nature's recycling channels. With time, other colonies will learn about them and their situation and record them in the historical documents that were passed from generation to generation. The governor and the assistant leader watched the colony members stop functioning until the last one.

The governor and the assistant leader were the last to remain and then upon their death, the colony's last message was frozen in a particle pattern.

We have no food.

After five days in the cinderblock hotel, Samuel was released. He sat in Stan Kraft's office, tired and haggard.

"Thank you for hiring the attorney, Stan." Samuel spoke in a low tone. "I don't know what I would do without your help."

"You would be doing time. More time." Stan lit his pipe and blew the smoke toward the ceiling. "And don't tell me that smoking is prohibited in here. I know."

"I never said a word."

"Now, you have to get your shit together, Sam. I am with you on this and we both could get in deep trouble. I am still thinking how to save our asses regarding the university's money. I have few ideas but I have to consult the attorney."

"Thanks, Stan, but you know what the saddest thing is?" Samuel dropped a piece of paper on his boss's desk.

"What is it?" On the paper there was a striking image of a dotted pattern. Stan puzzled over determining the type of structure. "Is this some sort of code? What is this?" He scanned the dense pattern more but couldn't figure it out.

"Look at the bottom, Stan. That's where my software translated this message."

At the bottom of the page there was one line, printed in bold letters.

We have no food.

"Yesterday, when I was released, I collected the petri dish from the police station," Samuel explained in a somber voice. "The cancer cells that we communicated so well with didn't have their regular glucose supply. That's their message. Their final message."

Stan looked with great disbelief. "They were aware that you were feeding them?"

"Yes. Here, look for yourself at the documentation I've compiled over the past few weeks."

Stan read the documents and examined the attached images. "This is amazing! Now I understand your passion. Many of the notes here are inconclusive and vague but if the rest is accurate and real, then you've discovered something that was never dreamed of."

"The main issue is how to communicate back and forth with them. The only way we could reach them was through feeding. They sent a message and we approved by dripping glucose. Limited, I know, but this was still a breakthrough. Now, it's all gone. This specimen was already in sync with us and now they've died. I'll have to restart the entire process with new HeLa cells."

Stan slumped back into his chair. "Are you sure these are not from interference of some sort? Radio waves, atmospheric anomalies? Something that bounces back from somewhere? Or even worse, maybe someone is playing a nasty joke on you? Have you ever thought about these possibilities?"

"Stan, we are dropping glucose and a minute later getting a message that they received food. We didn't even tell them that we dropped glucose. There is no way someone else is responding. We see these changes on the Photonic Microscope. That's why I am obsessed with it."

Stan remained silent. "This is big, Sam."

"Exactly. And the last challenge that I have to overcome is the two-way communication. I have to find a way to alter the molecules in such a pattern to create the modified DNA code message. That's the main challenge before us."

"Is Alisha with you on this?"

"She is helping. Also a guy from AlphaTron is with us all the way. I think we can continue there, with his help, without any more money schemes."

"Well, that's good news. You are enough in trouble without any more bank hacking. As it is, I hope that when your research is complete we'll find someone to take sponsorship and cover the costs. We are talking almost fifteen million dollars now, Sam. That's enough fraud to put you in jail for many years."

"When the research is complete, we will give these people jobs, Stan. I just need to continue my research until I solve the puzzle."

Stan released a long sigh. "Well, you are out of jail now. Let the lawyer work on your case. We bought you some time, but not for long. I'll think about who to get to help cover the costs and set you free."

"Thank you, Stan."

"Don't thank me yet. I don't know for how long the lawyer can save you. I'll work on my end of things."

Samuel looked at the petri dish on the table. "In the meanwhile, I'll create new specimens and start new communication." He shook his head. "Poor guys, we could have saved them."

Stan puffed more smoke clouds into the air. "Sam, don't get sentimental with cancer. They are one of the fiercest enemies of the human race."

The Adirondack Mountains, tall, evergreen sloped, and white at their peaks from the night's dusting were magnificent. Sam and Alisha headed up the New York State Thruway to Lake George. Winter was setting in and the so swimming and kayaking were out, but the hearty could still enjoy hiking and biking and a few nights in a cabin.

"I've never visited here before, Sam. You're right. The mountains and woods are simply magnificent." Alisha pecked his cheek as he drove north. "It was a great idea to spend the weekend here."

"The cabin is small—what real estate people call cozy. There's a fireplace though and a cord of wood stacked high in the back."

"We deserve a break after all we've been through."

"Yes, I need some invigorating mountain air. We need to rethink the project and there is no better place than upstate New York. I grew up near here, Alisha. I had an uncle in Glen Falls and we used to spend time there at least twice a year—summer and winter. The lakes are clear blue in warm weather and often they freeze over by January."

"That's sound like fun. You never told me about your uncle, Sam."

"His name was Patrick. He's gone now. Never married. Said that being alone is much better. He couldn't handle relationships. Too much energy, he claimed. He was funny." Samuel sank into memories. "But I loved him. He had a large and good heart. He was always happy, always confident. Those who knew him, loved him."

"What kind of work did he do?"

"Blue collar. He worked in a Corning factory all of his life. Simple worker, without any bold ambitions or goals. A basic, contented life was all he sought. I envy him."

"Sounds like a nice man. What happened to him?"

"Well, he was severely overweight and afflicted with diabetes. It was just a matter of time. But he lived fairly long life for a person with such health problems. He had a stroke at the age of sixty-five and passed away a few days later in a hospital. Although I was in medical school then, and an adult, it was a very sad day for me. I really loved him. All of his quirks, laughs, crazy ideas, and just joy of life. You never forget such moments, even when you were just a kid." Samuel wiped a tear.

"I am sorry, Sam." Alisha held his hand.

"He taught me to appreciate and love this area. Although he was heavyset, he loved to walk and hike. He took me everywhere. To the mountains, to the woods and to remote caves and streams." Samuel patted her hand. "I'll take you there."

"I'd love to see these places."

"Oh, yeah. All these places we shall see."

"Count me in."

"I already have!"

The road curled into the woods and became narrower.

"It's getting dark. Look how tall the pines are. I'll bet they go back to the eighteenth century." Samuel opened the car's window. "Breath in!"

Alisha opened the window and bracing air shot through the car in an instant.

"Soon we will be at our cabin. After we check in, we shall enjoy an elegant candlelit dinner with a view of the lake and mountains."

"I can't wait. We should come here more often, Sam."

"We will."

"It said that the Chateau on the Lake is more than just a hotel, it's an experience." Samuel raised a glass of red wine to the air. "Bon appétit!"

Their secluded table afforded a remarkable view of Lake George, and just outside was a patio. If it gets too cold there, a roaring fire inside will swiftly take off the chill.

Samuel ordered a private dinner for two out on the patio, just a few yards from the water. The table featured a cloisonné vase with a crush of pink carnations, and two vanilla-scented candles which flickered in the gentle air. A private server had already brought a pinot noir, which had been bottled near Lyon in 1972—an excellent year according to the wine steward.

Alisha raised her glass. "I am positively enchanted. You are full of surprises, Sam Daniels. What else you have planned for the evening?" She took a sip from her wine and gave him a meaningful look.

"After this dinner and an appropriate dessert, I am going to take you where my uncle took me many years ago for a less conventional dessert."

"Oh, I see. This time of night?" Alisha raised a brow.

"Especially this time of night." Samuel smiled. "This is one of the most beautiful times to explore the forest and the caves."

"Caves?"

"Yes, dear, caves. It's all been arranged." Samuel gave her a quizzical look. "Do you trust me?"

"Yes, I do. Of course."

The filet mignon was a masterpiece. Thickly cut, soft and juicy, brazed on the outside and quite rare inside, marinated in wine and mushrooms and served alongside asparagus sautéed in sesame oil. Generous scoops of house-churned vanilla ice cream topped with coconut and pistachios made for a rich dessert. Pleasant memories of schooldays accented the meal.

Alisha's green eyes sparkled in the dark as she looked into the still waters of the lake. Moonlight glistened over the darkened surface.

"You surprise me, Sam. I love this side of you. But I guess I should have seen it earlier. Your dedication, your belief, your passion to push the boundaries. You are truly amazing."

"Thanks, Alisha, but I don't think that I'm really unique. I just believe that we have to achieve goals in life. Especially when it comes to an illness that so many people die from every year. There's got to be a way to find a cure somehow. There's got to be."

"But the way you think, it is really different, Sam. It's unique."

"Well, that's how we find out-of-the-box ideas, isn't it? Now, with your permission, let me take you to one of the most exquisite places from my youth."

They made a quick change of clothes and footwear, and grabbed a backpack filled with flashlights, water, and a GPS unit. Samuel even had night-vision goggles that he purchased on eBay. The little path curled through the darkening woods.

"This wandering in the woods at night is kind of creepy. I would never do it by myself."

"This is only eight-thirty, Alisha. It's still early."

"How do you know your way around? Especially at night?"

"My uncle, remember? Here, let's stop for a minute."

Samuel kneeled. "Listen to the night, Alisha."

They both tuned out everything but the murmurs of the forest night.

"So what is the most reliable sense at night?" Samuel asked gently.

"I don't know."

"Your hearing. You can't rely on your vision; the visibility is limited. Trust your ears." Samuel put his finger to his lips.

And soon enough they heard the forest. A distant owl, crickets, and locusts. Far away a coyote called out.

"It is beautiful, but aren't you a bit scared to be out here at night?

"No, why? We're safe. There are animals all around us but they fear us and will keep their distance. Besides I brought a weapon, just in case."

They continued their journey into the night and soon enough arrived at the caves that yawned from the foothills of a mountain. The gibbous moon illuminated their path and cast a silvery outline on the rocks.

"It's . . . magnificent," Samuel whispered.

"Yes, it is. Exceptionally so. Alisha held him tight. "I'm still concerned about animals in the night."

"Oh, no worries, sweetheart. I've done this path many times as a child. No animals will bother us."

Alisha shivered in the night air and Sam put an arm around her.

"Here, we'll take this narrow path just to the rock up there." Samuel pointed a hundred years or so up the incline. "This leads to a cave that I don't think too many people know about."

The path had many rocks and roots but the way up wasn't terribly difficult. There were branches to help steady themselves and pull on when they came across sharp inclines.

Alisha looked into the maw of the cave and came to a halt. "I am not going in there."

"Sure we are." Samuel aimed an LED flashlight into the opening.

"What if there are bats in there?"

"No bats, I promise you. I've been in here many times and there were not bats at all."

He held her hand and led her into the cave.

"Shhh. . . Can you hear that, Alisha?"

She listened carefully in her tracks. "Yes. . . water?"

"Exactly There's a steady flow of spring water from the granite. It's practically intoxicating."

"I believe you. But where are we going?"

"I'll show you. We'll get there in a few minutes."

They continued into the cavern as their flashlights shot powerful beams of light that cast angular shadows from the rocks. Soon, they arrived at a large rock that seemed to block their way.

"What do we do now, Daniel Boone? Go back?" Alisha's voice was shaky.

"Look carefully. Things are not always as they appear to be!" The found their way around the large rock and just behind it there was a small opening. "Everyone that was here before probably thought the way was no longer passable, and turned around. Well, maybe not everyone but here it is, our secret cave. Let's go inside."

They crept into the aperture. Inside it was as though someone had hewn a chamber into the rock. The top had a low slope and the floor was smooth rock.

"It seems like nature created this place by pressure," Samuel explained. "Many years ago there was an earth displacement, due to an earthquake, I assume, which created this secret place. But the amazing thing is that we are not the first ones here. Look up here."

Samuel shone his flashlight above them. There were carvings in the rock. Drawings of some sort.

"Wow! I've seen things like that only on the History Channel. Look, there are many of them. Images of people, animals, and many other things."

"My uncle discovered it many years ago and took me here to show me. I don't think that anyone else knows about this."

Alisha stood as best she could in the cramped area and gently touched the images on the roof. "The images are carved more deeply into the surface than I thought, and I see red . . . and other faint colors. Who do you think did them?"

"I don't really know. There's not much known about the people that lived in these mountains in ancient times. My uncle assumed they were forbears of the Mohicans or Huron."

"This is amazing." Alisha's hands moved from image to image, her fingers running along the indentations and grooves.

"I have a plan for us." Samuel removed his backpack, laid it on the floor, and removed a down sleeping bag. Tucked further down was a bottle of Merlot. The sound of the cork reverberated in the chamber.

"Voila!" Samuel kissed her and ignited a flame. They kissed more passionately and kneeled onto the sleeping bag.

"Wait!" Samuel took out a candle and lit it with a match. The flame flickered on the rock surfaces, creating shadows and silhouettes, making the images seem to come to life. The scent of roses came as the wax melted and drifted upward.

"I love you, Alisha."

Within mere seconds they were taken by passion.

They laid together inside the sleeping bag, looking at the ceiling as the images danced about.

"This is so beautiful . . . an unforgettable memory, Sam. It was a little scary at first but you fixed it all."

"Memories, like little corners in our minds. Who said that?"

"Barbara Streisand, I believe."

"So right. We are made of memories. As a matter of fact, all the things that shape and create us are memories, if you think about it. Everything we know or do is based on memories."

"True."

"We enter our car in the morning and drive to work. This is based on memories. We remember how to drive. We meet our boss at work, this is memory based. We go to the supermarket to buy milk. It's also memory based."

"Yes. Every detail that we know is based on our memory. Since birth we learn things and they go into our memory."

"Exactly." Samuel remained silent for a while. "If we could just find that key."

Alisha gently caressed his face. "We will one day. I am very confident that we will. With your persistence, we will."

They lay there quietly.

"Sam? Did you ever look at the images in that corner?" Alisha pointed towards the far left corner of the cave. There were a half dozen red carvings.

Samuel shone his flashlight and they both got closer to the images.

"What is this?" Samuel whispered. "I never investigated too deeply in here. After all, there are so many images. My uncle thought this place was an ancient people's history. Something like an epic poem."

Alisha got closer to the lower part of the wall. "Look at this figure of a person. It looks like he or she was sick."

They carefully observed the images.

"I'll be damned, you're right. This person looks like he has some type of illness." He then pointed at another section of the cave.

"Yes," Alisha illuminated more parts of the drawings carved on the rock. She pointed at a figure lying on the ground. "This guy looks deceased. See the halo drawn above him?"

"Also look at the little shapes on his body." Samuel added. "Obviously there is an indication of disease in here but we don't know exactly what."

"Look here." Alisha pointed to another spot. "This young woman seems to have a lump in her stomach. She is drawn and weak. This may be a depiction of cancer."

"Or it is different artist with different perspectives and experiences." Samuel gave her a kiss on her cheek.

"Could be. But check this." She pointed to another image. "This one has his stomach opened up and a cloud of dots is coming out of it. That's amazing. I really think it is a depiction of illness."

Samuel observed the images more closely. "These dots are what interest me. What are they?"

"I don't know. Look here." Alisha pointed into another image of an old man that looked like he was sitting on the ground. "See, this man looks in pain. And this woman is giving him a potion to drink. A potion made of this." She pointed to a plant that was near hers. "It looks like this entire section may be an early infirmary of some sort."

"Yes. The question is, what disease is this."

"And what is the plan? What is this ancient medicine?"

"Who would imagine?" Samuel murmured as they took pictures with their cell phones. "I bring you here for romantic purposes and we end up doing archeo-medical research."

Alisha laughed. "There should be no contradiction, Sam. Working on this research means spending time together. It is very romantic for me. And besides, I am done with my observations for now." She turned off her phone.

Samuel took a last picture. "I am done with mine."

No more words were needed. They fell back into the sleeping bag.

Nikolai looked upbeat and reasonably well groomed. Sam was pleased on both counts.

"Hey Nikolai, any news?" Samuel was back at work in the Photonic Microscope chamber and eager to get back in the groove. Furthermore, he, Alisha, and Alex were able to use the magnificent device in the wee hours.

"Hey, you used to tell me that you are happy to see me and how great I am. And now this? Nikolai, any news?"

"Please? You already know that you are great and I need some answers quick."

Samuel sent Nikolai the images that they took in the cave for analysis. His powerful software tools could scan and identify objects in the images, then search the net for information about the objects. Era, characteristics, function, and any other detail that someone had uploaded.

"You guys are working every night so late?" Nikolai mumbled as he typed on an oversized keyboard. "Oh, looks like I have an ID on the medicine plant."

"No!"

"Oh yes, it is now clear to me. Based on the extensive information that all my programs provided, I can identify the plan with a high percentage of reliability."

"Nikolai. . ."

"Yes, I am getting there. The pattern recognition algorithm and the expert system that analyzed the image's pixels—and there are many pixels you know—reached a high probability assumption that most likely. . . ."

"Nikolai!" This time Alisha and Samuel both screamed.

"Okay, okay. Don't be so touchy."

"What is the plant, Nikolai?"

"It's the most common fruit that humans eat."

"Which is?"

"Nikolai gave them a surprised look on the 52" LCD screen in the lab.

"The plum tomato."

"Tomato?" Samuel exclaimed.

"Not just any tomato, but the *plum* tomato." Nikolai ignored completely their impatience and beamed happily to tell them the results. "My program is so accurate that it could find that the plant was not just a tomato plant but a plum tomato one. You know those small, long tiny, sweet tomatoes that you buy in the supermarket, which by the way I love. Yes, those ones. So it turned out to be a type of plant that was very popular among ancient tribes for its medicinal properties. They used to eat the fruit, cook its roots, and believe it or not, the plant's leaves are actually poison but mixed with other ground plants the toxicity becomes homeopathic."

"What are those clouds of dots that were coming out of the human's stomach?" Alisha asked.

"Ah, good question—and I believe that you'll like the answer." Nikolai's expression conveyed an unexpected earnestness. "That's why I would like to remind everyone that, owing to my contributions—the legality of which we shall discuss another time—I consider myself an integral part of this team, and not just for the hacking skills. How did you put it last time when we talked, 'exist' something?"

"Coexistence, Nikolai. We're Team Coexistence." Samuel spoke impatiently.

"Yes, that's it."

He became silent as everyone's eyes were on him.

"Well then, we are all in agreement. Nikolai is a valued member of Team Coexistence. But the question needs to be answered: What are the dotted clouds supposed to signify?" Alisha kept calm.

"Oh yeah. So at first I was very skeptical myself. I mean, the outcome of my programs looked a little too far off to me, but as I investigated the topic again and again, launching more analysis nodes across the web, it started to make sense."

"Oh, Nikolai! Please save us the agonizing suspense." Samuel held his head with both hands.

"Yes, yes, I am getting there. So my program detected a pattern that is defined as *mitosis*."

"Mitosis?" Samuel and Alisha couldn't hide their surprise.

"Indeed, my friends. After all, I am not a medical doctor but according to my program, mitosis is the process of nuclear cell division."

"Yes, we all know what mitosis is, Nikolai. Cancer is essentially a disease of mitosis - the normal 'checkpoints' regulating mitosis are ignored or overridden by cancer cells. But what? How?" Samuel had difficulties to even phrase his question.

"Nikolai?" Alisha interrupted. "What are you saying? That these dots are connected to mitosis? How? At what stage? There are a few of them?"

"Well, I don't know that much. Look, I studied the topic in regards to the dot pattern. During division, the nucleus of the cell divides, resulting in two sets of identical chromosomes, or organized DNA proteins. This process is almost always accompanied by a process called cytokinesis, in which the rest of the cell divides, leading to two completely separate cells, called daughter cells. There are four phases in the process: prophase, metaphase, anaphase, and telophase. There are a number of reasons for this process, including reproduction and replacement of cells, and problems with it can seriously damage or kill cells. It's often confused with meiosis, but the processes differ in several ways."

"All this is good. You've certainly done your research." Alisha nodded for him to continue.

"Cancer begins when a single cell is transformed or converted from a normal cell to a cancer cell. Often this is because of a change in function of one of several genes that normally control growth. Once these crucial cell cycle genes start behaving abnormally, cancer cells start to proliferate wildly by repeated, uncontrolled mitosis. This is done by a certain pattern—one identified by my program," Nikolai explained.

"Outstanding, Nikolai." Sam was elated that someone in another field was making such a valuable contribution. "So we know that cancer is dangerous cell growth. Maybe I'm a little slow at this time of night but can you relate this to the dots in the image from the rocks?"

"Well, as much as I hate to admit something that I don't know yet, I have to admit that I don't know—yet." Nikolai smiled to someone off camera. "Hi, dear!"

A lithe young blonde woman pecked his cheek and sat in a swivel chair next to him. Nikolai zoomed out to put her in the Skype video. "Who are you talking with—and leaving me all alone?" She smiled beautifully to the camera. "Hello, I'm Svetlana."

Nikolai smiled more warmly than Sam had ever seen before.

"As you folks in America see, I am a *truly* fortunate man!"

"Yes, Nikolai moved in with me a week ago, so now we are a couple. We live about sixty kilometers from his former residence. Bye for now." She kissed Nikolai more fully and began to stand up. "At last I got him all to myself. Well, almost to myself. He still loves his computer a little bit more!"

"What? Nikolai, you moved so far away to be with Svetlana? Why Nikolai? Why did you move to a different city?"

Nikolai looked like a mischievous kid that had been caught.

Samuel shook his head. "And you didn't even tell me. What happened? Were you traced?"

Nikolai released a long sigh. "Something like that. It became too dangerous and I had to take my leave."

"I am sorry, Nikolai. I hope the move works out for you and Svetlana."

"No, don't be sorry. Do you think that I'd leave the glory to you three? No way. I insist on helping you. Eventually, when everything is complete, we all will be famous and I am sure that the FBI will forgive our computer indiscretions! Let's get back to the topic, shall we? We still have one big mystery to solve here. The program clearly identified a mitosis process from the cave images. I don't know how those old guys knew about it, but it doesn't matter. There is still one thing to solve and it's a very hard one. The code key. There is definitely a code within these patterns, the only problem is that there is an exponential number of possibilities. Without the key, we can't translate the messages. That's why you can't communicate back with the cancer cells. You don't know the key. Given the fact that we have to develop a system that is affecting biological factors and electrical factors, this makes it extremely challenging. I am going with the idea of levels of EMF and chemical elements distribution within the culture, but I'll let my program, which is artificial-intelligence based, to decide. We are running millions of possibilities as we speak."

"They can communicate with us though. Why we can't communicate back in the same modified DNA code?" Alisha asked.

Nikolai anticipated the question. "Well, this unique DNA code will still be our interface and that's how we'll communicate with the cancer cells but we need to translate this DNA code into molecular structure so they can understand. That's how they communicate with us. They know how to manipulate the molecular structure to create a pattern of this ancient DNA code. We don't."

The four researchers of Team Coexistence now had a succinct idea of the task ahead of them.

"We have to find a key," Nikolai continued. "And we will. It is just a matter of time. I am working on a program now to create millions of tests, repeatedly. It should find the key, the only thing is that the run may take months, maybe years."

"Please continue your search. We'll continue with our efforts here. We'll have to be in touch every few days to compare notes." Samuel moved to end the Skype call. "Thank you again, Nikolai—for everything."

Nikolai squeezed his lips in a tiny smile. "No worries. We'll crack this one. I've faced harder challenges than this one. I'll let you know if I have news. Be well."

His image vanished from the screen and the graphs and charts of the Photonic Microscope took its place. The low hum from the photon beam was the only sound in the chamber.

It was Alex that broke the silence. "So what's next?"

The time had come and all conditions were ready. As it has been done for millions of years, cells started to divide. The group of cells that resided in a certain location for many years without any interference from the human system, started its process of multiplication. The cells did not just divide randomly into two cells; they had to distribute an exact copy of each of their chromosomes to each new cell.

The cells had to be very precise. Each chromosome contains thousands of genes, each essential to the proper functioning of the organism. It was vital that each new cell gets the same set of chromosomes that its parent cell once had.

Humans have about 120,000 genes spread over 46 chromosomes in each bodily cell. Each one of these cells is genetically identical to each other.

Each replicated chromosome was then composed of two identical parts—each copy of DNA is called a sister chromatid, held together by a centromere. These chromatids stayed together to keep the cell's organized structure.

Then a single cell was transformed, or converted, from a normal cell to an abnormal one. This happened because of a change in function of one of several genes that normally function to control growth. The cells had a name for this phenomenon. They called it 'the guardian of the genome'. This ancient process has occurred for millions of years in many types of hosts. Once one cell cycle genes start behaving abnormally, other cells start to proliferate wildly by repeating and growing. The abnormal cells ignored the usual density-dependent inhibition on growth, multiplying after contact with other cells are made, piling up until all nutrients are exhausted. But for now, they had plenty of food.

The abnormal cells proliferated to form a mass of cells. As the mass grew larger, it began to release proteins from the cells to stimulate new blood vessel growth. Very quickly, the mass constituted about one million abnormal cells. This was what called an uncontrolled mitosis—uncontrolled cell reproduction.

A new colony had formed. In the medical world there is a name for this mass. It's called a tumor.

The steamboat paddled slowly through the placid waters of Lake George, leaving a gentle wake that provided additional fun to children on smaller craft that day. It was Saturday, noon time, and Samuel and Alisha dined on the upper deck. The air was brisk, the sun was bright but weak, and the couple enjoyed their outing.

"This is becoming my favorite place, Sam." From the deck of a tour boat Alisha watched the reflection of the mountains ripple as the breeze raced across the surface of the water. "Look at the geese over there." She pointed towards one of the many islets that were spread across the lake. A dozen geese took to the skies and formed a perfect V. "Amazing symmetry. Internal guidance, I imagine." Alisha sent her hand and held Samuel's. "Thank you, Sam, for thinking of this day."

"It's my pleasure, Alisha."

A waiter appeared with two glasses of wine.

"Thank you." He raised his glass. "To us."

"To us!" Alisha gave him one of her most beautiful smiles. "I love you, Sam."

Sam took her hand. "May I invite you to see the view from the stern?"

"You may!"

They walked towards the back of the boat, wine glasses in hand, and leaned on the rail. The waiter brought out a pink rose and a covered plate. "Great service in this place."

"Is this dessert?"

"Something like that." Samuel smiled. He raised the cover and revealed a wrapped, ribboned presentation box, three inches cubed.

"But I brought nothing for you! What is this?"

"Please just open it!"

Alisha removed the bow and opened the box with shaky hands. Sunbeams struck the diamond seated atop a ring, emitting thousands of prism-like glints.

Samuel kneeled. Alisha covered her mouth.

"Alisha, I love you with all my heart. I hope you will join me for the rest of our lives."

He gently slipped the ring onto her finger.

"I don't know what to say! I . . . I . . . Of course, Sam. Yes, yes, of course. I love you. I've dreamed about this moment."

They kissed as several charmed onlookers gathered around applauded warmly.

"Sam, I have but one request."

"Up to half of the kingdom, my love."

She laughed. "My father always wanted to give me a traditional

Greek wedding. Could we please tie the knot in my home country? My family will be more than happy to cover the costs."

"Of course, my love. It sounds very exotic to me. Greece has the Mediterranean, ancient architecture, remarkable cuisine. Greece shall have us as well!"

"I'll show you its beauty."

He gave her another passionate kiss.

"Whoa! I suddenly feel dizzy." Alisha had to hold the rails.

"It's the passion, my love, the passion!"

"No, I really feel *very* dizzy, Sam." Alisha leaned on the rails and breathed in deeply, just as the boat swung to starboard to begin its return to the pier. It all happened very quickly. Samuel watched in horror as Alisha's eyes rolled backwards and she lost her balance and lurched over the rail. He tried to reach her but the momentum from the hard turn worked against them. He grabbed her sweater sleeve but in a moment she was falling overboard. The same people who were charmed by the young couple's happiness was now horrified by their unfolding tragedy.

"Stop the boat! Woman overboard!" Samuel shouted towards the staff members and the bridge.

He didn't think twice and jumped after her.

"Hi, handsome." Alisha whispered fraily as she looked up from the hospital bed.

Samuel sat near her and held her hand. "How do you feel?"

"Weak. Okay, but weak." She looked around at the puzzling environs. "Where are we?"

"We are at a hospital near Lake George, love."

"What happened?"

Samuel took a deep breath. "Don't you remember?"

"Vaguely. I felt dizzy."

"And then you fell overboard just as I reached for you. The water was rather chilly."

"I don't remember that. Sorry."

Samuel laughed and gave her a kiss. "No worries, I'm a good swimmer."

Alisha then became serious. "So I passed out. Why?"

"The doctors ran a battery of tests and we'll hear from them shortly. Then I would like to continue checking you back in New Haven."

Alisha smiled faintly. "I guess I got too excited from your proposal. You did propose, didn't you?"

"Yes, of course I did. And you accepted."

"Yes, of course I did."

A doctor entered the room. He did not look pleased. "You didn't just get excited. It didn't seem right to me and I ordered an MRI."

Sam and Alisha clutched their hands together as he held up an image of a head with a red circle around a dark object. He wasted no time.

"I'm afraid you have a brain tumor."

Samuel was in his office, late at night, trying to find a way to break the molecular pattern code. He seems to push aside the bad news and continue with more efforts in order to find a solution. A Skype window opened.

"Terrible news about Alisha, Sam." Nikolai's face was drawn and glum.

"I appreciate your thoughts, old chum. It came as such a surprise. Such things always do, I suppose. The cancer is exceptionally aggressive. Her lymph nodes have started to swell which means it has spread. It's progressing fast, Nikolai. It's terminal. She has a few months, no more. I have to find the way to communicate with the cancer. This is the only way to save her."

Nikolai released a long sigh. "I am sorry, Sam, but I have no news yet. I am working day and night to find the code. The pattern has so many possibilities it is worse than trying to pick a winning lottery ticket."

Samuel observed Nikolai's face. He was unshaven and worn out. "You don't do any of your own work anymore?"

"Nope. Now that I am practically in hiding, and living on Svetlana's salary, I have all the time in the world to try to break the code. But it is slow going, my friend, and it is very easy to give up. I have many days that I want to break all my servers here."

"No, please, Nikolai. You have to continue." Sam's voice cracked. "We have to continue. This is the only way that gives Alisha any chance. I can't believe it. I am an oncologist, Nikolai, I've seen many cancer cases in my life. I know the statistics. And what can I do?"

Nikolai didn't know how to encourage his friend. Then he took a deep breath. "I will continue, Sam. I will continue until we master this thing. If you have any piece of information that can give me some leads, please do so. Even if it is very minor it can give us a new direction because now we are searching the galaxy. We don't know where to go and we don't have any clue where our star is."

"I already established successful communication with a new colony of HeLa cells. I am able to read their messages but still unable to message them back. So for now it's one-way communication."

"What're HeLa cells, Sam?"

"Sorry, I forgot to tell you but all my previous specimens were of HeLa type cells. A HeLa cell is an immortal cell line we use in research. It is the oldest and most commonly used human cell line."

"Did you say immortal?" Nikolai wondered. "That's a fascinating term."

"HeLa cells come from cervical cancer cells taken in 1951 from Henrietta Lacks, a patient who eventually died of her cancer. The cell line is durable and prolific and is widely used in research. Typical cells survive for a few days, but not these cells. They lived for weeks and even months, so we named them the immortal cells."

"Wow, this is amazing. I should be a doctor, maybe. Maybe in my next life."

"Oh yeah, the HeLa cells were a major achievement. We developed a vaccine for polio and achieved other milestones due to the HeLa cells. In 1955 we even cloned the HeLa cells. Thank you, Henrietta Lacks. The human race owes you a great deal."

"It sure does. Sam, off I go to my computer program. I think that I may have a good lead and I would like to continue."

"Before I let you go, what does your program do?" Samuel took a sip from his coffee.

"Are you familiar with the genetic algorithm, Sam?"

"Yes, but only the basics. Tell me more."

"Are you sure? You look tired."

"Nope, I have all night, Nikolai. Please."

Nikolai took a french fry from the paper bag near him. "Actually the genetic algorithm mimics your cells' behavior. That's why its name is from the medical field and it's inspired by Darwin's theory of evolution. The algorithm is started with a set of solutions, which are represented by chromosomes, called a population. Here is the main idea in short: solutions from one population are taken and used to form a new population. This is motivated by a hope that the new population will be better than the old one. Solutions which are selected to form new solutions, which are the offspring, are selected according to their fitness—the more suitable they are the more chances they have to reproduce."

"Ah, this sounds familiar and makes sense." Samuel nodded.

"This is repeated until some condition is satisfied." Nikolai continued with a serious expression. "Now, this seems to be a perfect method to find our pattern. Well, not exactly. Since the genetic algorithm belongs to the field of artificial intelligence, it is heuristic-based and mimics the process of natural selection. This heuristic is routinely used to generate useful solutions to optimization and search problems. Now, a heuristic is a technique designed for solving a problem more quickly when classic methods are too slow, or for finding an approximate solution when classic methods fail to find any exact solution. By their nature, heuristics are error prone. I developed a smart derivative of the classic genetic algorithm that is much broader when it comes to search for patterns of dot clouds. I am hoping to find something promising.

"Samuel didn't get excited. He remembered that one of Nikolai's habits was to lecture people. He simply enjoyed going on and on, especially if he knew much more details about the topic.

"Okay, so what are your predictions, Nikolai?"

"The riddle is definitely of NP-Complete type which refers to nondeterministic polynomial time."

"I know what NP-Complete problem is, Nikolai: a given solution to an NP-complete problem can be verified swiftly in polynomial time, but there is no known efficient way to reach a solution in the first place. That is why NP-complete problems are often addressed through heuristics and approximation algorithms. I know the textbook term, Nikolai, but how do you address our problem?"

"Aha, I developed a unique Turing machine." Nikolai beamed like he'd won the Nobel Prize.

"What is a Turing machine, Nikolai?" Samuel braced for another lecture.

"A Turing machine is a theoretical machine used in thought experiments to examine the abilities and limitations of computer programs. In essence, a Turing machine is a program-thread that reads and writes symbols one at a time endlessly into a file. The dot structure is assigned to numerical dots and alphanumeric dots. An example of one of a Turing Machine's rules might be: "If you are dot 2 and you see dot AB, change it to #5 and move right.""

Samuel got lost. "What is the outcome, Nikolai?"

"The outcome is detecting a pattern among billions of dots. The program can assemble endless possibilities of patterns this way. Most likely the majority of them will be worthless." Nikolai got excited and his voice quivered. "But it would be enough to find one solution, Sam, only one. This one is going to be the key. This only one key will enable you to send messages back to the colony. A message that they will understand."

Nikolai's enthusiasm encouraged Samuel. "Didn't understand much of the last part, Nikolai, but what can I say? Make it so, by all means." He felt a burst of hope.

Alisha refused to stay in the hospital. Although her cancer was aggressive and in stage four, she insisted to come to work everyday and help Samuel. She admitted that she had high hopes with the research, which pushed Samuel to work long hours trying to find the key.

Alex from AlphaTron continued to help too, providing many nights of the Photonic Microscope usage. The CEO's wife had died recently of ovarian cancer and he felt the company should help out as much as it could.

Nikolai spent days and night trying to crack the code, and Samuel and Alisha continued other possible methods besides the dot cloud. Alisha refused to be relegated to the sick list and worked many hours with Samuel. She rested only after chemotherapy treatment. On Alisha's request Samuel moved in with her and they were together all day long.

It was late Friday night when Samuel and Alisha conducted numerous experiments without any success. Samuel stared at the flickering computer screen and Alisha rested on the couch.

"I don't think we're going to find the key," Alisha said in a low tone.

Samuel lift his head from the computer screen. "Yes, we will. It's just a matter of time, Alisha. We will find it."

"Maybe. . . but not in time for me, Sam. I have to accept this fact. And so do you."

They cuddled on the couch.

"I have to disagree with you, my love. It took me years to find the love of my life and I am not going to give up now. Not now, not ever."

Alisha hugged him to her heart. "The number of possibilities is endless. You heard, Nikolai."

"True, but we will find the key. My father once told me something. 'You never know how close you are to success, so keep pushing!' I think he was right."

Alisha didn't answer.

He looked straight into her eyes. "My love, I promise you. I'll never give up. I truly believe that once we communicate with cancer, we can find a cure. I can't explain just how but I know it. You have to stay strong until then. You have to. Please, do it for me?"

With tears in her eyes she promised. "I'll hold on, Sam."

"Good," he wiped his tears. "Because I really want to have a Greek wedding."

"I got it!" Nikolai's face beamed trough his exhaustion. "I am ninety-nine percent sure that this is the key. Man, that was hard, even for me."

Samuel and Alisha hugged in joy.

"You are what we in the states call *the man*, Nikolai. Tell us more."

"Again, it is ninety-nine percent, my friends, but this sure looks like the answer we've been searching for. I am uploading it into your FTP site right now. Listen, Sam, it is a highly complicated program so I'll need to go through it with you on setup. Once that's done, the operation is simple. Just type your message and the program will adjust the strength of your electromagnetic field and its polarity. It has to work with the electronics that control your EMF. This is it. You'll have to make sure that the culture is soaked in seawater for high conductivity. The combination of EMF and seawater will arrange the molecular structure in a pattern that they should understand. My assumption is that they are reading the cell's membrane pattern since that's the method that they send their messages. This will be translated into their modified DNA code as the interface. I don't know much about DNA but I know the basics. Up until the 1950s, scientists knew about heredity, but they didn't have a clue what DNA looked like. In order to learn more about DNA and its structure, they experimented with X-rays as a form of molecular photography. Although the official reward was given to scientists from England, I saw, as a child, the first drawing with the familiar DNA structure. My father conducted research of his own and discovered the DNA structure."

Nikolai slumped back into his chair. "No one knows that my father was the one who directed the first research. He has never been recognized for his work. Instead, he died anonymously. But with this, I hope to make his name as well known as it should be."

"Your father discovered the first DNA structure?"

"Check this out." Nikolai pulled out an old photo album and brushed the dust from it. He removed one photo and moved it closer to the camera.

On a yellowish paper they could see a pencil sketch of the now familiar DNA structure. Just below it they saw a few scribbles in Cyrillic-Russian.

"This is my father's name and signature." Nikolai was proud.

"Wow! Nikolai, I never knew!" Samuel all but stammered.

"No one did. Anyway," Nikolai brought them back to the discussion. "For my father's sake, we need to solve this puzzle. You will have to rebuild your electronic circuit with precise EMF levels. I am talking in one thousands of units. Can you do that, Sam?"

"I have to and I will. Let's work on the setup program and by tomorrow, I'll have the electronic circuit for my coils."

"Go and make the circuits. I'll go and take a nap. I didn't sleep for three nights."

"Thank you so much, Nikolai, we'll never forget this." Although Alisha was obviously weak, she smiled and Nikolai felt the warmth thousands of miles away in a Russian winter.

The cells cycled through their ordered series of events. This was required for the faithful duplication of one eukaryotic cell into two genetically-identical daughter cells. The precise replication of deoxyribonucleic acid (DNA) duplicated each chromosome as it was done for thousands of years. Subsequently, the duplicated chromosomes separated away from each other by mitosis, followed by division of the cytoplasm, called cytokinesis.

These monumental transformations in the chromosomes were accompanied by general cell growth, which provides enough material of all sorts, mainly membranes that were required for the resultant doubling of cell number. The cycle continues indefinitely in specialized cells called stem cells that can be found in skin or bone marrow, causing constant replenishment of cells discarded by natural physiological processes.

The repetition of the cells produced a clone of identical cells as the colony's main aim. The specimen was on a petri dish and was accompanied by intricate changes that led to differentiation into distinctive cell types, or ultimately to the development of a complex organism. In all cases, the DNA sequence of each cell's genome remains unchanged, but the resultant cellular forms and functions varied. This was created by the induced amount of EMF and its polarity changes. From the viewpoint of chromosomes, four distinct, ordered stages constitute the cell's cycle. DNA synthesis and mitosis alternate with one another, separated by EMF, causing pattern of growth. Every chromosome replicated to yield two identical sister chromosomes called chromatids that remain attached creating certain code.

This code was created within the colony's perimeter.

For the first time in the colony's history, they read a message came to them from outside their own.

"We are getting some type of communication, sir." The assistant leader was anxious.

"Interesting. What type of communication?"

"That's the thing, sir. Although we clearly understand it, we don't exactly know how to respond."

"Is the message in our perimeter? Is it clear and organized?"

"Yes, sir, and it's very accurate, almost too accurate."

"What do you mean?"

"The pattern and the sequence are perfect, without any error. Typically when there are so many particles, there are errors, but we clean up the message with an error correction protocol. This message has no errors at all. We've never encountered anything like this before."

"We already know about our host communicating with us through food. We are blessed to know that our host is friendly, but where is this message coming from?"

"We suspect that the message comes from our host, sir, but this is an astonishingly significant change. From nothing to a perfect pattern."

"This is good. We should not be too suspicious. They must have figured out our communication method. Not so primitive as we thought."

"I agree with you, sir. We thought the same. It is a good thing."

"But still, I see that you are not satisfied. Is there any problem?"

"Well, yes, sir. The message is perfectly constructed. The only thing is its content. We do not understand what they mean."

"Why? What is the message content?"

"The message is this."

We want mood.

"We are making progress. This is great." Samuel, Alisha and Alex were in the microscope lab communicating with the colony. Nikolai was on a conference call on screen. "There is a change in their message."

"Yes, but –" Alisha was puzzled. "What do they mean by this?"

We do not understand.

Everyone in New Haven was unsure what this meant. Fortunately, Nikolai had some thoughts.

"This means that they received our message. That's a good news but it looks to me that they didn't understand it. Two possibilities here: First, the message is completely unintelligible. Second, they can read it but the words make no sense." Nikolai rubbed his hands as he sunk into thoughts. "Now we have to fix the protocol."

"Wait," Samuel was excited. "You say that we cracked the code but not entirely. That means we're still missing something so they can understand our messages.

"Exactly. We found the key. The images that you guys found in the cave gave us the basic key. We can communicate in their language. That's means that we know their alphabet. We even know some vocabulary, at least some of it. We'll know more with time. I am not worried about vocabulary. We will use different terms then we will learn more words with time. But we still have something missing. I suspect that we are missing the logical sequence of the words and how to put them together."

"The grammar?" Alisha wondered.

"Not only grammar but also the logical combination of sentences." Nikolai's confident look encouraged the others.

"So what we send them does not make sense?" Samuel suggested.

"Yes. Each word is known to them but the sentence is not clear."

"The problem is that we don't have any way to let them know about this issue," Alisha pointed out.

"Which can be a problem. We are inadvertently confusing them," Samuel added.

"Or worse," Nikolai raised a brow. "We might accidentally communicate a wrong message that offends them or causes them to stop all communication with us."

"They might get mad at us," Alisha murmured.

"Well, imagine that your mother tells you: Dear, please take the garbage out. And you answer: Mother you are fat." Nikolai's explanation conveyed the problem but nevertheless caused everyone to chuckle. "This may introduce some problems, don't you think?"

A chime sounded, indicating an incoming message.

We want mood.

The message repeated twice before another message came through.

You sent we want mood.

Everyone looked at the screens in utter fascination. "We are receiving messages from cancer cells. This is the peak of my career in computer science, my friends. One day. . . ."

"Yes, Nikolai, one day." Samuel stopped him. "But for now we have work to do. We don't have time for glorious self-congratulation."

"Yes, sorry. I suggest not to communicate with them anymore until we find the logical key. Otherwise we can damage our relationship. What was the original message that we sent them?"

"We asked them if they need food. The message was: 'You want food?'"

"So we are not too far but still need a logical key." Nikolai concluded. "This is still a very complicated task. I have to quickly go back to the old drawing board."

"Wait, but they are not dumb; they may figure out this mistake," Alex suggested.

"True, they may figure this one out but it's our further messages that I worry about."

Samuel was stressed. "So we shouldn't risk further communication with them?"

"Not for now. Not until we find the cause for this problem." Nikolai was determined. "That's what I suggest."

"I agree with Nikolai. We can't communicate with them until we figure out the cause for the miscommunication," Alisha said quietly. "We may say something that they will not like and the idea of angry cancer cells isn't very appealing to me. *Angrier* cancer cells, I should say."

"It's the worst thing in communication—miscommunication. We need a cognition key," Nikolai concluded. "I'll start right away. I suggest that you also try to think about any possibility that we may have missed. We need all the help that we can get. Any suggestion will be looked into."

The joy of discovery dimmed, yet Samuel saw progress. He took a deep breath. "We will get there eventually."

Alisha's joy faded.

From the viewpoint of the chromosomes, four distinct ordered stages constitute a cell cycle. DNA synthesis and mitosis alternate with one another, separated by two phases of preparation and growth. During one phase, every chromosome replicates to yield two identical sister chromosomes that remain attached at their kinetochores. A period of apparent chromosomal inactivity follows the initial phase. Then the cells prepare for mitosis. In mitosis, the duplicated chromosomes separate into two equal groups through a series of highly coordinated events. First, condensed sister chromatids attach to the mitotic spindle at the center of the cell. The fanlike mitotic spindle mediates the separation of all sister chromatid pairs as the chromatids, now called chromosomes, move to opposite poles of the cell.

Each of these activities causes change in pattern which translates into a message to other colonies. The phase of cellular growth and preparation for DNA synthesis, occurs next. Thus a cell cycle proceeds with its changes and the two new cells' cycles continue through the same series of stages. Cells that no longer undergo mitosis include most neurons and mature muscle cells.

These neurons get organized in a unique order. Letters and words could be assembled and that is how colonies of cancer cells communicated among themselves for millions of years. The puzzle was perfectly assembled, yet there was one piece missing.

The logical content.

"We tried to do our best, sir. We re-assembled different pattern structures of the messages that we are getting, hoping to build the correct message, but without success." The assistant leader reported to the governor. "We can't trust that we fully understand our host's messages. Something in their method doesn't work."

"We can't understand them correctly." The governor continued. "This is no good but we don't have any other choice." He looked upwards. "They'll have to continue their study. Otherwise we'll never be able to communicate."

"Sir, can you estimate what the consequences will be?"

"It's hard to tell. Based on our historical documents that cover millions of years, we were not aware that our hosts were our food providers. They may also know something about the existence of our disasters and maybe they have knowledge of how to overcome them.

All I can tell is that establishing communication with our host is a remarkable achievement that we never had."

"May I raise the possibility that they may be hostile, sir?"

"Indeed the possibility exists but still I believe that we should make all of our efforts to establish peaceful communication with them. Every living entity has one common drive which is very powerful. This drive is the reason for extreme changes and decision.

The assistant leader looked at the governor, waiting for his words.

"The desire to live."

"Where did you say that you want to go?" Samuel looked at Alisha as though she had gone mad.

"The Area 51 gathering." Alisha observed his face with joy. "Trust me, you'll love it. Many people bring their camping gear and sleep at the desert for two days."

"And do what?"

"They search for UFOs and paranormal phenomena, of course."

"I knew about your science fiction passion a long time ago, sweetie, but I never imagined that you'd go this far." Samuel gave a meaningful look. "There is a difference between watching *Star Wars* and going camping with a bunch of –" Alisha's eyes filled with fire. "Science fiction aficionados. That just might be a little too much for me. Besides we have to fly to the other side of the country. We don't have time for this."

"Oh yes, we do. We have to wait for Nikolai's research. It will be good for us to take a few days off anyway. A break will only help. It's only for two days, Sam. Trust me, you'll love it. Please?" Alisha made a most sweet face.

Samuel released long sigh. "I know that I am going to regret this!"

Alisha jumped on him and covered him with kisses.

They flew into Las Vegas, rented a car, and drove eighty-three miles across enchantingly open desert to the mystery-laden Air Force base on the southern shore of Groom Lake. The weather was much warmer than Connecticut in the winter and that was both pleasant and therapeutic. Samuel tried to convince Alisha to stay one night in Las Vegas but she insisted on getting to the gathering as soon as possible.

"Trust me, you'll love it. There will be many interesting and amusing people at this event." She laughed loudly when he gave her a skeptical look.

As they were driving down Rt 375 to the airbase, they could see many cars that were also on their way to the gathering. They passed a few venerable multi-colored Volkswagen buses with decals of aliens on the windows and rear bumpers.

"Now look at all these counterculture people heading to Area 51. They're your kind of people, are they?"

"Yes, these events typically draw many New Agers and of course some downright weirdoes, but so what. For me it's just part of the fun." She enjoyed Sam's wrinkled brow.

"What's the plan?"

"We are all gathering in the open desert near the base, and camping there for two nights. People bring their tents and simply have fun all day long. At night everyone is trying to spot suspicious activity and unique aircrafts. You know, secret prototypes or alien craft."

"Aha! Now that's very . . . how to say it?"

"Cool? Adventurous? Simply fun?"

"I would not exactly put it that way, but sure. We're on an adventure. Eh, what the heck. I never experienced an event like this. Maybe some of the people will think *I'm* a weirdo."

"Thank you, Sam. I'm glad you're opening up to new experiences." She leaned against his shoulder as they passed a road sign saying they were ten miles from the meeting place.

They arrived to the camp area in mid-afternoon. Samuel stepped out of the car, used his hand as a visor, and looked out in great wonder. Tents had been pitched across the desert floor and seemed to stretch for miles and miles. Some people were driving poles deeper into the sandy soil, others were setting up lawn chairs and snacking on foods from vending trucks or their own provisions. A few signs had been posted. Some read, "Area 51—The truth is out there" and "Alien activities, we'll expose the truth." One banner especially grabbed his attention. "Volunteers for Mars settlement—Sign up here."

"Unbelievable!" Sam shook his head. "I feel like I've been transported back to the sixties.

"You have!" Alisha stood next to him and leaned against him. "So, I told you it's going to be fun. Just think about it as a huge fair. Come, let's find a place to pitch our tent. Wow, this place is much more crowded than last year."

"I'm sure the Nevada desert can hold all of us."

A tall man in his thirties wearing ripped orange pants, a floppy hat, and a neon yellow shirt walked towards them exhaling smoke plumes into the Nevada sky. "I can't believe it. Alisha? Is that you?"

"Joe! Smokey Joe! Good to see you. Yes, it's me. How are you, my friend?" Alisha and Smokey Joe hugged. "I see you still smoke those nasty cigars or whatever. How many times have I told you that they're not good for you. I'm a doctor, you know."

"Stop smoking? But that's why they call me Smokey Joe. It's my trademark." Joe laughed aloud and lifted Alisha into the air. "And how are you, little girl." Then he smiled to Samuel, exposing angled, discolored teeth. "And who is your friend here?"

"This is Sam. He's also a doctor—and we are engaged."

"What? That's great news!" Joe grabbed Samuel and lifted him in the air. "Welcome to the family, my friend. You'll have to treat Alisha with respect, otherwise you'll hurt her feelings as well as my own! But you look like a wonderful guy. Congratulations!"

Taken aback, Sam fumbled for a reply. "Yeah, of course. Nice to meet you, Joe." He straightened his clothes and took a few steps backwards.

Smokey became unexpectedly serious. "Wait, everyone stop. Everyone stop." Smokey became surprisingly serious.

"What's going on?" Samuel whispered.

"I am channeling, I am channeling."

"Shhh! Smokey is channeling." Alisha whispered to Samuel.

"*Channeling?*" There were limits on Sam's openness.

Smokey was quiet and motionless for several minutes while Sam. Alisha, and a few others all looked on patiently. Then he opened his eyes and gave them a big smile. "You won't believe it. I just channeled John Lennon. It was awesome!"

"Really?" Samuel couldn't hold himself. "What channel was it? Maybe I can tune in also."

Smokey's smile slowly faded away and he stared at Samuel hurtfully.

Alisha intervened as she tried not to burst into laughter. "Smokey, my friend Sam here is not familiar with the term and mistakenly thought something else happened. I'll explain it all to him later. And I'll see *you* later. Take care."

She took Samuel's hand and led him away. "Come, Sam, we have to build our camp for the night. Told you you'd like it here." Alisha coaxed a smile from her.

"Your friend Smokey positively reeked of marijuana, not cigars." Samuel told her later that night. "I'll bet the guy is high all the time. He would be a good post-doc research assistant to a good friend of mine back in New Haven. He's a psychiatrist, of course."

"Fuddy-duddy! Almost everyone here is high. There is nothing to get worked up about. They do no harm."

They lay outside their tent covered with heavy blankets. The desert retains little of the day's warmth and temperatures plunge after dusk. The skies were clear and the stars flickered in a million lights. People in nearby tents talked and laughed and peered into the sky hoping for a glimpse of a strange aircraft. The night breezes wafted the aromas of barbecues and popcorn and every now and then, the same vegetation that Smokey Joe liked so well.

Sam and Alisha stayed by themselves.

"You didn't tell anyone about your condition." Samuel held her a little closer.

"They don't need to know. I don't want them to know."

They watched the stars for few minutes. Far from a city, there were thousands and thousands of them.

"This, I must say, is an amazing view. I guess I never took the time at home to lay and watch the skies at night. These stars, just lying there like an endless, flickering blanket. Nevada could grow on me."

"Lake George and Nevada. . . . Sam? Do you believe that there is life out there?"

"There are billions of stars out there. It would be vain of us to think that we are the only intelligent species in the universe. Don't you think?"

"Yes, I do."

"It is a magical atmosphere, don't you think, Sam? I love these moments of searching the endless skies, searching for something."

"What are you searching for?"

"Anything out of the ordinary. Anything that will teach us something different."

"Wait, I think that I just saw something."

"Where, where?" Alisha leaned up and searched the skies but saw nothing.

Samuel couldn't hold himself and burst into laughter. "Sorry, I was trying to fit in with the spirit of the community here."

"You are not taking this seriously. I am not taking you with me again."

"Yes, you are." He kissed her and they continued looking to the skies. The moon slowly arced its way up from the horizon. "You know what? You continue watching for ETs and I'll cuddle here, under the blanket. I promise you, I'll listen intently."

"Sam . . . please. . . ." Alisha moaned. "Ah, you're *so* unscientific."

Alisha then joined him under the blanket.

The apparent simplicity of the particular alignment, division, and motion of chromosomes in routine cell division belies the intricateness behind it. The chromosomes were aligned in a certain way by the colony. Remarkably, the transitions between cell-cycle stages depended on one family of evolutionarily conserved proteins that act as enhancers, driving forces to direct the progression of the cell cycle.

These proteins are enzyme-regulated and catalyze the addition of phosphate groups to protein substrates. The key factor to regulation is the addition of one or more phosphate groups to a substrate protein so they can change that substrate's ability to do its cellular task. One particular substrate may be inhibited by such a modification, while a different substrate may be activated by the same type of modification. Due to their abnormal activity-cycles up and down during the mutated cell cycle, the proteins target specific cellular parts for phosphorylation, thereby causing changes in cell-cycle progression.

There is a unique cellular condition that has to be established and this has been going on for millions of years. When this unique transition occurs, an inactivation of normal mitotic occurs for a subsequent cell-cycles, when cells exit mitosis and proceed to the cell-cycle checkpoint activity.

A cell-cycle event occurred at a certain time during abnormal cycles. It was tightly controlled by regulating the activity of every chromosome division. Each protein was active only periodically during the cell cycle, with its peak of activity limited to the period during which it was needed. Regulated transcription of genes and regulated degradation of proteins provided this oversight and new sets of abnormal cells were generated.

The abnormal cells grew rapidly, invading normal cell structures, and at some point pushed their way into her brain. The brain consists of about 100 billion cells. Most of these cells are called neurons. A neuron is basically an on/off switch. A few hundred million neurons inside Alisha's brain were activated and this triggered an event.

An amazing event.

Alisha and Samuel lay near their tent. Samuel fell asleep but Alisha remained awake, watching the stars.

So many, such beautiful patterns.

All of a sudden she sensed something. A bright light flashed in front of her eyes. She didn't feel anything and for a split second she was out. Then she woke up and felt her toes tingling. Her entire being felt different but she couldn't define it.

Oh, my God! This may be it. I'm dying. I have to wake up Sam.

She tried to move but couldn't move a finger. Yet despite of the rising panic she thought logically. Her medical training helped her think things through.

I can see. And I can think.

She could move her head slightly.

I can see Sam. He is sleeping. I am not dead . . . and I am okay.

Her brain felt exceptionally sharp. Like she'd drunk a thousand cups of coffee. She felt that she could calculate millions of mathematical problems in an instant.

What's going on? I don't know but it is not too bad. Feels like I got more brilliant than Albert Einstein. What to do?

She tried to move her hand again and watched her hand moving in a very slow manner. She tried to move her foot. She could do it but again her body moved extremely slow.

Okay, so my motor functions are very slow but my brain feels extra fast. There is only one explanation. It's either I am having a seizure or it is my brain tumor. I am not going to wake up Sam. I don't want to stress him out any more than necessary

Then she looked at the skies above. Billions of stars. They are all sparkling at me.

Then something happened.

Wait! What's going on? The stars . . . I see lines connecting them . . . I see shapes . . . what are they?

Her brain analyzed the stars' structure. Information entered from the spinal cord and arrived at the base of her brain. From there it branched out like a tree with an enormous number of branches, twigs and leaves and went to the surface of her brain. Electrical impulses flashed into every one of the billions of brain cells and the information was processed at the speed of light.

She wanted to say something to Sam but then the image changed and she remained silent. Billions of flickering stars were gently moving towards her. She saw a bright dot in a distance. The dot looked like a tiny star, but wait, it was growing. There was no doubt. The small dot slowly neared her.

Oh my. . . . What is it?

The white dot grew and grew and then she saw a small figure floating in space towards her. As it got closer she noticed it had the shape of something familiar. But what? The shape stopped just in front of her. It was white, semi-transparent, and ameba-shaped with a soft finger standing out. It had two eye-like dots in the center and a gentle curve below that resembled a mouth.

Am I hallucinating?

"Alisha. . . ."

A moment of fear came through her.

"Do not be afraid. I mean no harm. We chose to take this shape from information in your brain cells. You have such a magnificent brain with so much information, so it was hard to choose." The entity had a gentle smile.

"Who or what are you?"

"We are the colony in your brain, Alisha. We know each other."

"Well, there goes my privacy," she murmured. Now something else took over. Enormous curiosity. She wanted to know all about this entity.

"I am glad that you are not afraid of us anymore."

"But, how do you know?" She asked and then immediately remembered the entity's home. It knows everything.

"We wanted to tell you something very important, Alisha."

She remained silent.

"We, the colonies, have existed millions of your years. We evolved from you as we both came out of the oceans. Wherever you go, we go with you. We mean no harm. We colonies have a purpose to our existence. Our purpose is to grow and expand."

"We know that. This is fatal to humans."

"Although we attempted to communicate with your species for millions of years, you were not ready for it. You were not developed."

"Many humans died because of your growth."

"Our expansion is for a reason, Alisha. We store information for the future."

"Information?"

"Yes, information. All of what we call particle evolution is recorded for generations to come. Furthermore, we fix particle mutations and prevent what you call diseases."

"You *prevent* diseases? How do you do that?" The doctor in her was alerted.

"We learn about many type of particles and those that can cause harm we find ways to fight and eliminate. We eliminated numerous numbers of what you call bacteria and viruses along the years. You were not aware of it. All of these activities are recorded in our archives. You call it our genetic code. We store it and pass it on through nature's cycle."

"So you prevent many diseases that could harm humans?"

"Exactly. Not in all cases do we succeed, but we are still at work. We grow only to store more and more information about our historical records. We tried to communicate with you before, without success. Your existence sustains ours. We now know that when you die, we also die. We are interconnected, and have been since the dawn of time."

"But still, because of you so many humans have died."

"We understand, and we want to change this. We are ready to communicate with you now, Alisha. We need to help each other. You can use the information that we've collected to eliminate harmful particles. We can work together."

Alisha remained silent. She didn't know how to respond.

"But first we need to communicate. You need the code. I'll guide you with the code that you'll need. Then we will be able to communicate. I am here to let you know that we are going to give you the communication code. Small steps, Alisha. Small steps."

The entity smiled and started to recede into the sky.

"No, don't go! There's so much more to know!"

"Small steps, Alisha. Small steps."

Lights flashed again. Patterns and shapes surrounded her, larger ones, more colorful ones.

"I see . . . I see . . . patterns, shapes, puzzles. Sam! Sam!"

Sam reluctantly woke up.

"What? Is it morning yet?"

"Sam, I see things." Alisha grabbed his arm. "I saw the most amazing things."

Her eyes remained transfixed on the skies. He looked into her eyes and saw millions of stars.

"Alisha, are you okay?"

"Yes, I am. I am not in critical condition, nor am I having a seizure. I am well aware of everything but all of a sudden I see things that I never saw before."

"What? What did you see, Alisha?"

Samuel checked her pulse. It was elevated but not overly so.

"I saw . . . I saw. . . . I can't explain now. I do believe that what I saw was due to my tumor but I am not sensing that I am in danger." She still was unwilling to look away from the sky. "No seizure or stroke symptoms."

"What did you see, Alisha?"

"I saw patterns in the skies. I saw lines connecting billions of stars. It was amazing! My brain was running at billions of gigahertz. I saw patterns. I need to write this down."

Samuel jumped out of the sleeping bag and rushed to the car for his valise. He brought back pen and paper. He noticed that Alisha was moving her hands slowly.

"Sam, no worries, I noticed this earlier. I have slow motoric reaction but I am okay. Just help me, please."

"Maybe you are experiencing a seizure, Alisha. We have to take you to a hospital."

"No, Sam. You know as well as I do that the nearest hospital is too far. Please let me try writing what I saw. I have a feeling that it will help us."

Connections were formed through dendritic spines, which are micron-sized protuberances of neuronal membrane that receive and initially process most of the excitatory signals transmitted in the brain. Due to the pressure of the abnormal cells, a significant increase of dendritic spines occurred throughout the brain. In addition, the number of synapses dramatically increased. Dendritic spines and synapses are the basis of communication within our central nervous system. As these increase, so too does the potential for connections and learning within the brain. Alisha's brain power received the sky's image and analyzed it with billions of iterations. Neurotransmitters were released in her brain and traveled through the synapses at a very high speed. As the exposure of a synapses increased, so does the response to the stimulus from the sky. The axon-receiving cells were aggressively stimulated to create more receptor cells and the process accelerated as Alisha's eyes scanned more of the sky. The stimulus became more frequent and initiated stronger cell connections.

The full human brain potential was unleashed, if only briefly.

Alisha's pen flew about the notepad and filled fifty pages with pattern schemas.

She could hear muffled noises. Then she saw blurred images. Slowly her vision cleared and she saw Samuel.

"Good morning, love." He kissed her. "Don't talk too much yet. Gain some strength first."

"Where am I?" she mumbled weakly.

"You are in a hospital in Rachel, Nevada. Apparently you didn't have a seizure. You were right. You were coherent but with very slow motoric reactions. Do you remember drawing this?"

Samuel showed her the notepad with all of her sketches. Alisha turned the pages without grasping what was sketched there. She saw many lines and shapes connected together in a wide variety of forms. There were also numbers in tables and drew dots that were marked with coordinates. She shook her head with great disbelief.

"I don't remember this at all. Furthermore, I don't understand anything of what is written here."

"That's what I thought." Samuel nodded. "My theory is that your brain took all your college mathematical knowledge and implemented it into a super-analysis. I tried to understand what you have written in these pages and I couldn't understand anything. It is *way* beyond me."

"Oh well," she joked.

"I am taking you back home tomorrow and we'll give you a CT and MRI, just to be on the safe side. Maybe we can figure it out then. But for now, I am happy that you are well. After you completed your sketches you stared at the skies for a few more minutes and then fell into a deep sleep. I tried to wake you up but couldn't. Then I brought you here and you came to this morning, about ten hours after the incident. It seems like your motoric features are back to normal, as though nothing happened. I think that you had some brain event. It is hard to know exactly." He caressed her head. "But we'll find out at home."

"But something extraordinary happened last night. The question is what."

"Wonderful people in this rural hospital, but they don't have the best medical equipment. We have all the necessary stuff back home."

"Yes. . ." She sent her hand and held his. Samuel kissed her hand and smiled to her.

"I will scan your sketches and send them to Nikolai."

"Oh, yes." Alisha smiled. "He may shed some light on whatever it was I wrote."

"Nikolai is the man."

The algorithm analyzed the patterns that Alisha sketched while in her moment. Each line and arc was scanned, digitized to millions of pixels, and virtually assembled within the server's memory. After the information was transferred from two-dimensional graphics, a second algorithm kicked in. It's purpose was to identify each combination of geometrical objects. It had an advanced geometrical analyzer that was based on unique methods and mathematical techniques to analyze objects and categorize them according to known shapes and objects. The program also assigned coordinates to each vertex, line, and arc. Although the servers had more than 128 cores of processors, the vast amount of calculations took days.

At first the program successfully identified known shapes like rectangles, triangles, ellipses, and polygons. Then it tried to understand if there was any logic behind the assembled shapes. Then it looked for patterns.

After three days of continuous processing, a pattern was found.

"Still our typography is not accurate."

Samuel was disappointed. It was their third day of using the translation program that Nikolai assembled, but their messages were still confusing the colony. Nikolai almost threw a soda can at his computer, and the atmosphere was gloomy.

Samuel tried to change some parameters in order to effect a change but it didn't seem to help. Alisha looked tired and Nikolai played a computer game. He said that this relaxed him.

"Well, anyone hungry?" Alex was the only one that still had some spirit at this point. "I brought some sandwiches and salad. Alisha? Sam? Anything?"

Samuel nodded and Alisha just waved her hand to show that she'd skip the offer.

"Okay, I guess I'll eat alone. What am I in the mood for? I think I'll have some salad. It is light enough for a late night snack."

"I think we can call it a night. I'm tired." Alisha rubbed her eyes and leaned back.

"And I am winning here," Nikolai said with unappreciated elation as he was seated at the game controls.

Samuel looked down at the floor. He raised his eyes and looked at Alex that was pouring dressing over his salad. "Hey, wait. . . ."

Alex stopped eating.

"What?"

"We forgot one factor. Something that we saw in the cave, Alisha."
All eyes turned towards him.

He pointed towards Alex's salad.

Nikolai returned to his game and Alisha rolled her eyes. "Salad?"

"No," Samuel's eyes sparkled and he was alert. "The tomato. The *plum* tomato. We forgot the plum tomato!"

'Yes, we saw the plum tomato in the cave's carving as a medicine of some sort."

"What if that's what's missing?" Samuel trembled from excitement.

Alisha was doubtful and so was Nikolai.

Samuel didn't wait. He rushed to Alex's salad. "Here, with your permission, I'll use one of your plum tomatoes." He grabbed one just before Alex plunged a fork into it.

"Wait, what are you doing, Sam?" Alisha raised her voice. "It may kill our colony. Are you sure?"

"There is only one way to know."

He took a deep breath and squeezed two drops of its juice onto the specimen in the petri dish.

All stared at the screen. Nothing happened.

"All is ready," Alex said as he peered at the screen.

Samuel typed in the graphic user interface of the program.

We are friends.

The Photonic Microscope sampled the specimen at a very high speed. The molecular structure of the cancer cells changed in a unique pattern. The results were transferred into the translation program. After about a minute, a chime sounded and an answer appeared on the screen.

We are also friends.

Three humans stared at the screen for a few moments, without believing their eyes.

Then they jumped for joy.

Who are you?

We are particles. Who are you?

We are humans.

Are you our hosts?
Yes. We are your hosts.
Are you feeding us?
Yes, we feed you.
We need food.
We gave you food.
We received it. Thank you.
You are welcome.

"We've successfully established two-way communication with cancer, Stan!" Samuel rushed into his boss's office and sat down, giving off a sigh of exhalation tempered by exhaustion. "We should be able to get all the necessary funding and forget about the money that we stole."

"*You* stole, Sam. Not *we*. *You*." Stan lit his pipe and exhaled high into the air.

"I'm sorry, Sam, but we don't have anything substantial. The transmission can come from who knows where. It will be hard to convince anyone differently, especially in the medical world."

"I know how it sounds but it is a reality, Stan. Now I have the task of establishing a relationship with the cancer cells."

"Ha! Don't tell this to any of our psychiatrists. They have rooms for people who talk like you."

"I know how it sounds, Stan, but I will prove it to you. I'll do us all proud."

"Yes, but assuming that you really make it. We're—*Hmmmm. You're* still communicating with only this particular HeLa specimen, Sam. There are many types of cancers, many types of abnormal cells, how do you plan to handle all these? There is plenty of research to do still. It is too early to expose this on an unsuspecting medical community."

"I don't know yet, Stan, but the first mission is to learn about each other. We both need to learn."

"This achievement of yours is mainly technological, Sam. We can't really prove that it is medical. There is no immediate utility to it."

"Currently, yes. But that's ultimately my goal."

"And how exactly do you expect to do it? You'll just ask the cancer cells what's the cure? What can we find to kill them?" Stan grinned sarcastically.

"No, I actually have another plan. I will try to tell them about the damage that they cause to humans."

"And they will just listen to you and back off, eh? Sam, are you listening to what you're saying?"

"Yes, I am."

Kraft tamped more tobacco into his pipe. "I don't know what to say, Sam. This sounds completely out of our scope. It will never go through. This will not save your neck from the law either. You'll need to come up with something better than this."

Samuel remained silent.

"You'll have to come up with a cure or at least a treatment."

"I have a different approach."

"Well, if it is really as you say, and you *can* communicate with cancer, you'll have to discover their weakness. You'll have to find out their weak spot, Sam. In other words you'll have to figure out how to kill cancer. Then it will be worth something. Then and only then will you have a chance to be saved from your bank fraud."

"I have to disagree with you, Stan. My approach is completely different. See, cancer existed for millions of years. If they are a living entity then there is only one way to avoid the damage that they cause us. Every living organism wants to live, to exist. Cancer is no different than any other living organism. Unfortunately, its existence kills humans. Exactly like people in war. If you try to occupy and control a nation, it's bound to explode eventually. Everyone wants to be free. Everyone and everything wants to live. If one entity's existence interferes with the existence of another entity, there is only one solution—that both entities find a way to live side by side."

Stan exhaled pipe smoke into the air and looked at Samuel in an expression of wonder, as though he was looking into the very embodiment of naivety.

"It's called coexistence. These two entities will have to coexist with each other. If we build more powerful weapons to use against them, they'll build more powerful weapons to use against us. Coexistence is the only way to deal with cancer, Stan. It's the only way."

"So let me understand you correctly. You are going to explain to cancer cells that they are killing us and therefore we have to cooperate with each other." He shook his head. "This is crazier and crazier. Even if your idea is brilliant, it will be extremely hard to convince the medical world, practically impossible."

Samuel nodded. "I agree with you on that. That is why I do have to find a cure. The world will not care how I got the cure and through what means; all they care about is that we got the cure."

"True, but do you really believe in your sci-fi idea of coexistence?"

"Yes, I do. I think it will work." Samuel looked intently into his boss's eyes.

Stan looked back lengthily. Then he shook his head. "Coexistence, coexistence."

"Good news, sir. We are successfully communicating with our host." The assistant leader reported with great satisfaction. "They solved the particle issue and now we are receiving clear, understandable messages that we can respond to."

"This is very good." The governor was pleased. "What kind of information do we share?"

"We just started our communication. We already informed them about food and they provided substantial quantities."

"This is even better. Now we know that they are friendly. We need to let them know that our goal is to grow and expand."

"Yes, sir. We also need to learn about them."

"I agree. We need to know how to help them. If they provide us food, we need to find a way to be of some benefit for them." The governor was logical.

"Indeed, sir. We'll start with teaching them about us and we'll learn about them."

"This is fascinating. This will be the first time in our history that we established communication with our hosts."

"Yes, sir. We also thought to ask for their help against the disasters that happened to our species. Maybe they know how to prevent them or even to fight them."

"Good idea. The deadly clouds, the poisonous storms, the meltdowns. All the information on them has to be transferred to our host. They may have already encountered these disasters in the past and know how to protect against or avoid them."

"Also continued food supplies, sir. As we expand, we consume more food. We need to ensure that we receive food on a regular basis."

"Yes, very good. I think it is a very good development for both species. Let's be dedicated to communicate with our host to the best of our capability to ensure a fruitful relationship for both."

"We are on it, sir."

"One more thing."

"Yes, sir."

"We need to document these events in our historical documents. This is important to pass to other colonies."

"Yes, sir."

"Keep me posted. Dismissed."

We are living to expand our colony.

Yes, we know.

Could you ensure regular food supply?

Yes, we can and we will.

Thank you.

Are you familiar with our deadly disasters?

No. What are they?

Our historical documents mention deadly clouds that randomly start, out of nowhere. These clouds kill our particles by the millions.

We understand.

We also have other type of disasters that we would like to tell you about. Currently, we don't have any way to fight them.

We understand.

Did you encounter these disasters?

No. We never encountered them.

What is your organizational form?

We are called people. People are groups of humans. A human is a large group of particles like you. What are you?

We are called particles. We are a colony. We have one governor and many assistants. We have one assistant leader that reports to the governor. All the rest are working particles.

We have many humans on a large planet. You can say that this planet consists of many colonies of humans. We have many countries, again like many colonies. Each country has its own government which is like one governor and assistants. We are very similar to you.

What type of food do you use?

Very similar to yours but with more variety.

We are glad that we established contact.

We are also glad. It took us long time to find the way to contact you but now we succeeded.

We assume that you are much larger than us since you are our hosts. Are you able to see us?

Yes, we can see you. We are much larger than you. You are a million times smaller than us.

What is million?

A unit size. A million means many units.

Understood. That means that our entire colony is very small. How do you see us then?

We are using a mechanism that magnifies on a very large scale. An instrument is a device. Like a particle that does some operation.

Understood.

How come there are many words that you recognize from our world and some that you don't?

Every colony is formed with historical information that is

stored from long time before. We don't know exactly how the information got there. We assume it is from our hosts.

So you learned your vocabulary from your hosts along the years?

What is years?

Long time term.

Yes. That is what we assume.

Understood. There is so much information that we like to know about you and we assume that you would like to know about us.

Yes. How do you understand our structure?

It is a long story.

What is a story?

It is like telling you about something for a long time. Like historical document. We have learned about particles. We call this subject chemistry. We know how you work and function.

This is very good.

Yes. That is why we know how to provide you food and what type of food you need.

Understood.

We even know further. We learned about your operations. We have a special field that is dedicated to particle study. It's called medicine.

We have to teach each other many things.

Yes, many things.

Do we have the time? Does your organism live long or short time?

We live long enough to teach and learn from you.

This is very good. Are we going to live long enough to learn from you?

Yes. There are many subjects that we want to communicate with you.

Yes.

I have a question.

Yes.

You communicate in a code that we know. We call it DNA Code. This is a very old DNA Code. How do you know it?

According to our historical records one of our oldest colony learned it from its host long time ago.

Probably someone in ancient Egypt. It is one of the oldest human colonies.

Yes.

We didn't know. We will need your help with some subjects. We will help you also.

This is good. We will be glad to cooperate.

Yes. We will work together as one team.

Yes. As one team.

So do you think that an ancient Egyptian had cancer and that's where they took the DNA code?" Samuel asked at the table.

Sam and Alisha were having dinner at the Hard Rock Café, New York City, a short drive from New Haven. They both liked the vibe, the musical memorabilia, and the food. Although not considered gourmet, still the food was decent and the portions ample.

"We don't have any evidence of that. They didn't know about cancer then and in any case there were many deaths that weren't known to be from cancer. If someone died there was no effort to come to a definitive conclusion on the cause."

"True. All too true."

"I still can't believe that we are talking with cancer." Alisha shook her head. "Sometimes I think about what Stan Kraft told you. What if he is right? What if someone else is communicating with us? I don't know, even aliens make more sense than cancer."

"Can't be, Alisha. You saw for yourself. We give them drops of glucose and they say thank you. The only possibility is it's from the cancer cells. They called themselves particles. So what? Naturally they don't use exactly the same terms and vocabulary as we do, although I must say that I am fascinated that they do know many of our terms. Apparently they learned them from humans."

"You mean cancer victims."

"Yes. I am puzzled how they can transfer what they call 'historical information' to colonies across time. I wonder if there is a gene that somehow released through waste to nature and then back to cancer colonies. If you think about it, that is the only way they could transfer information along the years."

"It makes sense. Cancer produces proteins or genes, these are flushed out of our bodies through the sewage system back to nature. We eat the plants, animals and so forth, and cancer gains the information stored biologically."

"Exactly."

"Uhh!" Alisha's face contorted as severe pain seared her head.

"What is it, honey? Headache?"

"Yes, very bad!" Alisha was getting more and more severe headaches. After her last chemotherapy session there was an improvement in her tumor, and it shrunk impressively. They were hoping that she is on the path to recovery but frequent headaches caused them to be concerned.

"Tomorrow you have an MRI. I am sure there will be good results."

"I'll be okay, Sam, just give me a few minutes. It always goes away after a short while."

"It is time. I will communicate with our colony tomorrow about who they really are and what they are doing to us."

"No, Sam, please. If you go ahead too fast, we may alarm them and they'll not communicate with us anymore. Let's proceed slowly. We need to learn about each other and gain a strong level of trust before we can break the truth to them." She massaged her temples for a moment and seemed refreshed. "There! I already feel better." Alisha began to enjoy her chicken salad.

"Still, I think in the next few days I'll start with the slow process of letting them know the truth. They are already very friendly with us. I don't foresee any problems asking for their help. We also don't know if they *can* help. But we have to go ahead." He held her hand. "It is important for you, love."

Alisha lowered her eyes. "I am not sure that there will be time. We both know I'm stage four."

"No!" Samuel's voice raised. People at other tables looked over.

Sam calmed himself. "There is always time. We'll not lose this battle."

"Look, Sam, I know that you are more passionate about this research because of me, and I love you for that. We're both oncologists. We know the statistics."

"Stats are mere generalizations, with limited applicability to individuals." Samuel's lips pursed. "We *will* find a cure."

"Yes, I believe that there is a high chance of it. All I am saying is that it may not be there for me. Sam, we don't even know how to provide a solution. What do you intend to tell them? We need a cure for me?"

Samuel was in deep thought. "I haven't thought about that yet. I'll think of something. But the first phase will be to let them know the reality. I am not giving up. Please don't you give up either."

Alisha smiled through her tears. "Not everything is in my control, but I'll not give up."

Their hands held each other's tightly.

"I must say, Sam, this is truly impressive." Stan Kraft looked at the printouts. "You have full conversations with them. I still can't believe what I see."

"Oh yes, we are talking with them every night for almost a month now. They know our names, our profession, and even our personalities—well, to some extent."

Stan raised a brow. "So you told them that we are medical doctors? Oncologists?"

"We told them that we are researchers to find cures for diseases. They understand the concept. They shared with us chemistry and cell information that we never knew before. Material on mitosis and records. Stan, with their help we can find a cure for many other illnesses. For example, based on some of the information that they shared with us, I believe that we can make a breakthrough with diseases such as HIV. Look, I wrote some of the chemistry in the documents. They are very bright little guys. They also learn fast."

"It's fascinating, and it's all good. One question still remains. How are you going to deal with their existence? They are cancer cells. Good cells gone bad. They just don't know it."

"Yes, I'll have to explain to them and it will be the time soon. Now that they know about us, I believe that they are ready for the news. Also they are really becoming good friends."

"Good friends? Please, Sam, have you forgotten why you are doing this?" Stan laughed caustically. "Ultimately, you need to find a cure for them. In other words, you need to find something that will kill them."

"Well, I had a different idea."

"Yes, I know your idea. You already told me. And I have a hard time believing it. I tend to believe in finding their weaknesses in order to kill them." Stan looked straight into Samuel's eyes. "Let's be realistic, Sam, all the rest of your ideas are sci-fi, and increasingly like romantic novels."

"Every organism wants to live. Mosquitos, germs, bacteria, and viruses. Yes, many of them cause us to get sick and die."

"And therefore, we kill them first. In many of the cases, this is our only strategy." Stan continued in a cold tone. "We simply don't have any other way to protect our species."

"Yes, I know."

"Cancer is one of the most deadly scourges of our age. But then I don't need to tell you this, Sam. You are an oncologist. We all know the stats."

Samuel remained silent.

"You know it as well as I know it, Sam. We can't think about them here. If you are really communicating with cancer, then you'll have to trick them." Stan then smiled. "Then you'll make history. Imagine the fame and glory that will be all yours. You, Samuel Daniels, found a cure for cancer. Unbeatable, Sam, unbeatable."

"Yes, it will be."

"I have to attend a meeting now. Let's talk again in a few days." Stan stood up and extended his hand to Samuel. They shook hands uneasily.

"Good luck, Sam. Go make me proud."

Samuel, we have few questions for your group.

Yes.

We already mentioned before about the disasters that are deadly for us.

Yes, I remember. The deadly clouds, the storms.

Yes. Did you check if you know anything about these?

Alisha is asking if you know the chemical structure of the clouds or the storms.

Yes, we have records about the exact particle changes and the boundary deformation.

Send these records to us. We may be able to analyze the information and help.

We are sending the information now. From our historical information we can tell you that colonies experienced massive changes that killed the majority of them.

Do you know what started these disasters or when they showed?

According to our information there was no record why these events happened. They just happened.

Still, we think that something triggered them. Since your location is within our bodies, for every change there must be a reason—biological or chemical reason.

Nothing that we know.

Did you made any changes in your structure of any sort?

No.

Did you change your feeding schedule or type of food?

We have no records of this.

Did your particles engage in some sort of activity near these disaster's initiation?

We checked with our governor and there were a few changes around times when the disasters appeared. The next events happened and then shortly after the disasters occurred.

What are these events?

Access of food which initiated colony growth above the normal rate. Typically the colony's mortality rate balances the growth rate and is steady. Sometimes there is a sudden growth that exceeds the particles mortality.

What happened then?

The colony starts to grow. There is always risk in the growth. The risk is exhausting the food resources. In case there is no more food, the colony starts what we call selective elimination of particles.

Please describe.

We have to eliminate particles in order for the others to continue living.

Continue with the colony's growth.

When a colony has excessive food resources, and other reasons, the colony started to significantly grow.

What else?

If the colony is large enough or ambitious, they even send particles to colonize other areas.

Then these disasters start shortly after?

Yes.

There was a delay in the communication. Then Samuel's message arrived.

We know what these disasters are. We also know their source and better of all, we know how to stop them.

This is very good. Could you please teach us how to stop them?

We need to take a break now. We would like to continue tomorrow at the same time.

Yes. Thank you for your help.

Goodbye for now.

Goodbye.

"I looked into the chemical elements and compounds that they sent us. It's an exact match." Alisha was unhappy as she poured a cup of coffee.

"We know exactly what these disasters are." Samuel looked at his microscope. "We can of course save them."

"Now we consider Stan's words. Since we know that they are able to deliver their biological history to their next generation or other colonies, if we provide them with an information how to avoid or overcome their disasters, we may risk our ability to fight them."

Samuel looked at her like he didn't hear well. "But Alisha, they are cooperative. They are working with us nicely."

"Sam, I see how things are going. These cells do not know that they are our enemy and one of the worst one. What if we give them ideas how to overcome these disasters and they don't cooperate with us. They can transfer this information to all other types of cancers."

"Alisha, this is nuts. Besides, this is in our control. We will not give them any information regarding these disasters."

"That's exactly what everyone would say about our discovery. But still, here we are."

"Wait, what are you saying? What information can they use against us?"

"Sam, you know that what they call disasters are our medical treatments against cancer. The deadly clouds are chemotherapy, and the storms are radiation."

"Yes, but we'll not give them anything. What we can do is to simply stop these treatments if they cooperate."

"We are dealing with an intelligent life-form. More intelligent than we dared imagine. I am afraid that it will be enough for them to figure it out. And what if they evolve, based on our information to sustain chemotherapy and radiation? Then we'll leave the human race even more vulnerable to cancer."

"Oh, I don't know about that, Alisha."

"Sam, we are talking with cancer every day. They know who we are, they know our names. They learned our vocabulary in what? Two months? We are talking with them now almost as we talk with humans."

Samuel remained silent. There was logic in Alisha's words. What if they did disclose information that may give cancer the potential to win out against their medicine? They proved that they are very intelligent and can learn quickly. How do they know that their intentions are friendly?

"But we forget that we are still have one major advantage in this situation."

Alisha waited for his words.

"We have them on our petri dish as a sample. Worst case we can simply eliminate the entire specimen and they'll have no opportunity to send the word out to other colonies. I say we take the risk. We'll offer life for life. If we learn to work together, I am sure we can find a way to coexist."

Alisha released long sigh. "I guess you are right. We are in a better situation than they are."

Samuel approached Alisha and hugged her tightly. "Look, sweetie, I really get the sense that they are friendly for real. I want to find a cure. I want to heal you. I want to live with you for the rest of my life."

Alisha released a long sigh.

"What?" Samuel sensed that she wanted to tell him something.

She exhaled lengthily and looked at him. "Do you remember when we were in Area 51 and I had that brain episode?"

"Yes, of course. Smokey Joe and the rest."

"While I was having this brain event that caused me to write all the schemas in the notebook I saw something. I didn't want to tell you because I was not sure that it wasn't my wild imagination."

Samuel held her shoulders. "What did you see, Alisha?"

"The colony appeared to me in a shape of an entity. An ameba-like entity."

Samuel didn't understand at all and his expression conveyed it.

"It told me that it took the image from my brain so I'd not be scared. That's true. I always liked ameba shapes. I thought that they would be cute figures for children's comic books."

"Okay."

"The ameba-like entity talked to me. It said that it is the colony and it would give me the code."

Samuel was fascinated. "It was the colony. This explains your ingenious schemas. Why didn't you tell me?"

"Well, because it sounds crazy, even to me. Maybe it was a figment of my imagination. How can I know, Sam? I have a brain tumor." She was close to tears.

Samuel hugged her to his heart and they both sat on the little couch.

"It told me that the reason that they expand is to preserve their DNA history of how to fight diseases. They store the biological information of bacteria, viruses, and ways to fight them. They pass this information through nature's cycle. All throughout the history, they find bad bacteria and ways to eliminate them. They eliminated many that we probably don't even know about."

"This explains how we found cures for other diseases from cancer research." Samuel nodded. "Please tell more."

"It said that now we are ready to communicate. Now we need to find a plan to work together. It said that it is giving me the communication code."

"And it did. This is amazing." Samuel's faces illuminated. "They want the same thing. That's exactly what I was thinking about. Coexistence."

"Sam, I am not sure it was not just a result of the tumor pressure. It may happened because you already told me. There could be millions of reasons. You know hallucinations can happen, especially with brain tumor patients."

"Yes they can, but not this one, Alisha." Samuel gave her a kiss. "They want to communicate with us. They want to work together. We just have to find the way quickly to help you. I love you."

She kissed him passionately and sat back on the couch.

Today will be a very important discussion, governor.

We are ready, Samuel.

First, we taught you our terms and about us. Now it is time to tell you why we started these efforts to communicate with you. Please feel free to stop us if you have any questions.

We will.

We humans have known about your species for many years. You live inside our bodies. We are the hosts. This fact, you already know.

Yes.

What we didn't tell you is that your existence is not good for humans. Your colonies live within humans in two types. One we call benign, which is harmless. The colony lives as a group of cells without expanding to other organs. The second one called malignant.

Yes, we are familiar with this, as you taught us. There are passive colonies and there are active colonies. For example we are an active colony. We grew rapidly. We live to expand. Passive colonies live only to exist.

Yes, we know. The passive colonies are harmless to humans. They live in peace. The active colonies are a problem to humans.

Why?

The human body is constructed of what we call cells. You call them particles. The active colonies are abnormal cell growths within our bodies. They are regular cells that got deformed somehow and now grow in an uncontrolled manner.

This is their main life purpose—to grow.

We understand. The problem is that as they grow, they damage the human body.

How?

The uncontrolled growth eventually spread from the one colony to the rest of the human body. The active colonies create new colonies in important body organs. This eventually consumes the human, and he or she dies.

There was a long delay. The atmosphere was tense. Samuel, Alisha, and Alex stared nervously at the large screen. All waited for the response. At length, the chime came.

"The moment of truth," Samuel mumbled.

We cause death to humans?

Unfortunately, yes. There are many types of colonies and not each one causes an immediate death; but if we do not treat these colonies, eventually they'll cause death to the human host.

We were not aware of this effect on humans.

Yes, we know. Many human doctors and researchers are constantly searching for what we call a cure.

What is a cure?

A cure is some type of chemical element or material that will stop the cells' uncontrolled growth.

This means killing the growing cells.

Sometimes. What you call the deadly clouds and the storms are actually our ways to fight your growth. It is our way to save our humans.

Again there was a delay as the cancer cells learned this new piece of information.

Understood.

We were not aware that you are intelligent organisms. But we are not mad or upset with you. We understand that this is the way your species lives and exists. But we want to save our species.

It is understandable. We want the same.

Our communication is part of a research to find a cure. I, Samuel, am a researcher and specialist on your type of colonies.

Proceed.

We even invented a name for you. We call you cancer. Cancer is one of the most deadly diseases for humans. Millions of people die every year from cancer. We don't have a cure for cancer.

What about the deadly clouds and storms?

These are treatments only. As you probably can find out in your historical documentation, these treatments do not work all the time. Sometimes we succeed in stopping the spread and the human is cured, and in other times we don't and eventually the human dies.

We understand.

We could say that we are enemies.

Yes, you could.

There was a silent delay.

But our group thinks different. We believe in working together. Proceed.

For many years we fought each other not because we wanted but because we both wanted to protect our species' existence and continuity.

We are the source of your deadly disasters. It is unfortunate.

There was another silent delay. Samuel was the first to break word of their intentions.

Yes, and we understand that. We want to work together with you. We want to find a way to let you live and let us live without causing death for you or us. Do we have your agreement to work together?

There was a pause. Samuel continued.

We believe that in the current condition we are fighting each other in order to survive. Many of us, and many of you, die in this battle that has existed for many years. I say, let's stop this war. Let's combine our knowledge to find a way to live together peacefully. This is the only way to survive.

Still no response. Samuel wiped the sweat from his forehead.

We would like to talk among ourselves. We will take a break and talk again tomorrow.

They all looked at the screen with great disbelief and growing anxiety.

"Well, at least we considered this possibility seriously." Alisha observed with obvious uncertainty.

"I can't believe it. They actually asked to have a discussion among themselves." Samuel scratched his head.

"Guys, we should not be too surprised. We already know that these are intelligent life-forms. From my point of view, this was expected," Alex noted.

"Don't take it so hard, Sam." Alisha sounded like she was giving a lecture in the university. "What did you expect? That they'd jump out with joy and offer us the cure? They have the right to discuss this. After all they were just informed that we are their enemies. We are the creators of their deadly disasters."

"We have been fighting them over the years. Given that we are the host, and in control of their food and therefore of their very lives, this must be unsettling news. I am sure that they are well aware that their lives are in our hands. I mean, they ask for food and we feed them." Alex turned off the large screen. "I guess we'll have to wait for tomorrow to know."

Samuel remained there still staring at the dark screen. He eventually stood up. "I don't know. I guess I expected immediate cooperation but if I think about it, you guys are right. It must be a shock for them, as it is a shock for us."

"Let's go home. We are all tired," Alisha suggested.

There was no argument.

"These are very disturbing revelations, sir." The assistant leader was clearly anxious.

"Indeed. I didn't expect such news at all." The governor was also uneasy. "So it turned out that we are causing the humans to get sick and die. We are a *disease*, as they define the term."

"But we cause no harm, sir. It's our destiny to grow."

"Yes, but I can see their point also. We grew uncontrollably, killing them. Their normal cells don't do that. They are living and dying at a rate that doesn't cause any harm."

"Yes, sir."

The governor was in thoughts. "This entire communication between us and them is the result of research."

"A research to find a cure, sir. The research aims to kill us."

"Indeed, but this is understandable. We would have done exactly the same. As a matter of fact, we do this with external cells. We consume them in order to survive and continue to grow."

"They are in control of our food, sir."

"Yes, so we are depending on them to start with. If they don't feed us, we die."

"So if we kill them, eventually we die also, sir. Their bodies provide our food."

"Exactly. We have to exist together. Otherwise both species will eventually die. Further, these humans seem to be very intelligent. If they continue their research, they may develop a lethal chemical that will kill us and not them."

"Indeed, then our species will be eliminated, sir."

"I think we don't have too many alternatives. We have to work with them in order to survive."

"But sir, what about our ancient code? The code that enjoins us to be independent and continue to grow? We have to obey the code, as we all have for many years."

"The code is worth nothing if we can't survive. If the humans activate the disasters, we are dead anyway. Also if we kill them, we die too. Remember we depend on the food that they provide."

"There is another option, sir."

"What?"

"We have the adaptation feature. We can learned their chemical particles and pass the information to other colonies. With time we'll be able to develop an immunity to their disasters, sir."

The governor didn't answer immediately. "You are suggesting war."

"Yes, sir. A *larger* war, actually."

"They are further advanced than we are. They are feeding us. If they stop feeding us, we'll die. That's one reason. Second, I agree with the Samuel human. All living entities want to live. We and our hosts are no different. Working together will bring much better results than tricking or fighting each other. It just makes more sense."

The assistant leader remained quiet. He didn't like the governor's judgment. "And our code, sir?"

"Our code will have to change. We'll make a note in our historical documents."

"But we don't even know how we'll be able to do this, sir. How will we be able to solve the conflict? It looks to me like we are in power in the long term. You heard the Samuel human. Millions of people die every year by us. The strong survive!"

"You keep forgetting." The governor was determined to effect a change in outlook. "If they don't survive because we kill them, we also do not survive. We are joined in life and death. If they live, we live. If they die, we die. But I do want their commitment to stop the deadly attacks on our colonies."

"With all due respect, sir, we have no way to know if they'll do so."

The governor didn't answer immediately. "We'll have to take the chance. I do believe in the idea that every living organism would like to live. This include us and our hosts. I've made my decision."

"What is it, sir?" It was clear that the assistant leader was unhappy with the governor's explanation.

"We work together."

After a delay the assistant leader replied. "Yes, sir." There was a strict order in colonies. The governor was the ultimate ruler.

"Dismissed."

SIMPLICITY IS INGENIOUS

Alisha waited for the students to take their seats in the lecture hall. It was her first bi-weekly class at Yale Medical. She looked at her watch. It was time.

"Good morning." She turned to the large board and wrote the lecture topic. "Today's topic is 'How do healthy cells become cancerous.' A healthy cell does not turn into a cancer cell overnight. Its behavior gradually changes, a result of damage to between three and seven of the hundreds of genes that control cell growth, division, and lifespan. First, the cell starts to grow and multiply. Over time, more changes may take place. The cell and its descendants may eventually become immortal, escape destruction by the body's defenses, develop their own blood supply, and invade the rest of body."

A hand was raised and Alisha pointed to give permission to speak.

"Why is cell growth a problem in cancerous cells?"

"Good question. A cell is continuously receiving messages, both from its own genes and from other cells. Some tell it to grow and multiply, others tell it to stop growing and rest, or even to die. If there are enough 'grow' messages, the next stage of the cell's life starts. In a cancer cell, the messages to grow may be altered, or the messages to stop growing or to die may be missing. The cell then begins to grow uncontrollably and divide too often. The cell's growth create what we call a mass of cells which caused damage to healthy cells. The mass invades healthy tissues, consuming their food and resources, and eventually causes their death."

Another hand shot up. "You mentioned invading healthy tissues. Could you please elaborate?"

"Most normal cells in tissues stay put, stuck to each other and their surroundings. Unless they are attached to something, they cannot grow and multiply. If they become detached from their neighbors, they commit suicide by a process known as *apoptosis*. But in cancer cells, the normal self-destruct instructions do not work, and they can grow and multiply without being attached to anything. This allows them to invade the rest of the body, traveling via the bloodstream to start more tumors elsewhere. This process is called *metastasis*."

She paused to write outlines on the board.

"Now how long do cancer cells live for? Every time a normal cell divides, the ends of its chromosomes become shorter. Once they have worn down, the cell dies and is replaced. Cancer cells cheat this system; they retain their long chromosomes by continually adding bits back on. This process . . . allows cancer cells . . . to live forever."

Alisha felt a dizzy spell. She held the table in order not to fall. She took few deep breaths. The dizzy spell passed in a few seconds. A few students noticed her momentary infirmity. She continued.

"Another important topic is missing checkpoints. Every time a healthy human cell divides, it copies all its genes, which are bundled up into forty-six chromosomes. This process has several checkpoints to ensure that each new cell gets a near-perfect copy. But in a cancer cell, these checkpoints are often missing. The result is chaos: parts of chromosomes may be lost, rearranged or copied many times, and the genes are more likely to acquire further mutations. Some of these may allow the cell to escape other checking and repair mechanisms."

Another hand was raised.

"Why don't cancer cells die normally?"

"In normal cells, gene damage is usually quickly repaired. If the damage is too severe, the cell is forced to die. An important protein called p53 checks for gene damage in normal cells, and kills them if the damage is too great to repair. However, in cancer cells these checking mechanisms are defective. Cancer cells often have an altered p53 protein, which does not work properly, allowing cancer cells to survive, despite their dangerously garbled genetic material. This leads to abnormal cell structures that do not contribute to the human body but ultimately damage it. When a person is healthy, every part of the body has just the right number of cells: the birth and death of each one is carefully controlled. Any cells that start to multiply too much, or in the wrong place, are either stopped from growing or forced into suicide by apoptosis. In cancer cells, these instructions are either missing, altered, or ignored. So cancer cells . . . escape destruction, and continue to multiply . . . in an uncontrolled way."

Another dizzy spell stopped her. This one was worse than the first one. She held the table again waiting for it to pass. It took long minutes until she could regain her powers and continue. More students noticed this time.

"Why it is very hard to find a cure for cancer? In other words, why are cancer cells so powerful? All the cells in our body usually work together as a community. But if a cell acquires a gene mutation that makes it multiply when it should not, or helps it survive when other cells die, it has an advantage over the others. Eventually, the abnormal cells . . . acquire mutations in more genes, causing uncontrolled growth. These abnormal cells . . . have a competitive advantage over normal cells. This is like natural selection in evolution, where a species that produces more offspring has a better chance of survival. Ultimately the stronger species . . . wins and the healthy cells die."

The auditorium started to spin. Alisha held the table and breathed deeply. This time the dizziness did not pass. On the contrary, it got worse. She could hear concerned students talking in the background. The lights became too bright and then a blessed darkness took hold.

"Where is Alisha?" Alex asked quietly when he saw Samuel arriving by himself to the lab.

"She's in the hospital, in a coma." Samuel answered laconically.

"Oh no! I am very sorry to hear that, Sam."

"Well, we'll just have to double our efforts." Samuel started with the hardware and software preparations. "Tonight is very important for us."

"Yes, the colony's decision. I am sure it will be positive."

"I really hope so." Samuel started the translation program.

Hello, are you there?

Yes.

Did you discuss the subject?

Yes. This is the governor. I want you to commit not to use the deadly disasters against us.

We will not use the deadly disasters.

How will we know this?

Our working relationship has to be based on trusting each other.

We can wait for next generation to confirm. We have time.

But I don't have the time. Alisha is not here today. She has a brain colony. She is in a hospital in critical condition.

What does critical means?

Means that she can die. Her life is at great risk.

There was a delay.

We will help.

Thank you.

Samuel released a long sigh. "This is good news." Then he looked at Alex. "But what's next?"

Alex shook his head. "I don't know."

Samuel thought for a short while. "I'll start with any information that they'll give me."

Let's start with information about your structure. Send me the particle pattern.

We are sending the information.

Governor, thank you very much for your help. I mean it deeply.

You are welcome, Samuel.

Samuel looked outside the window in Stan's office. It was a gray December day and a half foot of snow covered the grass of the campus.

"I am very sorry, Sam. I can assure you that she is getting the best treatment we can offer. You know that."

"I know. It's just so unfair. We are so close to a discovery." His voice broke and he lowered his eyes.

Stan stood and patted Sam's shoulders. "Look, you are really making tremendous strides. I read your emails every night. I'll back you up as much as I can and I'm holding the law off better than I thought. Seems the DA's office has more than one person who's lost a loved one to cancer. Maybe you'll find the information to help Alisha."

"I intend to. Currently, I'm studying the material that they sent me. The thing is, it is exceptionally complicated, especially with the differences in terms and syntaxes. I am working day and night trying to figure out their stuff, and I understand only maybe twenty percent of it. It will take years." He sat back in a forlorn manner.

Stan walked back and forth. "It will be a long time before we learn anything significant from them. I guess we thought it would all happen quick and easy."

"Nothing's as easy as it seems, Stan. Absolutely nothing."

"Never underestimate your achievement. You've done something that will place your name in the pantheon of modern science. But as with every major discovery, it will take some time to learn its practical implications. We'll find a way to work with cancer and maybe prevent it or cure it. I also believe that this research will open the door to curing other diseases."

"In normal circumstances I would be very happy to embark on this journey. I would have all the time in the world. But for now I need something quick. Otherwise, I'll lose Alisha."

"You know, Sam, you already said the keyword. I have a friend who's an engineer. He has this one quote that he tells me frequently—simplicity is ingenious."

Samuel looked at him without grasping the meaning.

"Typically I play the devil's advocate, Sam. Not this time. This time we need something simple and quick. I'll help you. Send me all the information that you have and I'll try to figure out something. Another pair of eyes may help."

"Thank you, Stan. You are a true friend." Samuel's mood brightened.

"Let's not waste time. Back to your desk, Sam Daniels!"

Samuel returned home late that night. It was December 31, New Year's Eve, and he felt desperately alone. Alisha remained in a coma at the hospital and all evidence pointed to her imminent death. His colleagues prepared him for the worst. It can happen any day now, they said. The tumor is too deep. No operation will be able to save her. In fact, an operation has a higher chance of killing her than saving her.

But he already knew this. He took a quick shower and sat in his living room. The TV was on. Without any passion he watched how the world was preparing to welcome the New Year with great exuberance. In about an hour the big ball in New York City would drop and a new year will start. He felt numb. Alisha was not there with him. He so wanted to be with her that night. The cancer cells sent him pages and pages of information. He spent all of his time trying to figure out the details, without much success.

He poured himself a glass of wine and stared at the TV.

I'll never find any answers in time to save Alisha. Stan was right. It's too big of a task. What did I think? I stole millions of dollars and soon I'll be put on trial. Probably leading to jail time. But the worst thing is losing Alisha. She's dying, she's dying.

He switched channels without even looking at the images that flashed before him.

The phone rang. He didn't notice until the fifth ring.

"Hello?"

It was Stan Kraft.

"Sam, do you want to come to my place this evening? I have a few friends over. I know it's a late invitation but if you leave now you'll make it before the ball drops."

"Thanks, Stan, I'm tired. I'll stay home."

"Sam, don't sink down now. We all need you. The world needs you. Alisha needs you."

"It's hopeless, Stan. I'll never figure out these millions of pages in time. I failed. I failed Alisha."

"No, Sam, you didn't. You are doing an amazing job. If there is one person in the world who can do this, it's you, Sam."

"Thanks again for supporting and encouraging me, Stan."

Stanley remained quiet. "I'm coming over."

"No, you have guests."

"I am not leaving you alone on New Year's Eve. What food would you like me to bring?"

"I am not hungry, Stan."

"Never mind. I'll be there shortly."

Samuel hung up the phone. His eyes glanced indifferently again to the TV. It was local New Haven news about rough weather in Europe and resolutions for the New Year. He poured another glass of wine.

The news shifted to Africa.

"Johannesburg is bracing for a massive invasion of killer ants."

His father, an entomologist, at times in Africa, had an obsession with killer ants for many years. He was there now, engaged in a project to find a hormone that would contain them. He was always considered an odd bird among fellow entomologists, not only there in Africa, around the world. Samuel talked with his father every now and then over Skype.

"I guess the apple doesn't fall far from the tree." He always used to joke with his dad. "I'm also considered to be an odd bird in my field."

"Why killer ants?" He always asked his father over the past few years. "Don't you have any more interesting insects to research?"

"I'm fascinated by this smart, yet vicious species, Sam." He told him. "They live in communities of billions, underground, and for an unknown reason, one day they decide to come out and relocate. No one really knows why. When they relocate, it is the most deadly journey for all of their surroundings. They will eat everything in their path. They can swarm over a human and eat him in less than an hour. Trees, animals, vegetation, everything goes. Entire villages are wiped out. They are unstoppable. So far. We can contain them by building a fire lane. Tractors clear a wide path in which we light fires in order to force them on a detour. In other cases we dig ditches and fill them with water, but they're clever enough to overcome them. They jump into the water in masses. The first and second layer drown but the rest cross the water on top of the dead."

"Wow, they're diabolically clever."

"Yes, that's why I'm working on a new hormone development. See, I found that these ants produce a unique hormone when they decide to relocate, and another hormone when they decide to settle and go back into the ground. I'll solve the hormone mystery and we'll be able to control them."

"Well, good luck with that."

That conversion was months ago but it stayed with him. Now he was watching events unfolding far away on the TV.

"Johannesburg is bracing for a massive invasion of killer ants. They've already killed large numbers of animals and humans over the past week. The danger is moving towards major cities, the first one is Johannesburg. Experts estimate their numbers at 500 million—an unimaginable quantity."

Samuel opened his laptop and logged into Skype, checking the time in South Africa. It was morning and his father might be near his computer. His Skype number rang and his father soon appeared on the screen.

"Hi dad, how are you? I see on the news that there's a lot of commotion in your area? Are you okay?"

His father's face beamed. "Yes, lots of commotion but this is my day. Right on time. I completed a sample of my hormone last week and this is an excellent opportunity to test it."

Samuel became alert. He knew his father could be careless.

"Dad, look, you have to be careful. On the news they said that there are more than 500 million ants in the army. They can kill you in an instant."

His father played with his large mustache. He always reminded me Einstein, Same hair, same large mustache, and puckish look.

"As a matter of fact, you just caught me before I went out the door. I'm going to treat the killer ants with my new solution. I call it the 'Peacemaker'."

He held up two plastic spray bottles. "With these babies, I expect to simulate the settling code and they should all stop their onslaught and dig their way underground."

"But dad, for this you'll have to be very close to them!"

"Yes, I know." His father gave him a wide smile. "I have prepared a suit for this reason. " He held up a white medical suit, reminiscent of a space suit or biohazard attire.

"Dad, I don't trust that suit. Please don't do it. Find a safer way to get near the ants. What if they don't respond to your hormone spray as you think they will? What if they become even more aggressive?"

"No worries, Sam. Remember, I am the expert. I'll be near the ants in about an hour. Will you still be awake?"

"Yes, I will."

"Great then. If I have cellular connectivity, I'll Skype you so that you can see my great achievement live. You can even put me up on YouTube!"

"Dad, please."

"Sorry, son, got to go. This is my show. Talk with you shortly."

His smiling face vanished from the window.

A knock came at the door and Stan entered without waiting for permission. He was dressed casually in jeans and a ski jacket and he held a takeaway box.

"I brought you chicken kabob over rice from the Dish Dash Restaurant."

"Thanks, Stan." Sam's voice was largely indifferent.

"Don't say thanks, just eat." Stanley took dishes from the cupboard and spooned out the Middle Eastern fare.

A half hour later, the station was redoing the report from South Africa.

"Watch this. Can you believe it?" Samuel pointed towards the TV.

A helicopter shot showed a large dark cloud moving eerily over jungle expanse. The cloud moved on, leaving nothing but empty land where only a few minutes earlier there had been lush vegetation. They could see antelopes and zebras overwhelmed as the large cloud struck then falling to the ground as thousands of venomous bites paralyzed them.

"My father is there."

"What the hell is your father doing there?"

"He's an entomologist. His obsession is ants—especially killer ants."

"Seriously?"

"Yes. For the past few years he was conducting a research about them. He developed some kind of hormone."

"Impressive."

"Impressive but crazy. He wants to spray his concoction on the ants. He says it'll stop them."

"This is good."

"I am afraid that he'll get eaten by the ants. He's careless when it comes to safety."

"Did he get his research funds legally? Just kidding. Give him a chance."

Samuel took the plate and ate quietly. "Good kabob. Thanks, Stan."

"Hey, I'll join you. I didn't eat much myself." He made himself a plate and sat near Samuel and watched TV. "Happy New Year, Sam. Let's brainstorm and save Alisha. We can do it."

Samuel looked at his friend. Stanley was not dressed in suit and tie and did not sound official. Instead, he was a friend.

"Thanks for being here with me tonight. And Happy New Year to you too."

"We'll make it, Sam. I just know it."

"Yes, we'll make it."

"We are providing them with all the information, sir." The assistant leader wasn't pleased.

"You do not agree with me?" The governor was blunt. He didn't know any other way.

"No, I don't, sir."

"You believe that we violated our code."

"Yes, sir, I do."

The governor didn't answer immediately. "These hosts have done something that was never done before. As our colonies existed for many time periods, they never achieved what we did. We communicate with our life source. These hosts are our life source and by establishing a friendship with them, we will ensure our continuity."

"We are their enemy, sir. I am afraid that by disclosing all of our information they'll be able to develop a new disaster to kill us completely. They are the reason for our disasters. They invented them in order to eliminate us. They said so themselves, sir."

"True, but we know that these disasters killed many colonies but not all. Many colonies survive and probably sometimes develop resistance. That means that these disasters are not efficient. We are still expanding. These disasters do no not kill all of us."

"That's why the humans continue to search for ways to eliminate us permanently, sir."

"We would have done the same in this situation, wouldn't you say?"

The assistant leader remained silent.

"The only way to ensure our specie's future is to cooperate with our hosts. Otherwise, I predict that eventually they'll invent such a disaster to eliminate us once and for all. We will continue providing them all of the information that we have and in parallel we have to think about ways we could live together without hurting each other."

The assistant's leader continued to remain silent.

"Did you hear me?"

"Yes."

"Yes, sir. I am your governor!"

"Yes, sir."

"Dismissed."

Sam and Stanley were uneasy as they watched Sam's father's Skype transmission.

"No worries, Sam, as you see I am wearing the protective suit. Nothing can happen to me."

"Dad, I don't trust that suit. It can tear as you hit something. It just doesn't look strong enough."

"Sam, relax. Watch, you can clearly see how the ants are progressing from the east towards me. As they arrive to the open field, I'll get closer and spray them with my hormone."

He aimed his phone towards the hills to show a dark spot covering the ground and progressing ominously towards him. The phone automatically adjusted the camera's zoom, and they could see animals trying to escape from the swarm but getting caught nonetheless and thrashing about until the poison took hold.

"Your father is a bit incautious," Stanley mumbled. "Can you urge him to get out of there?"

"Dad, listen, you have to keep back. Please. It is too dangerous."

"And lose the opportunity of a lifetime? No way! In a few minutes I'll scamper towards the open spot there where I'll have enough room to spray the hormone on hundreds of the critters. As they communicate with each other, I expect all of them to start searching for a new nest."

The camera jumped with a front view as his father ran to the open field, towards the approaching swarm. They could hear Samuel's father swearing.

"What's going on, dad?"

The camera moved downwards and showed, near his right knee, a five-inch rip. "It got caught in this bush but that's okay. I brought a little duct tape. I'll fix it very quickly." The phone was put aside and Sam's phone screen was filled with sky. "This will do. Anyway, I am not worried. My hormone will change their behavior. You watch." He aimed the camera on his face. "Today, I'll make history."

Samuel shook his head. "I can't believe this."

"Here they come. The moment of truth is arriving." His father aimed the camera on the swarm then on a plastic spray bottle that he took from his bag. "This is a breakthrough; this is my Peacemaker!"

"Just please be careful. If the ants do not respond immediately, run back as fast as you can."

"Everything will be okay." His father was panting more and more. Sam and Stan could clearly hear the eerie hum and buzz of the swarm. Samuel's father increased the zoom. "Now we can see them clearly. These are what we call the driver ants. The scientific name is Dorylus, safari ants, or siafu."

"He would make a good teacher." Stanley made light to break the tension.

"An eccentric professor, yeah!" Sam spoke into the phone again. "Thanks, dad, but we don't really need to know all this information. We need to see you running away—as fast as you can. What'a the scientific term for get the hell out of there?"

"Son of a gun, I guess I didn't seal the rip well enough." The phone dropped and now they could see his father taking off the suit.

"Dad, what are you doing?" Samuel shouted.

"I didn't seal the rip well enough and the ants got in. I have to take it off in order to get rid of them. Ouch! They're biting me all over!"

"Dad, just get the hell out of there."

They could see him brushing away a few dozen ants from his trousers. "There, now it's much better. I've been bitten by these before. I can handle it. It'll be a bit trickier but I'll have to spray the ants and back off quickly."

The army was only a few feet away when he began spraying in wide arcs as his arm moved back and forth. "There you go! Take in the Peacemaker, little guys. You'll know what to do."

He finished the first bottle and then the second before scooting back a few yards to gauge the results. After a full two minutes, it was clear that the army was unimpressed and peace had not been made.

"Dad, you've done all you can do. Now run away."

"Patience, my boy, patience. Let the ants get the idea. It can take a few minutes."

The swarm continue moving forward. Sam was near panic.

Then it happened. The dark cloud began to slow then become still. The camera zoomed in on the vanguard.

"They're rethinking things." His father's voice trembled with excitement.

COEXISTENCE

The massive army actually started to back off. Then something more amazing happened. The dark cloud began to fade away.

"They've burrowed holes in the dry ground and are building a new colony. This is it! I did it, I did it!" The camera bounced up and down as his father jumped for joy like a young child.

Within half an hour there was no sign of any ants. The massive swarm that had been probably half a mile wide, completely disappeared into the ground.

Samuel laughed in relief and shook his head. "Dad, you are the craziest scientist I've ever known. But you did it. Congratulations!"

"Amazing." Stan raised his glass in a toast. "Here's to your success."

His father's smile lit up the phone screen. "Time to celebrate the New Year!" He held up a small champagne bottle and poured a portion of the amber bubbly into a plastic cup. "Son, aren't you and your colleague going to raise a glass with me?"

"Sure, dad."

Stan handed Sam a glass of wine and they all raised their drinks into the air. After the moment of joy, Samuel became wistful.

"I wish I was as successful as you, dad."

"What do you mean, Sam? In a way what I've done here is very similar to what you do. You are trying to conquer the most deadly diseases in the world. You are dealing with one of the biggest fears of the human race."

"Yes, I know but I guess I hit a dead end this time. My research is stuck."

"Did you look into the obvious?" His father looked straight into the camera. "A simple approach?"

Sam closed his eyes.

"Wait a minute!" Samuel sat up straight.

"What?" His father and Stanley responded together.

"This is it. Dad, you just gave me the solution—or the path to the solution. You were right. Your ants are like my research. As long as cancer is benign, it's harmless." He jumped with joy and hugged Stanley. "Okay, Sam. I'm not sure just what I did but good luck—and I'll be here if you need anything."

"Dad, you are the best."

Samuel dialed Alex's phone number. "Alex, meet me at the lab in half an hour."

THE PLAN

Governor, I have a plan. A plan to save Alisha and many other humans. Also it will be good for your species.

What is your plan?

You are in a static status in regular times. Not growing.

Yes.

And then you start to expand and grow.

Yes.

As long as you are static, without expanding, you are not a risk to us, your hosts. You are living as a colony inside us and do not damage our bodies and cells.

Yes.

The problem starts when you start to expand and grow.

But the code of every colony is to grow. Even if not immediately, then at some point in time.

Here is my plan: If you live in static colonies inside us, then there will be no need for the deadly storms anymore.

There was a pause as the governor was thinking.

Yes, you are correct.

Because as a static colony your existence does not harm humans.

There was a delay in the colony's response.

These are good news. We found a way to exist without hurting humans.

Yes. All I need from you is to settle and remain in non-vital organs of our bodies and then you can live there peacefully without damaging us. Our bodies will provide you all the necessary foods and we can both live together.

This is something to think about. What if we expand in small amounts?

There must be no expansion. Any growth turns you into a malignant form causing damage to our bodies.

What if we move to a different location along the stream?

What you call stream is called blood in our language. This is the problem. When you expand and build new colonies along the blood stream, it causes even greater damage and eventually kills the human faster.

We understand.

This is the time when we are creating the disasters, trying to prevent you from settling in other body parts of our bodies.

We understand.

If you could limit your existence to certain locations in our bodies, which we will guide you to, you could live there without any interference—and so will we. We will not release any disasters, and you can live peacefully and so will we, for the rest of our natural life.

This is a good plan. I like the idea of living together without causing any death to either. We will have a discussion and conclude it in our next meeting.

This is good. I will talk with you tomorrow.

Yes, goodbye. But one more thing, Samuel?

Yes?

Do you love Alisha?

You know this thing we call love?

Yes, somewhat. We sense it at times. It has a chemical substrate.

Yes, I do love her.

I see.

"This is a good plan. I would like to implement it on our colony." The governor was satisfied.

"Sir, this is against our code. We are supposed to expand and grow."

"But then we are causing damage and the host will kill us with the disasters. We already discussed this."

"I say, we stop our communication with them immediately, sir."

"They will stop giving us food and we will die."

"At least we will be able to transmit to future colonies about their mission to fight us. We can also guide them to continue to grow. Eventually, sir, we will win."

"I predict the opposite. The humans will continue fighting the colonies, as they do now. Eventually they'll invent a major disaster that will kill us all."

"Sir, this is a risk that we'll have to take."

"Not on my watch. I am this colony's governor. I decide our future. Tomorrow we are giving them our answer. It will be positive."

"Sir, as the assistant leader, I object."

"As the governor, I overrule your objection. This is according to the rules of the colonies. Overruled!"

"Yes, sir."

"Dismissed."

We accept your plan.

This is very good news.

"Yes!" Samuel's jubilance reverberated through tiled walls of the lab. Alex and Samuel exchanged hi-fives.

"Wait, this is only the first part. I still need them to help me with another vital matter." Samuel's eyes sparkled.

"With what? They already agreed to work together. This is it. There will be no more cancer."

"I still need to save Alisha and I have the idea how to do it."

Governor?

Yes.

I would like to ask you for your help, please.

Yes, proceed.

Can you send a message to other colonies, asking them to retreat from one location and move to another?

Yes. We typically send messages to expand but we can send messages to gather in another location.

And can you ask a colony to leave one location, move to another and become static?

It was never done before but technically it can be done.

I call it a cure.

What do you mean a cure?

A cure, in our language, is when we find a solution to a problem. In the medicine world we invent an element or particle of some type that causes our bodies to feel better.

Understood.

Currently there are many people around our world that have colonies inside them. These humans are fighting the colonies and many of them will die. If we could transmit inside their bodies to all colonies to move to a non-harmful location and become static, we will save these people's lives and the colonies as well.

Understood.

The colonies will relocate themselves into other locations, become static, and stay there. The humans will feel better and will not use the deadly disasters against the colonies. Everyone will be happy.

And that will be a cure for humans.

Yes, governor, but also no more disasters for the colonies. A cure against the deadly disasters.

Yes, we will be able to live together, side by side.

Yes.

Governor?

Yes?

Here is my idea. You will prepare message particles and we will inject these particles inside human bodies with expanding colonies.

Understood. Our particles will carry the message through your blood stream to the colonies. Am I correct?

Exactly, governor. Once the colonies receive the message they will relocate themselves to other organs and become static. Problem solved.

Good plan. We will cooperate. Please prepare a description of the non-vital organs to be relocate to and become static.

Will do it now. Please wait.

We will. Is this related to your idea love?

Yes, it is. Very much so.

ASSASSINATION

The assistant leader prepared an emergency pattern change. He made a local emergency change. He prepared it as he always did when they had to sacrifice cells in order to benefit the rest of the colony. Only the governor had the authority to declare an emergency structure change, but this time the assistant leader prepared one on his own.

He created a protein called p53. This protein checks for gene damage in cells and kills them if the damage is too great to repair. The assistant leader created an emergency change in only one location—the governor's location. He caused significant damage in the governor's base structure. When he releases the p53 at that place, a defective structure will be identified. The result will be almost immediate. Obeying the rules of many years, without any questions or concerns, the governor will be destroyed.

"This is remarkable, Sam." Stan looked at the recent correspondence printouts. "So are you saying that the cancer cells will prepare a message to other colonies to relocate somewhere else?"

"To a non-important area to be precise. I am thinking a foot, toe, anywhere. Once there, it will become benign."

"And they can tell other colonies to become benign?"

"They called it a static colony. Yes, they'll cooperate to prepare a message to existing colonies to relocate themselves."

Samuel smiled in joy. "This is it, Stan. That's what I was looking for. It's a cure for Alisha." Then he said quietly. "It is a cure for cancer."

"You should call it the Coexistence Serum."

"Exactly." Samuel took a sip from his coffee. "Science never dreamed of this."

"The cure will turn cancer from a monster into a personal pet?" Stan appreciated his own wit.

"No, into a partner. This venture will open a whole new world of possibilities. What if this colony can help cure other illnesses? They may become the internal helper with our body's health problems. Think about this, Stan. The HeLa cells contributed mightily to find vaccines for other diseases. Now, that we know their language, many researchers, around the world, will continue communicating with these colonies, trying to find cures to many other viruses and diseases—this time, as our helpers."

Stan shook his head. "You are right. This will be the dawn of a new age in medicine. An era where we can communicate and work with other organisms to find more and more medical breakthroughs. Amazing!"

"Indeed. But first I am on my way to the lab now. I prepared a message with a description of harmless body parts to relocate the colonies. I need to make sure that the colony understands it. Then I'll have to conduct some basic tests before using the Coexistence Serum on humans."

"Well, you'll have to conduct extensive testing, Sam. It can take some time. We don't want to cause more harm by relocating these tumors to places that they'll cause more damage. We're not sure they're pets just yet."

"I agree." Samuel looked in deep thoughts.

"What?"

"I am just not sure if I have the time. Alisha is fading fast."

⌣⟶

"Why they are not answering?" Sam was concerned.

Governor, are you there? Can you see our message?

Samuel checked the specimen on the petri dish. He dripped a few cc's of glucose on it. Then he checked the coils and the computer program. Everything seemed to be functioning.

"We just talked with them yesterday. Something's gone wrong."

"Let's continue." Alex suggested.

Are you there, Governor? Governor, can you see our messages? No reply.

Do you need more food? Are you there?

Sam and Alex looked at each other in confusion and growing anxiety.

"Our governor is dead." The assistant leader communicated with hundreds of assistant cells. "I killed him. He wanted to cooperate with our hosts."

The other assistants remained quiet. The entire collective knew about the communication with the host. The messages had spread. The worker cells didn't participate in leadership decisions. That was the task of the assistant leader and the governor only.

The assistant leader also knew that he cannot become a governor. By the code, if the governor dies, for any reason, then the assistant leader will replace him as the leader but he'll never receive the title governor.

"We followed the communication between us and the hosts." One assistant cell spoke. "It made sense to work with our hosts. They are our food providers. If we cause them harm, they bring the disasters on us, and we die."

"Yes," spoke another assistant cell. "It is better working with them than against them."

"This is against our code. The humans want to be superior to us. They are trying to kill us for many years, without success. We are still here, aren't we?"

"The humans are constantly seeking to create new disasters to kill us. As the governor said, they'll eventually find one. When they do, we will be killed. There will be no way back."

"Now we have a chance to live together with the humans. This is our chance to make peace," said another assistant cell.

"But at what price? We will have to give up our living purpose. What are we worth without fulfilling our purpose to expand and grow?"

"The governor was weak and unwise. Now we will continue to grow and expand. We will also prepare a message to other colonies not to establish communication with our hosts and not to cooperate with them. All they want is to destroy us. I am now your leader and you'll have to obey my commands."

The colony remained silent.

"We have plenty of food. We start our growth immediately. Dismissed."

"I don't understand what happened, Sam. They stopped talking with you?" Stan and Sam had a hurried lunch at the Medical Center cafeteria.

"Yes, all communication has stopped. I don't get it. I can't get anything for the past few days, Stan."

"Did you check if they have enough food and enzymes?"

"Yes, everything is good. The specimen is alive and well, but uncommunicative. The equipment is good. My EMF and the translation computer program. Nothing is awry."

"I wonder what's happened then."

"As much as I hate to think this way, they may have decided to disengage from us." Samuel scratched his head.

"But why now? After they already talking with you for months? It doesn't make sense."

"I am puzzled also."

They ate their lunch quietly, mulling over various explanations, none of which was entirely satisfactory.

"I visited Alisha last night. She is in a deep coma in the ICU. She can die any day now." Samuel said what Stanley already suspected.

"Look, Sam, there must be a harmless reason for this breakdown in communication. When was your last message from them?"

"A few days ago. The governor liked my idea of coexistence. He promised to cooperate and asked for a list of organs where they can build benign colonies. The day after, they didn't answer my messages anymore."

Stan took a forkful of his salmon filet and noticed it was cold. Sam's cellular phone rang. He spoke briefly then turned back to Stan.

"That was Alex. I asked him to examine the specimen if he passed by the office today. The specimen has grown over the past few days. No doubt about it. And it's grown more so than in recent months. You know, I do believe that I have a reasonable explanation. See, if the culture is alive and growing, this leaves only one possibility to the sudden disconnection."

"What?"

"It's their decision."

"And why would they decide that?" Stan looked at his watch as he had a lecture to give in fifteen minutes.

"Well, Stan, we know that they have a structure. They have a governor and a group of assistants. This opens the way to differing opinions."

"Differing opinions?"

"What if one part of their governing code says to grow and expand, no matter what. And another part of their governing code says to obey the governor, no matter what."

"Then they have dissent." Stan nodded as he tried to imagine this almost political scenario in an unfamiliar and unlikely locale. "Are you thinking of a revolution" A coup of some sort?"

"We know they have various components and a complex code. We simply can't rule out this possibility."

"Well, even if this has happened, there is nothing that we can do about it. As much as I hate to say so, it is in their hands now. Wait! I didn't mean to say they had hands! Maybe you should start with a fresh colony."

"Can't do that. It will take me months to train them how to communicate with us again."

"Not necessarily. This time you already know their language and codes. It will be much faster."

"The communication part, yes. It will still take months to teach them our terms and medical definitions again. This colony already knows it."

"I have to run. I have a lecture to give in five minutes. Sam, one thing you have to keep in mind. Alisha's right. If by any chance they are able to send a message to other colonies about us, it can damage our cancer treatments and medicine. We don't want to lose the few weapons that we have. I say if they don't answer your response in the next few days, destroy them."

"Yes, I was just thinking about that, reluctantly. Even the little information that we shared with them can be used against us in case they are able to send messages to other cancers, which of course we think they can do."

"Yes. Continue for few days and if there is no answer, you have no choice. Incinerate the specimen."

Stan left a twenty on the table and left the cafeteria. Samuel looked after him as he vanished among the sea of students.

The colony was built and maintained by many hundreds of millions of working cells. There were only a few thousand assistant cells. The assistant cells were in charge of the colony's operation, including when to divide and when to modify the structure. They were also decided who received the food in the colony. In case of emergency they would be the last to be sacrificed. They reported to the assistant leader cell.

"I supported our governor's opinion," one assistant cell told the other.

"I also supported it. Most sensible," said the other.

"I don't think it is good that our leader killed the governor," offered a third one.

"This was never done before," added a fourth.

There was no communication for a while as they performed their maintenance duties.

"If we do not act, the host will stop providing us with food."

"Worse, they'll kill us. They will send the disasters. We already know that we are inside them."

"It is better to cooperate with them."

"I agree."

"I agree."

"I agree."

The agreement repeated millions of times.

There was no communication for a while.

"But our assistant leader is in control now."

"What should we do?"

"The leader forbids us to communicate with the humans."

"This is not good."

"I agree, this is not good."

"I agree, this is no good."

The communication repeated itself millions of times.

"We have no choice" said one of the assistants.

This time there were no repetition for millions of times. An intelligent collective reached a conclusion and they were about to execute it.

Samuel sat quietly on vigil near Alisha's bed. Lights flickered on the monitoring equipment and an occasional beep could be heard. It was just after dinner time and the intense care unit prepared for the night shift.

She has such a peaceful expression on her face. Like nothing is bothering her.

He kissed her hand.

"I miss you, Alisha." He stifled his sobs though he was sure no one could hear. "I was so close to saving you . . . I reached an agreement with the colony but now I lost communication with them. I'm so sorry, so sorry."

A nurse entered the room to check Alisha's values. She then approached Samuel and handed him a cup.

"It's coffee, no sugar. Would you like something to eat, Sam?"

"No, thank you, Trudy."

She smiled and left the room.

"I am not giving up, Alisha, I am not giving up." He kissed her forehead and left for the lab.

Governor, can you read this message?

No response.

Can you read this message?

No response.

Alex knew something had to be done. "It's been a long time since we heard back. Too long."

The colony indeed might have to be destroyed.

All these past months of work and training. If I destroy this colony, I'll have to start from scratch. It will take months again. Poor Alisha.

"I am going out for some a quick walk outside, Sam. I'll be back in a few." Alex patted Sam on his back closed the door behind him, leaving Sam in the chamber and the whirring instrument.

Samuel looked at the equipment around him housed in what was a second home for the past months. He looked at the petri dish in the Photonic Microscope chamber. He had had so many hopes.

He sat there and stared at the screen without the will to do a thing.

The assistant leader was just about to check the perimeter when thousands of assistants approached, wordlessly. He could feel a substantial structure change and instantly knew what it meant. An emergency change was being created and it involved him. He could immediately feel the density of p53 protein and knew he was about to disintegrate. He knew this because he had done the same to the governor.

"You are making a mistake."

"Our governor was correct. Our only way of surviving is to work with our hosts."

"Our hosts are an enemy. We can't believe them. They'll destroy us."

The assistants didn't communicate anything. The leader understood. He was not sad or unhappy. Every cell accepts death just as it accepts life. It is in their code.

"I hope that you are correct. Because if you aren't, you are responsible for our extinction."

No response.

"Who will be your leader when I am gone?"

"We will consult our host."

"A sound choice. You put all of your trust in him. Now he will have to help you."

"As we will help him."

"Farewell and good luck to the colony. Long live our code."

The p53 synthesized into the assistant's location. Within seconds he ceased to exist.

Samuel looked at his watch. It was almost three am. He looked once more at the culture in the petri dish.

"You could have saved Alisha. But you disconnected from the outside world, and from me."

He shook his head.

"The right thing to do would be to destroy the specimen. They can send messages to other colonies. I have to destroy them."

He opened his medical box and took out a vial of sulfuric acid. A few drops and everything will be dead in a matter of minutes. After that, he'd put the sample into the incinerator for complete annihilation. He held the eye dropper over the petri dish, feeling like a prison warden about to end the life of a condemned man.

"Maybe I should try one more time. Dad said to never give up."

He stared at the computer screen for a few minutes before entering another message.

Governor, are you getting this message?

He was waiting for the soft chime that was heard every time that the system detected an incoming message.

No sound.

This is Samuel trying to communicate with you for the past few weeks. Can you read my message?

No chime, no motion on his screen. No hope.

"This is it. I tried, Alisha."

He took the dropper with the lethal acid and held it over the Photonic Microscope specimen tray.

"Goodbye, guys." His fingers had begun to squeeze the dropper when a chime sounded.

Samuel quickly moved his hand back but a drop of the acid nonetheless fell on the petri dish's perimeter, producing a puff of smoke and a powerful stench as the acid burned into the cotton substrate.

Hello, Samuel.

His mouth remained open. He ran to the keyboard.

Governor, I tried to contact you for many weeks. Why did you stop communicating with us?

An assistant leader killed our governor. He didn't want to cooperate with you humans.

"I'll be damned," Samuel mumbled in shock. "I was right."

Who is in charge now?

Us, the assistants. We agreed with our governor. We killed our assistant leader. We have no one in charge now.

They have to have a leadership authority, otherwise communication and cooperation would be much more difficult. Samuel bit his lip. He had an idea. It was risky but options were few just then.

Who are you?

An assistant.

You are in charge from now on. I make you a new governor.

There was a moment of silence.

The protracted pause made Sam wonder if he had triggered another revolution in the colony. Minutes passed, excruciatingly. Then a chime sounded.

We all agree. I am the new governor.

Samuel released a long sigh.

Very good.

Then he had another idea but wondered if it might be too much for one day. It might add another level of confusion and cause mistrust. But as he thought more about his idea, he liked it. It was something he learned in one of his psychology classes in med school. The new governor needs a stronger identity. He was just now nominated into a governor and probably doesn't know what to do. He maybe even be scared. Sam wanted to increase the new leader's confidence by giving him an identity. Something that none of the other cells has. Sam would give him a name.

In our world, we are providing identification for every humans. For the most important ones especially. For leaders. We call it a name. I will give you a name now. Your name will be. . . .

Samuel thought frantically. He hadn't prepared for this. What name he should give him?

Abraham.

There was a moment of silence. Sam again wondered if he'd miscalculated.

It is a good name. I am now Abraham.

Very good. From now on I'll call you by your name. You will call me by my name—Samuel.

Agreed.

Now, Abraham, time is important. I need your urgent help.

I agree to help.

I created a list of locations that your governor asked me for. These locations are safe parts of our bodies. Your colonies can move to these locations and this will cause no harm to us anymore. Do you understand?

Yes.

You will need to prepare a message to all colonies to relocate immediately to any of these new locations.

Yes.

Since the message will come from you, the colonies should do what you said. Am I correct, Abraham?

Yes, Samuel. We will use a Supreme Message. Supreme Messages are to be immediately obeyed by all colonies. It is in our code.

Please prepare your message in particle form. I will need to take these particles and place them in another host body. The message will move with the blood stream and reach all other colonies that exist in this host's body. Will this method work, Abraham? Will the host's colonies be able to receive this message?

I believe it will work, Samuel. This is a good plan to communicate with other colonies.

Samuel exhaled long sigh. "This is it. Showtime."

This is very good, Abraham. This is very good. I am sending you the locations now.

With shaky hands Samuel typed the short list of locations and description into the outgoing message field which then would be processed into the colony's language.

Then he pressed enter.

Samuel stood near Alisha's hospital bed. It was after midnight and staff was settling down into the nightshift. A nurse checked Alisha's vitals and smiled to Sam as she left. He'd worked all day long to prepare the serum—the Coexistence Serum. The small quantity of the mixture in the syringe looked milky and thick.

He didn't ask the hospital to approve the procedure; they'd never allow it. He was operating completely on his own. Alisha's face was calm, peaceful, accepting. Her eyes were sunken and her now gaunt form seemed to be sinking into the mattress and bedding.

He thought her chances were very slim. With the message that was contained in the syringe the tumor that spread into her brain should remove itself and move to another organ to become benign. This was the Supreme Message, as Abraham, the new governor of his colony, told him. How much of this was science and how much was hope, Sam didn't know.

"Alisha, do you allow me to inject this?" he whispered.

She didn't respond. He held her hand.

"Alisha, do you want me to inject you with the Coexistence Serum?"

No response.

"It contains a message, a message from Abraham."

He thought he felt her hand weakly press his.

"Alisha, it's Samuel. I am holding the Coexistence Serum. Would you like me to inject it into you?"

No response.

He gave her forehead a soft kiss and injected the serum into her IV tube.

"We'll know soon. We'll know soon."

Samuel sat near Alisha, holding her hand and talking to her. The full moon night shone with all of its glory above the clear skies. He fell asleep sitting near Alisha's bed.

Mitosis happens in the adult human approximately 25 million times a second. An irregular mitosis started inside Alisha—one that happened moving along the bloodstream. Obeying the ancient code, cells detached from the primary colony and drifted down her bloodstream. The cells must move through the wall of a blood vessel to get into the bloodstream. After entering, the cells were swept along by the blood to an unknown destination. The assumption is that these cells were stuck somewhere, usually in a very small blood vessel called a capillary. But these cells were actually navigating themselves to defined destinations.

They penetrated the wall of the capillary and entered the tissue of the destination organ. There they stopped their journey. They continued to multiply but in a controlled fashion.

The journey was complicated. Many of the cells did not survive it. Out of many millions of cells that reached Alisha's bloodstream, only one survived to form a secondary colony, or what is called in medical terms—metastasis.

Some cells were killed off by white blood cells in her immune system. Others cells died because they were battered around by the fast flowing blood. But the journey eventually was completed. The older colony completely disappeared and a new colony formed. The new colony was mandated by the governor and its growth was directed not to exceed a certain amount. The new colony was static, or benign.

The new colony received plenty of food from the host. They were satisfied by the conditions.

Samuel and Alisha hugged on the warm sand and Alisha kissed him on his lips. Samuel closed his eyes as Alisha kissed him all over his face with boundless love.

"Sam . . . Sam. . . ."

Her voice became louder and he opened his eyes.

The sunshine and the blue water disappeared. He was still in the hospital of Yale Medical. His head was on her bed.

Reality hit him in a flash. His heart sank, though only for a moment.

"Sam, I feel good, much better. I am weak but hungry as can be. Well, I haven't eaten much recently, I suppose."

Samuel had tears of joy in his eyes.

"No, you haven't. We'll dine together."

FORTUNE AND GLORY

Alisha and Samuel lay on their beach chairs on Paradise Beach, one of the most beloved beaches of Mykonos, Greece. They were married one week ago in a traditional Greek wedding, with the help of Alisha's family. They were spending the last days of their honeymoon, enjoying the beautiful weather, before going back to the US.

They held hands as they watched the calm sea stretching out to the horizon.

"I still can't believe what we went through." Alisha took a sip from her retsina.

"Did that really happen?" Samuel turned to her with a bewildered smile before kissing her.

"It happened all right. Here, I have living proof." She led his hand to her left foot. Just above her heal, he could feel a small bump no larger than a rye seed. "This is my tumor. It used to be in my brain and now it is in my foot."

"Way less harmful."

"I can't believe you thought up this idea." She looked at him with love. "You are definitely special."

He gave her a look. "Special? I hope you said it in a good way."

"Only."

"How does it feel to have fortune and glory?"

He kissed her hand. "All I wanted was just to have you back. I was selfish."

"No, no! You were obsessed with this research way before I got sick. You wanted to find a cure. You wanted to save people you didn't even know—and you did it. Millions of people around the world are getting better every day because of you."

Samuel looked at the horizon where a large cruise ship slowly made its way into the Mediterranean. "Yes, I did want to find a cure. I wanted to do it in a different way."

"You did. Your approach led to the Coexistence Serum. You are aware that you made history, aren't you? Your name has entered the annals of history as the man that found the cure for cancer."

"It is not really a cure, it's a . . ." He searched for the right word. ". . . an arrangement? An agreement?"

She grinned. "Call it as you wish. It is a cure. Patients with cancer recover very rapidly, almost immediately. You have almost 100% recovery rate, even with terminal patients—and even though most physicians don't fully understand the serum. Look at me. I was terminal. And now I'm on a beautiful beach with a handsome man."

"I am just happy to be the one who helped find this solution. You know, Stan is still in shock and I think that he still doesn't believe that this is happening—and will not for a while. It is hard for him to grasp that we are actually talking with cancer."

"He still talks of them as though they're aliens."

"Yes, but these aliens are a whole world of opportunity. This is just the beginning. Now we can start many research projects using their help. We already developed vaccines based on the HeLa cells. With these guys on our side, who knows what tomorrow may bring."

"You're right, Sam. They can become valuable helpers inside people. They are insiders with access to bodily chemistry and functionality."

"Exactly. They can become our personal medical helpers. Isn't it a grand idea, Alisha?"

"I have another grand idea. Let's go swimming."

They ran into the warm, azure waters of the Mediterranean Sea.

"We owe a lot to Stan. He saved your ass with the authorities and mollified them with your promise of prompt reimbursement from serum revenues." She swam and he followed her.

"And I'll always cherish him as a good friend."

They swam back to the beach and lay on the warm sand, getting dry in the sun.

"I could live here." Samuel laughed.

"Why don't we? We have money now. We can do whatever we want."

Samuel laughed. "You know me, I have to have new projects at all times. We can't just quit right now."

"I am not saying to leave it all behind. Just take a break for a few years."

"What did you have in mind?"

"I don't know. Maybe children?"

"Aha, so that's your master plan?"

She gave him one of her beautiful smiles. "Yes, it is."

"Let's take a walk on the beach." He took her hand and they ambled down the shoreline.

Seagulls soared and squawked above them as they walked hand by hand, sinking their feet into the wet sand.

"You know, Alisha, there is something that I didn't tell anyone else."

"What is it, Sam?" She was surprised from the turn in his mood.

"You were the one to advise us about the risks in case there was no cooperation, remember?"

"Yes, and you almost destroyed them, just before they established communication."

"Correct." Samuel was in thoughts and took a deep breath. "They already proved to be an intelligent life-form."

"Yes."

"What happened when intelligent life-forms, like humans, made governments and so forth, Alisha?"

She didn't see where he was going.

He straightened his eyes to hers. "Individualism. Opinions. Controversy. Strife."

"Ah. . . . And?"

"Different opinions, Alisha. We already witnessed two assassinations in the master colony. These are living entities. They think, and although they have a very primitive form of government, they still have varying opinions." He stopped his walk. "One of them can think differently, exactly as it happened with the assistant leader. For all kind of reasons he didn't want to cooperate with us, and so he killed the governor."

Alisha remained quiet as fingers of fear slowly crawled up her back. "Then the others killed the assistant leader in order to re-communicate with us."

"They killed the new leader and turned to us for help."

"We've seen many similarities in human history. Julius Caesar, Caligula, Lincoln, Rabin. . . ." she murmured. "It goes on and on."

"It can happen again. The only question is when." Samuel said in low voice as they continued their walk. "I already asked Stan to prepare an isolated laboratory. We can continue to research drugs and methods to eliminate cancer. We have much more knowledge now. This is highly confidential, Alisha."

"But this is against our agreement with the master colony."

"I know, but we have to be prepared for the worst." He then stopped and hugged her to his heart. "You are at great risk my love and I don't want to lose you."

"So you'll conduct research based on the information that they are sharing with us."

"Yes."

She lowered her eyes. "We have much better chances to find a cure now. They are giving us all the information."

"We will never use it against them, Alisha. This is just a precaution."

"We are *lying* to them."

"We are protecting us from any bad cells that may screw it all up!"

"What if they discover it?"

"All specimens will be destroyed. Nothing is going to go through our sewage system."

She released a long sigh. "I guess I see the logic in it. Although my conscience says it's wrong."

"I don't like it either . . . but it has to be done."

"Now, can we forget about this unpleasant topic and jog?" She smiled naughtily.

Samuel jumped like a little child and they raced along the golden beach.

Samuel, Alisha, and Alex shared the Nobel Prize for medicine the next year. The Coexistence Serum became a veritable cure for cancer. The master HeLa specimen remained at Yale Medical for further research and development of vaccinations and drugs. All around the world the medical community initiated research in many directions to find out more about viruses and bacteria.

Nikolai got his own computer lab and was helping the medical researchers around the world.

Although Samuel and Alisha became quite wealthy, they continued a simple life. They built a modest home in New Haven and continued their work with the master cancer cell colony. There was a whole new world to learn about.

The world's fear from the most deadly disease was ebbing.

Over the years, the Coexistence Serum became as common as the flu shot.

ET TU, BRUTE?

Abraham led the master colony to a comfortable existence. They were put in comfortable incubation conditions and received regular nourishment. They worked with humans to research more biological phenomena. They also received vital information about their own structure and biological behavior from the humans. This gave them information how to have new life purpose now that growth was forbidden. The colony seemed to be satisfied.

Assistant 5,345 performed his routine as commanded. He supervised cell division by mitosis and made sure that the DNA was replicated and copied correctly so that each new cell received a complete set of 46 chromosomes. He was not the only assistant that supervised the 3 billion cells that had to be replicated every 4-6 hours. He also ensured that the DNA double helix was perfectly suited for replication since each strand can serve as a template to produce a shape opposite to itself. He performed his duties meticulously and without complaining.

But Assistant 5,345 was not satisfied. He never related this to any of his colleagues but he didn't like cooperation with hosts. He believed that the cancer cells were the stronger species and they could survive the disasters made by humans. He didn't do anything, though. The colony was satisfied.

It would be very easy to create a DNA mutation to cause uncontrollable growth. But other assistants could very quick eliminate these mutations and contain the situation. The only way to gain control would be to have his colleagues' cooperation. He'll have to convince the majority that he is right and Abraham is wrong. Then they'll have to spread the message to other colonies.

They can do it in a clandestine way. The humans have no way to know. They have to introduce something into the message that they give, what the humans call the Coexistence Serum. They'll provide serum but with a hidden code. With time, everything is going to revert to the same situation before communication was established. In the meanwhile, he did his job as required in a large colony like theirs. He'd continue to do his job and duties as an integral part of the biological community.

He will be patiently waiting for that one day. It was in the code.

Printed in the United States
By Bookmasters